FATE FROM CIRCUMSTANCE

The House of Renault
Volume 1

Jason Wayne Carr

RoseDog Books
PITTSBURGH, PENNSYLVANIA 15238

RoseDog Books
585 Alpha Drive
Suite 103
Pittsburgh, PA 15238
Visit our website at *www.rosedogbookstore.com*

ISBN: 979-8-88683-538-0
eISBN: 979-8-88683-537-3

For my family, my inspiration – All my love

PROLOGUE

Oran, Algeria, 1961

Standing amidships just outside the cabin of his twenty-foot fishing trawler, Uharu, resplendent with all her nets and other tools of the trade any fourth generation fisherman required, Hadj reached back inside, grabbed his binoculars, and placed them into his passenger's outstretched hand.

The early morning sea was calm. The mid-spring weather pattern forming overhead was typical, and welcomed. The aura of tragedy and loss that had accompanied his passenger onto his boat was significant, and unfortunate.

Saying nothing to him, not knowing what he could say, Hadj returned to the pilothouse to change course to a more northwesterly heading. Hadj did so because he knew this to be the quickest route out of the Golfe d'Oran, into the Mediterranean Sea, and into international waters—and relative safety. In another ninety nautical miles or so, once the coast of the Iberian Peninsula appeared on the horizon, Hadj would then head northeast towards the southern coast of France.

Abdenour Hadj, an Algerian of Meghrebian descent, was a small, robust man with aged eyes and a pepper-colored beard. He was an excellent sailor, a good husband and family man, and an even better friend. As he kept one eye on the horizon, he kept one on his passenger. Hadj understood the man's pain, and understood the meaning of the debt he was about to repay.

It had been his passenger and longtime friend, Maurice Renault, who had brought the two murderers to Hadj's front door all those years ago. He'd hunted them down and then delivered them to answer for the deaths of the Algerian's infirmed parents. They were seventy-year-old children of the sea who had done nothing but voice their neutrality in the ongoing civil war; and yet, they were ruthlessly murdered in cold blood for harboring such an unpopular opinion. When revenge was called for, and no trace of the murderous soldiers could be found, it was Maurice who had thrown them to the ground at Hadj's feet and then simply walked away. A long and interesting relationship then flourished, with Sophia Renault often acting as the arbitrator between them while they argued about politics and the potential independence of Algeria.

A simple note left in his mailbox earlier this morning was all Abdenour Hadj had needed to justify his being here right now, grateful that he could finally fulfill his debt to his dear friend. And although they would be square, Hadj would take it upon himself to maintain Sophia's grave until his dying day—this he would do for his friend without request.

Maurice lifted the binoculars to his tired, bloodshot eyes and looked back at the city of Oran, the city that had been his home for the last fifteen years. He could just make out the commotion at the Filaoussene Jetty on Quay #1, in the Bassin de Ghazaouet, and could only guess that it was the colonel's men flailing about in their continuous and frustrated attempts to locate him. Satisfied they couldn't no matter how hard they tried, Maurice lowered the field glasses and handed them back to his friend. He then walked aft to sit on a small bench seat where his satchel lay on its side.

He opened it and took out the packet of documents and tape recordings. Having remembered where his former resistance leader, Capitaine René, was now living, Maurice addressed the packet appropriately. He would give it to Hadj for mailing once they arrived in France. Maurice knew the package would make it, but only if his own name wasn't on it.

Next, he took out a letter pad and a pen. As he started writing, the tears instantly began. Fearing not only the words he would have to write on the blank pages, he also feared for the life of his daughter. He feared for her safety and he feared that her ability to carry such a hefty burden, the Renault family burden, without knowing exactly what it was or why it was, would be too much. Maurice knew that, at least for now, fate was against him. And Elena Renault, his daughter and only child, would now become the last remaining purveyor of the history of their branch of the Renault family. He put that thought aside; he had other things to tell her first.

Maurice had to tell his daughter what had happened to her mother without giving too much detail. He couldn't reveal the truth behind Sophia's death and his chosen sacrifice, but he knew he had to write something down. Most of all, he needed her to be protected. At some point he would need to write a second letter to his cousin Jean Francois, the man with whom Elena was staying in America. Maurice struggled to string the words together in his mind, causing an even greater flood of tears.

Maurice had demanded Sophia go with Elena to America, but his loving wife would hear nothing of it. She informed him she would stay by her husband's side throughout it all. For that, Sophia had paid the ultimate price. It would be agony for him to be away from his daughter, just as much as it would be torturous on his soul to be apart from Sophia.

Might I be overreacting?

It didn't matter. And besides, he couldn't take the chance. Maurice wasn't sure if his father-in-law, the colonel, was reckless enough, or truly sadistic enough, to use his own granddaughter as leverage. Maurice didn't know how long it would be before he could see Elena again—if ever. He would miss his life in Algeria and he would miss his home in the Legion, but most of all he would miss his Sophia and his Elena.

He began as simply as he could:

My Dearest Elena,

Please know that I will always love you. It is with immense sadness that I must tell you that your mother has died in Algeria...

CHAPTER 1

Gretna, Louisiana, 1996

On the scale of things, Elena was emotionally overjoyed yet co templative in her revelry as she sat in her bedroom trying to keep her watery eyes from smearing the recently applied and ultimately unneeded cosmetic changes to her persistently youthful face.

The revelry was not for her own accomplishments, though; it was for her son's—and she was so very proud of him. He was a good boy and an endearing son, and brave in every sense of the word. She stopped to reflect upon his eighteen glorious years, years horrifically altered by an extraordinary event that was completely out of his, or her, control. She wondered if life would play another malicious trick on him. No, she thought, one incident like that had to be enough. She turned to the last page of the letter in her hands. The last page was always the hardest to read, always the saddest to repeat, but was a memory she couldn't live without. It seemed cruel torturing herself like this, but she read it anyway.

For now, remember your mother and remember my love
for you. I will always keep you both close to my heart.
Adieu. Your loving father,

Maurice

She constantly read the words, over and over and over again, remembering every line and every phrase. So much time had passed since the day her uncle, Jean Francois, had brought her this letter. The paper was now a dingy, whitish-yellow shade of its original papyrus beige. The smell of the ink and the ocean once so ingrained within the porous valleys of the delicate textile had long since evaporated. Regardless, it was a treasure from a former life that she clung to religiously—and much too tightly sometimes.

Elena remembered being excited to see it that first day, all those years ago, but quickly realized something was wrong. The letter was unopened, but Uncle Jean's posture said it all because he had received his own letter from Maurice. Jean's expressionless face and the sadness in his eyes would become an unwelcomed harbinger of many a crying night for Elena Sophia Renault-Bassett.

She had always wished for the Ts in her married name to be pronounced silently—she liked to think traditionally. But the Americanization of her husband's surname, with the added hard pronunciation on the final syllable, was simply an unfortunate consequence of modernity. Her mother-in-law didn't mind; and of course, what she thought and said were gospel around this house. Elena put all other thoughts aside as she sighed heavily, knowing today would be the last time she would read the letter alone. It was finally time to tell Sebastiane, her only child, the story of his grandfather—what she knew of it anyway.

Elena didn't know the whole story, but what she did know she hoped would be enough to soothe his mind and assure his heart that he wasn't the only member of the Renault family to have an experience like he'd had. The letter in her hand was only part of that story, but it would be her starting point. It was time he knew of his other family's history. She had waited many years to tell him, a couple of years longer than she'd wanted, but that hadn't been her fault.

She looked up at the picture of her son stuffed into the frame of the vanity's mirror and smiled, gratefully. At a shade over seventy-three inches tall, with medium brown hair, dark hazel-colored eyes, a slender face, and a muscular physique, he was the absolute spitting image of his grandfather. When Elena compared his recently taken graduation picture to the dated emulsion just below it, a forty-eight-year-old wedding photo of her mother and father, it was like looking at the same person. It was a pleasant reminder of what her life once was. She peeked down at her watch.

Oh goodness! Is that the time already?

"Sebastiane Maurice Bartholomew Renault-Bassett," Elena shouted, tauntingly. Surely he was ready to go, but a little pleasure in playfully tormenting him couldn't hurt. He was graduating today after all, and she couldn't hide her joy. He had academically overachieved at school, and had come a long way over the last four years.

From across the second-floor hallway and up the stairs to his attic-space bedroom, Sebco—a nickname given to him by his father—winced from the use of his entire name. A slightly audible ouch escaped his lips as he gazed into the full-length mirror hanging on the back of his closet door.

Well, I've done it now. My whole name and it's only, what, eight o'clock in the morning! Like this tie isn't hard enough.

He continued to fool with the maroon-colored, silk tie. It was an incredibly good match to his cap and gown, complete with white tassel and the requisite plastic number 96 hanging from the button in the top center. Becoming more and more frustrated at his continued failures he finally finished—for the third time—when he noticed his mother walk into the room. Turning to face her, he could instantly see her beaming smile showing her perpetual pride in him. He stood erect like a soldier on inspection day, and her smile turned to a wry smirk as she approached.

She immediately went for the tie and began to fiddle with it. He let out a joking sigh, thinking he'd finally gotten it perfect, but a mother's prerogative always outranked any feelings of accomplishment he might have garnered at affixing his costume appropriately. As she looked up at him, a twinkle of tears began in her eyes.

Today, you are truly a man.

She continued to fiddle with the tie, finally saying to him, "Sebastiane. I am very proud of you. You have come through a lot. And for all intents and purposes, you're a better man for it."

"Yes, ma'am." His eyebrows dipped just a little and his expression changed ever so slightly to one of serious introspection.

Elena continued, "Your father and I just want you to enjoy it. All your hard work has paid off. Now, well…" a slight pause, "…just enjoy it." Her statement finished, she also finished with his tie.

The touch of seriousness on Sebastiane's face preceded his response. He thought of himself as quite the orator when he needed to be, although some thought him to be overdoing it. However, his selection of words and phrases, acquired from the pseudo-classical education his mother had intertwined with his regular schooling, a voracious appetite for reading, and a wide range of sincere facial expressions and candid body language that accompanied everything he said and did always combined to portray exactly what his thoughts conveyed.

"You, Father, and Grandmother Donah have always been here for me. You've been here for the girls since that day as well," he began. He reached for his mother's hands and held them softly in his, and then continued, "Yes, I did the work. And yes, I was the one who faced the nightmares and overcame them. But without you three, I'm not a hundred percent sure I'd be in this most enviable of positions, a position from which I can return the favor and show all of you how much I appreciate everything you've done for me." Sebastiane continued to stare at his mother, his expression changing to one of thankfulness. "You were firm when it was required. You were lenient without my request. You allowed me to share our home with Heather and Sarah and made me feel at ease when they needed me, even when I had almost nothing left to give."

He paused before continuing, giving her enough time to interject, "We did what we could. We knew—"

He stopped her words with an appreciative shake of his head, and said, "Thank you," and then quickly changed his expression to one of gratitude mixed with a slight hint of hopeful finality. It was an expression that he hoped would make her change the subject.

Elena realized she was harping on the situation. Not on purpose, of course; she was just trying her best to remember this look in his eyes and forget the one of absolute nothingness in them from four years ago. To survive something so violent at such a young age was something she had marveled at. The fact that he'd come through it at all, let alone so easily, was truly remarkable to her. But he was his grandfather's grandson through and through, and she thanked God for it every day. She easily read his demeanor and changed the subject.

"Your father is coming home to pick up Mother Donah and myself, so you go get the girls and we'll see you there."

His face, ever so serious, regained its liveliness. "Yes, ma'am."

With a grin and a calm step, he grabbed his truck keys and his Nokia flip phone from the table next to his bed and then put out his arm to escort his beloved mother back downstairs so she could finish getting ready. At the door to her bedroom, he smiled and kissed her on the cheek. She smiled back and motioned for him to go. He then continued down the stairs, out the front door, and jumped into his 1961 Chevrolet C-10 Apache pickup truck.

In immaculate condition, with limited mileage and no rust, the truck had been purchased for seven hundred dollars from a family friend by his grandmother as a present on his sixteenth birthday. Sebastiane was extremely grateful, but paid out of his own pocket to have it repainted in its original Mesa Tan color scheme so as to cover up the rather interesting choice made by its previous owner—that of Crystal Green.

He turned the wheel left as he backed out of the driveway so he could go north. Once in the street, he stopped, shifted into drive, and then headed away. He took the left at 6th Street, and then another left onto Lafayette Street. He grinned, excitedly, as he continuously fiddled with his tie in the rearview mirror. There was no real need to concentrate on the road—he could do this trip in his sleep. Next was a right turn onto 9th Street, and then the stop sign at Weyer Street three blocks later. The girls lived just four houses down on the left. Seeing their house and remembering his mother's words made him sink deeply into the truck's leather bench seat, awash with the unfortunate memories of the day four years ago that had changed everything.

Wow!

His mother's comment from earlier—you've come through a lot—had outflanked his defenses and only now made him flinch inside. The nightmare had hovered around and within him for what seemed like an eternity, but eventually stopped its uninvited advances long ago. Now when it did try to resurface, he just let it roll off his shoulder. Still, the way she said it had seemed a little apprehensive from his point of view, but was from her perspective probably, he guessed, just a prideful anecdote of motherly endearment in his ability to overcome adversity. His graduation from high school on this very day, his enduring friendship with Heather and Sarah Prescott, and his ability to compartmentalize his thoughts and feelings were all a testament to his strength of character. It was a strength he'd used to defeat his fears. It also helped him to keep the prowling lion in his mind at bay.

Now when he thought of that day, he only wondered why, why was he able to do what he had done? To his utter dismay those thoughts wouldn't leave him alone. Actually, it was never a question of what he had done, it was a question of how he'd done it. He didn't cower at the horror of the situation, nor did he freeze in fear from the violence that had possessed him.

I did what was needed, no more no less, right?

His thoughts remained positive as he stared at the stop sign at Weyer Street, but the lingering hole in his mind, his actions on that day—what he did on that day—reminded him of one simple and as of yet unobtainable truth.

With the compartmentalization of his thoughts and his innate ability to consistently control his external emotional state, he presumed there must inevitably be a price to pay for his actions. This price, Sebastiane believed, was to be his life's burden, one to be borne alone and kept from the outside world so as not to infect it. His actions on that day and his ability to compartmentalize them gave him control over those actions and their consequences. And so he had been afforded the ability to restrain himself, never allowing the actions of that day to resurface.

However, because of his innate ability to control his visible emotions, he also believed he would never know the truth behind the how of what he had done. Externally, all was well. Internally, life was just something Sebastiane figured he'd constantly struggle with because of it. He detested having to lockup certain things deep inside, encasing it all within an unknown pain and suffering, and then entrenching it all behind mountainously high walls of manufactured regret, and finally dangling it all at the end of a very long rope constructed of hopeful redemption. It was a malaise that manifested as a lack of confidence, something he hated just as much as the nightmares.

Fortunately he was young, and hoped life would provide him the opportunity to make amends. Unfortunately he was untrained and uninformed, and therefore wrong—he just didn't know it yet. The burden he would have to carry for these, as of yet, unknown abilities was not something brought on by his own actions or indiscretions, but was an accumulation of the actions and choices of the past—a past only one person could explain. That one person was someone he had not met. And since he hadn't, the realization he would come to much later in life was that his burden and the price he thought he had to pay for it were in fact one and the same. They were not individual things but were a simultaneous, coexistent mass. They were brothers but not siblings, always together and impossible to separate. This realization was the unobtainable truth he couldn't yet contemplate.

Still staring across the void at the stop sign, Sebastiane's unfocused mind allowed the images of that day to float to the surface. He tried to fight them, but gave in to the hope that today would be that one last time. So, for this one last time he set his mind adrift. And wander back his mind did, back to the days when a young man thought himself invincible. It was a time when most young men believed that real life, its trials and responsibilities, were things that happened later. It was a time when youth meant everything and nightmares became a thing of the past. It was a day that had encapsulated a horrifyingly unfortunate event, transfixing an imprint into the memories of a fourteen-year-old boy who had almost killed that bastard.

CHAPTER 2

Gretna, Louisiana, 1992

"Outstanding! Well done! Now, go, go, go!" shouted Coach Jerry from the sideline. Coach Jerry, Juan Javier Antonio Rivera to his mother, was flabbergasted by his young star's ability to play the game he himself had grown up trying to perfect on the streets of San Juan, Puerto Rico.

The kid just knows how to do something by seeing it once.

It was an amazing skill set, one in which Coach Jerry hoped might propel Sebastiane into a possible career. For now, it was a true pleasure to just admire his star player's instinctive ability and swift recovery from a deftly performed and magnificently executed slide tackle against the opposition's star striker. The tackle was from behind, but not through the legs. Using his cupped foot and ankle, Sebastiane slid feet-first, stopped the ball, popped up with it at his own feet, and took off back up the field. The striker went flying through the air, landing on his belly just outside the eighteen-yard box, and rolled dramatically to shield his pride from his own coach at being dispossessed just so. His coach frowned. Coach Jerry smiled.

"That's a yellow card. Come on, Ref!" The cry came from the opposition's bench, accompanied by moans and groans from many orange-shirted parents cheering on their garment-matched children.

"Damn right no yellow card, jackass," Sebastiane uttered to himself as he went on the offensive. He yelled, "Brandon!" And with a precise twenty-yard pass, Sebastiane put the ball right at the feet of his advancing teammate.

Sebastiane then sprinted forward down the right-hand touchline as Brandon juked towards the center of the field, around one defender, and was now looking to pass. As a different defender came up, hampering Brandon's midfield progress, he quickly realized the only spot to put a pass was deep into the right-hand corner and let a teammate run onto it. This Brandon did. And there was Sebastiane, outrunning all the others to catch up to it to maintain possession.

Collecting the ball while angling his head up to evaluate his options, Sebastiane looked into the center of the field. He was running out of real estate with only ten yards left to the end line. He had to pick out a target, fast. Two of his teammates, one flashing toward the middle of the goal area, the other covering the back post, were both available. With a strong and controlled out-swinger, he sent the ball into the area.

The goalie froze, not sure whether to come out and get it or to hang back and... too late. Anticipation from the crowd grew as Ibrahim, waiting at the back post, stuck out his left foot and angled the delivered cross into the net.

Cheers erupted from the stands. Ibrahim jumped up and down as the rest of the team mobbed him. Sebastiane began jogging back into position for the restart when Ibrahim looked over to his teammate and nodded. A sly grin was returned. The score was now 3-1, with what had to be only seconds remaining on the clock. The whistle blew not thirty seconds after the restart, ending the game.

A mad, mosh pit of players congregated in the middle of the field. Jumping up and down, they started chanting, "We're number one... we're number one!"

Coach Jerry and a majority of the parents ran onto the field to join them. When they stopped celebrating, Coach Jerry singled out his star player. "That was amazing, Sebastiane. You are beyond your years, and I hope you stick with this game—one goal and two assists." To the rest of the team, Coach Jerry proclaimed, "Can I get an MVP?"

"You damn skippy." The exuberant and singularly timed reply was shouted by the whole team, and was accompanied by a big cheesy smile from Sebastiane. It was the team's joking expression—basically it was a *yes, sir.*

More high fives were exchanged and louder yelling echoed throughout the park as Coach Jerry pronounced in as loud a voice as he could muster after all his yelling during the game, "Ladies and gentlemen, friends and family, I present to you the Jefferson Parish Parks & Recreation Department's, thirteen and fourteen-year-old soccer champions—your Westbank All-Stars!"

"Yeah!" erupted from players and parents alike.

Coach Jerry looked around and saw only one thing missing. He motioned for Sebastiane to come back over, and asked, "I saw your mother, but what about the rest of your cheering section?"

"Not sure," replied Sebastiane. "Probably couldn't get a ride over. Their uncle was going to bring them, but knowing him he was probably late so...." He ended his statement with a shoulder shrug, gathered up his bag and water bottle, and his shiny new trophy, high-fived his coach, and sprinted to his mother's waiting car.

Elena had watched the whole game, and had participated in the cheering from the stands, but was now walking to her car very quickly so they could hustle home. Of course she knew exactly where he wanted to go; definitely not home, and not out to celebrate with the team at some pizza place or other fast-food restaurant, but straight to the girls' house.

Sometimes Elena wondered if her son was with Heather and Sarah too much. He would soon be a man, and only the Lord knew what was going on in his mind. She knew he had at least kissed Heather, and presumed that quite possibly they had done other things—she wasn't naive. She had taught him well, though, well enough for him to understand that if he didn't completely respect either of those sweet girls she would have grounded him for the rest of his life—not to mention what his grandmother would have done to him. That threat in and of itself would probably have been enough. However, Elena also saw to it that her son had gotten the traditional rendition of the *birds and the bees* from his father. Those two things combined would more than likely guarantee he was not sexually active with anyone, let alone Heather and Sarah. Also, she reflected, dating either one of them would most likely end their friendships. For Sebastiane, she knew he would never allow that to happen.

Ever since he'd met the Prescott twins he'd been enamored by them. Nancy Prescott, their mother, did her best to be as good a mother as she could, and it hadn't been easy for her. Her underprivileged upbringing in southern Mississippi had led to a rebellious and not-so-unintentionally, unplanned pregnancy at the age of seventeen. She'd decided to escape to New Orleans with her deadbeat boyfriend who had then inevitably strayed and then abandoned her with three-month-old twin girls. Too proud to go home, Nancy had done what she needed to. She struggled with everything—from putting food on the table, to keeping a roof overhead, and sometimes even buying clothes—but eventually got lucky and fell into a job as a legal secretary with a large corporate law firm in the downtown New Orleans Central Business district.

In the beginning she still struggled, and sometimes even worked a second job to make ends meet. But even when the pay got better, she still worked both so she could send her girls to a better school. That better school ended up being the same well-respected, relatively inexpensive private academy Sebastiane attended. She even got help from her pseudo brother-in-law, David, when he came to visit from his oilfield jobs in the Gulf of Mexico. He would stay with them and help with the girls. If he couldn't, they would end up at the Bassett household doing homework or just playing in the backyard until Nancy would pass by on her way home from work.

Heather and Sarah Prescott were actually very sweet and very respectful girls. So far neither of them had shown a propensity towards any of their mother's youthful mischief. And when Nancy Prescott and her twin girls came over for barbecues and crawfish boils, they always helped Elena prepare the tables and chairs—and of course, helped with the cleanup.

Identical not fraternal twins, with cotton-top blonde hair that exposed hues of light brown as they'd aged, uniquely blue-grayish eyes, and matching wardrobes, which made it virtually impossible to tell them apart, it was no wonder Sebastiane acted like a lovesick puppy and a big brother protector all at the same time.

The car door slammed shut as Sebastiane jumped in the back seat of his mother's four-door sedan. He asked, "Can I stop by the girls' house just for a little while, please?"

With eyes towards the sky and an exasperated exhale she agreed, "Yes. Just not too long. Your father mentioned something about going out to dinner tonight, okay?"

"Yes, ma'am."

After a ten-minute drive, in which Sebastiane had enough time to change, Elena came to a stop on the corner of 9th Street and Huey P. Long Boulevard to let him out. Practically flying out of a still-rolling car with his trophy in hand, he yelled, "Be home in a few."

Elena rolled down the driver-side window and shouted at him as he walked away, "Rappelez-vous, venez à la maison bientôt. S'il vous plaît."

When his mother used her native tongue, Sebastiane always answered in kind and did as he was told, "Oui, ma mere. Je le ferai."

Sebastiane strutted down 9th Street with a spring in his step and a peacock's tail spread wide and filled with pride.

They're going to love this.

He always beamed from ear to ear when Heather smiled at his accomplishments. Sarah usually just rolled her eyes and would say something like—*was there ever a doubt.* He couldn't wait to show them his newest prize. Then, suddenly, a puzzled expression crinkled up his face as he tried to figure out why they weren't at his game.

He should have brought them over to the park. They should have been there, late uncle or not.

As he continued walking up the street, Sebastiane's puzzled expression festered into something akin to that of a morbid darkness accompanying the fear of learning a horrible truth. That expression changed yet again, matching his internally growing uneasiness, when he saw Sarah sitting on her across-the-street neighbor's, Mr. and Mrs. Domenici's, front porch. He picked up the pace and was in front of her and Mrs. Domenici before they realized it.

Sarah initially jumped, then began wiping away the flood of tears from her eyes to see who it was. She relaxed when she realized it was Sebastiane, but only a little.

Mrs. Domenici, with her frail, eighty-year-old body, was curled around Sarah like a protective cloak, hoping against hope that her wisdom and experiences in life would help hide the shame the little one must be feeling at that moment. She also hoped that the cloak would hide her own culpability with what had occurred, and with what had always been occurring, inside the Prescott house just across the street. The old lady finally looked up and said, "Sebastiane. Young man. Come here and sit."

He looked down at her and asked, "What's going on?" He shifted his gaze. "Sarah? You good?"

Sarah didn't answer but started crying again as she buried her head deeper into Mrs. Domenici's shoulder. The old lady began to sympathetically rub the young girl's back and hug her more tightly. Sebastiane leaned down to ask his question again, but Eloise Domenici put out her hand, signaling restraint.

Suddenly, Mr. Domenici shouted confidently from just inside the open front door, "I called. They'll be here any time now. I called the—" As he exited the house onto the porch, struggling to pick up the front legs of his walker over the threshold so he didn't trip and fall, Mr. Domenici stopped cold and went quiet when he noticed Sebastiane. He averted his eyes away from the young man and down to his wife as if trying to hide the same untold truth, and finally said, "I called the police."

Sebastiane's reaction was instantaneous. "What! Why did you call the police?" His eyes shifted from the old man back down to his friend, "Sarah?"

It was only then that Sebastiane noticed the broken piece of twine knotted around Sarah's left wrist, as well as the dried blood on it and the matching dried blood around her mouth. Then, a truly horrendous thought entered Sebastiane's mind. "Where's Heather?"

He started to lean down again, but Sarah looked up at him with empty, expressionless eyes. Her continuous crying, and now shivering, began to resonate like an earthquake in his bones. Internally Sebastiane didn't know what he was feeling. His senses seemed to want to go into overdrive. Before he knew it, his adrenaline kicked in. It not only ignited a spark within him but began over-fueling all of his internal mechanisms with a deliberately strange and otherworldly intoxication of strength, awareness…and something else entirely. The adrenaline he called upon for his soccer games gave him the ability to outrun and outthink most any opponent—but that was sports. This was something completely different from anything he'd ever experienced before.

What is this? What is going on?

Whatever it was, it exposed raw feelings and unquantifiable sensations within him that instantaneously boiled over into an unknowable glare of uncontrollable rage.

Mrs. Domenici saw it first. "Don't you go over there, young man. Don't you dare! The police are on their way, and—" She stopped mid-sentence and looked to her husband with fear-filled eyes as the young boy completely ignored her, turned, and began walking purposefully across the street to the Prescott home.

CHAPTER 3

Hearing no further shouts of protest, Sebastiane continued across the street, up the driveway, and then up the three, small steps to reach the front door of 931 9th Street. The silence was deafening as he slowly entered the house.

The Prescott family had lived here since he'd known them, and he'd spent many a night sneaking into and then out of it when the girls wanted to watch scary movies or just talk. He saw nothing as he entered. He left the front door ajar. Pausing to take in the scene, he moved forward and to his left to bypass the empty front room. Seconds later he arrive at the full-length corridor that stretched all the way down the left side of the structure—the main feature of the modest, shotgun-style home. He peeked cautiously around the corner. He saw nothing out of place, and saw no one. He paused again, listening for any hint of sound or movement. Nothing. His heart was racing. His mind and his actions, however, were calm, cool, deliberate, and collaborative. No thoughts of how or why, just purpose. And no fear.

THERE!

The faint wisps of someone sobbing uncontrollably, muffled to near incoherence by the presence of hands covering the face. It was coming from one of the back bedrooms. He made his way towards the source of the sound with movements that were silent and exact. He was completely unaware he was even purposely avoiding all the creaks of the warped, wooden floorboards as he continued down the corridor.

As he passed the small kitchen and dining area, he noticed the other end of the bloodied twine from Sarah's wrist knotted through the refrigerator door handle. He took note of the butcher block full of old and worn knives stashed on top of the cabinet on the far wall. He noticed the telephone cord was ripped from the wall. He also noticed a kitchen towel with duct tape stuck to it laying in the middle of the floor. He continued on.

The faint wisps had become more pronounced now and he heard... splashing water! It seemed to be coming from the 'Jack and Jill' bathroom that separated the girls' bedrooms, so he passed the door to Sarah's room and stopped at the door to Heather's. Glancing to his left, toward the back door and their mother's room at the end of the corridor, he saw no movement. He reached out for the antique-looking, crystal ball-shaped, acrylic knob on Heather's bedroom door and turned it slowly to the left because Heather had told him it wouldn't make any noise if it was turned that way. He didn't think it, he just did it.

Everything was coming at him now in a much slower motion than the last forty-six seconds had. He was consciously unaware of the fact that every second of his continuing advance had been preceded by a logical, determined thought process acting like a computer algorithm in his mind. This meticulous, analytical precision led to a definition of purpose that had culminated in conclusive actions and had allowed him to enter the house, walk silently and swiftly down the corridor, and then enter Heather's room without being detected.

As he slowly pushed the door open his eyes immediately locked onto Heather. She was sitting on the bed, head in her hands, right arm around and through the metal frame of the headboard as if clinging to a life preserver. And at that moment, he knew. He knew the truth of the lie that had hidden itself inside the Prescott home all these years.

All those times he'd noticed an emotional indifference from them, either at school or at his house, when they weren't really joking with anyone or simply trying desperately not to look at him, as if doing so was somehow wrong and possibly even shameful, came to the forefront of his understanding. He could never quite figure it out before and never asked, but now he knew. The combined feelings he had inside, the helplessness and worthlessness he was experiencing at having not protected them from this, locked up his muscles. Vengeance mixed with pure rage began to overtake him.

The splashing stopped. Then, a very gentle, menacing, and eerily satisfactory whistle came from inside the bathroom just loud enough to penetrate its closed event horizon. Heather's head popped up at the expectation of what was to come and Sebastiane could see the intense fear in her eyes. He could feel them pierce his soul as they swiveled past him towards the bathroom door. Suddenly, she glanced back at him. Her look of fear recast itself into one of uneasy relief, hidden behind an expression of perceived inevitability at what was going to happen to her even though he was there.

~

Sgt. Davis and Patrol Officer Anderson's police car came to a screeching halt in the middle of the street in order to block traffic. Both men quickly exited the vehicle while placing batons in already overburdened utility belts. Anderson surveyed the scene before looking over at Mr. Domenici. He asked, "Sir, you called 9-1-1?"

"Yes. He's in there," answered Alfred Domenici, as he pointed at the Prescott house. "The other girl, Heather, is in there too. And so is a boy, Sebastiane...a friend of the girls."

Another police car with two more officers pulled up opposite the first, blocking off the street in both directions. An ambulance from the volunteer fire station just down the road followed, sirens blaring as it arrived. Two paramedics exited the typical-looking red-and-white van. The young female EMT grabbed her medical kit and ran toward the Domenici home knowing exactly the type of emergency call that had come in over the radio. As a woman and a paramedic, EMT Melissa Downs knew her first priority was a reportedly molested little girl; no, a young woman, she realized, when she arrived at the porch steps. Steven Habers, a younger-looking but more experienced emergency medical technician, sought out the officers already on scene.

Sgt. Davis started giving commands, "You, Habers, is it?" he asked, looking down at the name tag and gesturing with his forefinger and thumb. "Stay behind us and wait for us to call you in. Got it?" With a head nod, Habers took up his position. Davis then looked at Anderson, "Partner? It's your turn, buddy. You're primary."

Davis continued giving orders to the other officers on the scene, directing one towards the back of the house and the other to stay as backup in the street. The officers drew their weapons, hoping not to have to use them but secretly wanting to inflict some sort of damage on what they had been told was a child molester, and began their approach towards 931 9th Street.

~

Across the room from where Heather was cowering in fear, with Sebastiane still standing at the room's entrance, the door to the bathroom slowly opened. Both sets of youthful eyes fixated on its movement. With a stunned realization, and a confused understanding of who it was, Sebastiane recognized Nancy Prescott's brother-in-law, David James Bourgeois, exit the bathroom. He was almost completely naked except for two things—a small towel around his waist, which he was currently staring down at and trying to fix, and a collection of cheap-looking gold chains around his neck that all but covered up his unsightly mass of chest hair.

Uncle Dave, as Sebastiane knew him, wasn't but five foot nine. With muscles randomly covered in tattoos, and built like tank armor from all his years on the oil rigs, he was a grotesque sight with black, slicked-backed hair, a small forehead, and sunken brown eyes under even thicker eyebrows. He had a curved nose, and a thick, wiry mustache. His small mouth and yellowed teeth kept whistling, portraying an exuding sexual satisfaction over one fourteen-year-old girl—and lustful desires towards the other.

David James Bourgeois looked up to see the tussled, soiled sheets on the bed, saw his next victim staring right back at him, and became aroused. His whole body tingled with anticipation. He rubbed his hands together, menacingly.

Well, time for seconds. Probably the last time anyway. I need to find something younger next. These two are a little too old for my tastes. After I get back from my Nigeria contract, maybe I'll move to Florida. They got cute little beach bunnies with cute little daughters all over the place. God only knows I don't want to get AIDS in Africa, so the next nine months are out. Better make this one count.

His self-absorbed, sadistic attitude had made him oblivious to the fact that someone else besides his prey was in the room, and to the sirens outside that had just stopped.

Sebastiane had noticed the sirens, but his mind told him not to concentrate on distractions; his focus was to remain on what had become the target of his rage. His body flexed ever so slightly in anticipation of what was to come. The distance between himself and the sadistic conqueror was calculated to be a mere seven feet. Sebastiane covered it in less than a second. He planted his left foot in the carpet and swung his right leg up underneath the towel. The strike landed exactly where intended.

David James Bourgeois's lungs moaned. They tried to grab at the air escaping from them when the pain from the strike reached his brain to tell him something was wrong. He fell straight down onto both knees after being lifted off the ground by the power of hatred and revenge.

Heather screamed at the unexpected and sudden violence. She screamed louder, thinking Sebastiane was in danger, when he moved in closer to her attacker.

As his target toppled forward in agony, Sebastiane grabbed at the mass of gold chains around David James Bourgeois's neck and pulled them upwards and outwards to keep him upright. Sebastiane stared at him, not saying a word, as the bastard opened his eyes to see who it was that had inflicted such abominable pain upon him.

Through an agonizing cough and another attempted gasp for air, a request for mercy and a feeble excuse for his actions fell on deaf ears, "Wait! I can explain."

Sebastiane grabbed tighter at the mass of gold chains, infuriated by any attempt to justify the hideousness of his actions and the damage inflicted upon his friends. "Explain this," whispered Sebastiane angrily, as he threw back his arm to begin his next bodily assault.

~

Both Anderson and Davis heard the screams of what their minds were telling them was a young female and decided to throw caution to the wind. They could see that the front door was ajar, and both entered the house at a steady pace with Anderson in front. He swept right to check behind the door while Davis continued left and then straight ahead, pausing only to get his bearings. At the entrance to the long corridor, they paused when they heard something.

THUD!

The sound came from the back of the house. Both officers moved forward, weapons up, scanning for signs of movement. As Davis approached an open bedroom door, he could see a young girl sitting on a bed with a look of utter shock on her face. He advanced into the bedroom with Anderson in his wake, turned right, and saw a young boy standing over a man who was on his knees and being held up by something around his neck—a wincing pain etched on his face in blood. The young boy had his right arm cocked back, so Davis quickly holstered his weapon and lunged forward to stop it.

Sebastiane had already landed his first punch right into David James Bourgeois's nose and left orbital socket, breaking both; his head had jerked backwards from the blow and his nose spewed blood. When it fell forward, his neck not having the strength to keep it upright, Sebastiane tightened his grip on the gold chains and pulled David James Bourgeois's head back up for another blow.

As he threw his right arm back, Sebastiane felt something grab and lock onto his forearm. Something was trying to stop the momentum he needed to inflict more pain. Instinctively, Sebastiane twisted his arm clockwise, dropped his body weight slightly, and pulled his arm down to free it from the viselike grip. Once free, he lunged forward. Sebastiane landed a round-house to the side of the bastard's face, separating the temporo-mandibular joint and knocking two teeth down his throat.

Without the counterweight anticipated by grabbing on to and holding the boy's arm, Davis lost his balance and fell backwards into Anderson. Both men then fell backwards into the bedroom doorway.

"Shit!" yelled Anderson, as he dropped his weapon and tumbled into the doorframe, knocking his head on it. The blow was enough to stun him but not stop him. He reached out to find his weapon before continuing into the fray.

Davis had been in fights before, losing some but winning most. Undaunted by the setback, he collected himself and then paused to wonder why he needed to stop what was happening. Guessing correctly at who was who in the scenario before him, he thought he should just let the kid beat the crap out of the pedophile—but he couldn't. Davis was an officer of the law and sworn to uphold it for all, even those who might eventually be found guilty. When Davis made it to his knees, he lunged forward while screaming, "A little help in here…."

The request for assistance was answered by EMT Habers, who ran in from the front, and by Officer Wilms, who kicked his way into the house through the back door.

With his third punch, Sebastiane aimed for the solar plexus. He wanted to knock out all the remaining air from David James Bourgeois's lungs and paralyze the diaphragm to prevent him from breathing in any more oxygen. As the punch barreled forward, Sebastiane's right leg was pulled back and out from under him. His left leg followed, and his punch lacked any significant power as he fell towards the floor. He let go of the gold chains and landed on the floor in the push-up position.

Intuitively, Sebastiane turned his body counterclockwise and used his left foot to lash out, making contact with Davis's forehead. Doing so caused the officer to lose his grip, again. With his leg free, Sebastiane continued his turn, landed in a crouched position, and found himself staring right into a very vulnerable and ironic piece of anatomy. He lunged at it with an open hand, grabbed at the exposed flesh, and clenched his fist as hard as he could.

Forced to release his grip on the young man's right leg due to the kick to his forehead, Davis was lying flat on the ground and clutching his head. This allowed Anderson, back on his feet now, to jump over and dive on top of the boy. Anderson's added weight forced Sebastiane's arm down just as his fist clenched, tearing David James Bourgeois's scrotal sac wide open.

The pain unleashed a bloodcurdling scream, announcing to Habers and Wilms that something drastic was happening inside the bedroom that required immediate attention. As they entered, Wilms angled to assist Anderson while Habers started towards Heather. He immediately changed direction when he saw the spray of blood and the source of the screams coming from the other side of the room.

"Stop hurting him. Stop! Please!" screamed Heather, as Anderson, Wilms, and Davis began to gain an advantage, by pure numbers only, and were finally able to restrain Sebastiane.

Habers found his way around the pile of humanity and began to assess the damage and try to stop the bleeding. Seeing what had been torn away, Habers moved quickly. More personnel entered the already crowded bedroom as Heather continued her verbal protests.

A third EMT, not quite knowing where the blood was coming from, raced towards the girl sitting on the bed and began trying to check her over. As he did, she pulled away, continually screaming and flailing at him. She didn't want to be touched. He backed off.

It took every ounce of their combined strengths for the three officers to keep the boy from wriggling free. Anderson shared a look of amazement with the others. Their returning glances asked the same question.

Why was it so hard to keep this kid down?

The three officers, after considerable trouble, finally got two sets of handcuffs on the boy; one securing his hands behind his back, the other around his ankles.

~

With its finality—a finality that had started with emotional rage and violent confrontation, continued through a physical rampage, and had ended with an overwhelmingly vengeful crescendo—the hidden and unknown inner persona of Sebastiane Maurice Bartholomew Renault-Bassett paused, confronted its imprisoned status, accepted it, and became compliantly calm. From release and exposure to subdued and quieted, this unrealized persona crept back down through the dark recesses of Sebastiane's mind and retreated into the depths of his subconscious to hide itself from being seen.

Behind wide-open eyes, eyes searching for answers to the truth of what had just occurred, Sebastiane's inner persona smirked in retrospect at a job well done before it disappeared. It gave no other signs or explanations as to how or why, nor did it show any other recriminations for its appearance. And now, with its job completed, it rested, peacefully, like a babe in a manger. It would only come out again when needed or when required to do so—but only when threatened, or asked.

Released from the clutches of the unknown entity that had possessed him and his actions, Sebastiane looked at Heather and saw that she was safe. He smirked at her ever so slightly, and then smiled at her thankfully.

Heather stared back at him, not quite understanding what she was seeing.

What is that look on your face?

She finally found the ability to exhale in exhausted relief and began crying tears of muted joy when Sebastiane smiled at her.

Relieved, Sebastiane closed his eyes to search for the truth of what he'd just done. He found nothing. There was no answer and no explanation. This thing, this unknown capacity for vengeance through violence, acting like some all-powerful beast from ancient folklore or a creature from a children's book used by parents as a moralistic fairy tale, entering from places unknown and ready to pounce at a moment's notice, had gone deathly silent. He couldn't feel it. He couldn't see it. He couldn't ask it the question, how? Or why? He wanted answers. He needed answers. Nothing replied.

CHAPTER 4

Things were calm now. The buzz of activity outside the Prescott home had morphed into a panic parade of neighborhood onlookers held back by police-tape barricades and straining to see what was happening—all were speculating furiously. Inside the house, final preparations were being made to clear the situation.

The soon-to-be guest of the Louisiana State penal system had been stabilized for his trip to the ER where a valiant but vain attempt by the hospital's vascular surgeon wasn't enough to save the right side of David James Bourgeois's manhood. His jaw, teeth, and nose would eventually heal.

Nancy Prescott had been in the breakroom at her office getting coffee when her name was called over the intercom. When she arrived at the front desk, her heart sank. She was brought home by Orleans Parish police detectives at the request of the Gretna Police Department. Now, she clutched on to her two girls as tightly as she could, under the watchful yet hypersensitive supervision of a Children's Protection Services Officer, as they sat on the Domenici's front room couch.

Sebastiane was still under restraint inside the Prescott home. Thinking a change of scenery would keep him calm, he had been moved to the front room by the officers. He was sitting on the couch, blood on his hands, arms, and shirt from the struggle. He was staring unequivocally at the one called Sgt. Davis whose attention was focused elsewhere.

Davis was flanked by Anderson as Wilms stood guard just outside the front door. Anderson had his hand on his holstered sidearm, and Davis noticed. "Hey, partner. It's time to calm down. You okay?"

"How big do you think Wilms is?" Anderson jerked his head in the direction of the front door, his eyes never leaving the general direction of the couch.

"I don't know, two-hundred twenty, two-hundred thirty pounds maybe," answered Davis, wondering why the question was asked. "He looks to be the same as you, maybe a little smaller, but not much."

This time Anderson directed his question, tainted slightly with distrustful admiration, towards the young man on the couch, "How old are you, kid?"

The reply came via a contemptuous, cold, calculating, yet controlled glare that seemed to penetrate directly through Anderson's eyes and deep into his soul, all the while showing absolutely no fear and no remorse. Lasting just long enough, Sebastiane returned to staring at Davis and left Anderson with the unsettling feeling that someone had just walked over his grave. Sebastiane wasn't trying to be belligerent—not on purpose anyway. He was simply trapped in his own thoughts, still seeking explanations for what he had done and how he had done it. And why, why was he so comfortable with it?

What did I do?

Sebastiane was asking himself the same questions over and over again. He closed his eyes to relive the entire experience one agonizingly slow second at a time. As the end of the replay culminated in his mind, he squeezed his hands. Finally, he released them and relaxed. Overwhelmed by a sense of moral justification, and yet unable to quantify the abilities he'd used to render the judgment dispensed, Sebastiane quickly devised and then constructed a compartmentalized state of mind. On one side he would consider the implications of his actions; on the other, he could allow himself to cope with it and move forward.

Hide whatever this is and whatever it can be deep inside, and never let it out again.

He opened his eyes to a new world, a world now defined by a failed realization disguised as self-restraint. Sebastiane believed that through introspection he had control over what just happened.

Wilms leaned inside the door and motioned to Davis, "The kid's parents are here."

"Okay. Let them in," replied Davis, hoping the parents would continue the calming trend.

As Elena came in the front door, Davis motioned for her to keep her distance. She disobeyed, went straight to her son, and wrapped her arms around him. Edward Bassett came up to Davis and quietly asked what was happening. Davis, foregoing her refusal to comply with his order to keep her distance by acknowledging a mother's need to protect her child, took the father aside to fill in the blanks.

Elena leaned back to look into her son's eyes and vaguely recognized something within them. Her son stared back, hoping for a sign of understanding and explanation. The explanation she wanted to give him couldn't come, not here, and she knew that. Her understanding of his need for forgiveness for what had happened and what he'd done was maternally automatic, though; and yet, at the same time, she chastised herself for not telling him about this—about his grandfather.

She didn't know much about the Renault family history, but enough of what she did know may have prevented her son from ever having this look in his eyes. It was a look she remembered from one night in particular when she lived in Algeria many years ago. It was the night she had seen the same look in her father's eyes and overheard the explanation to her mother about how he had handed some criminals over to a man named Hadj.

If she'd told Sebastiane about his grandfather, Elena's eyes began welling up, maybe, she thought, maybe she might have been able to prepare him for this. But no, it wouldn't have. She realized her son's actions would not have been any different. Her father, she'd come to realize, had only explained what he had done for the man named Hadj, not justified it. Her mother's acknowledgment of that fact, with a soft kiss on his cheek and a gaze of acceptance stating that her understanding was not an act of absolution, had nevertheless brought the life back to his eyes that night. Elena kissed her son gently on the cheek.

This is my fault.

She should have prepared him for this. She could have given him what he needed, maybe. Elena trapped her guilt behind a smile, realizing she was too late. She wanted to tell him even now, but couldn't. She would have to wait until he was free from the fallout of this incident, hoping for his sake that it would be over sooner rather than later. She asked, "Can we take him home now?"

Sgt. Davis answered, "We have finished questioning him, but we'll need to follow up at a later date. You should be hearing from one of the detectives in the next day or two."

Davis motioned for Anderson to remove the hand and ankle cuffs. There was no point in keeping this minor in custody let alone taking him into the station. Davis actually felt some deference towards the kid. Hopefully it wouldn't scar him for life. Hopefully, he would never do this again. Davis tried to imagine what this young man would be like when he got older and something like this happened again. Davis shook his head to clear the thought.

When Anderson finished with the cuffs, Sebastiane stood. With his mother and father at his side he walked out through the front door and left behind the life of an ordinary, everyday fourteen-year-old boy. As he watched the ambulance pull away with his two best friends inside, he took a deep, satisfying breath. He thought to himself that regardless of whatever came next, he knew he had done right. And because of that feeling of justification, henceforth and unknowingly, Sebastiane Maurice Bartholomew Renault-Bassett had just accepted his expected position as the next hereditary contributor to the ongoing chronicle that was the Renault family legacy.

CHAPTER 5

Gretna, Louisiana, 1996

HONK! The acoustical frustrations blasting from the car behind him snapped Sebastiane back to the present. He apologetically raised his hand at the driver of the Chevrolet Cavalier in his rearview mirror who was trying to turn right. Sebastiane accelerated up the street and then came to a stop again in front of 931 9th Street.

As he exited his truck, he saw Heather standing at the front door, waiting. When he got to her, she jumped into his arms. A big, fat kiss on the lips and a genuine smile of adoration coaxed his reply, "Hello to you too, dear. Graduation Day awaits. Everyone ready?"

"Smart-ass," she replied, as she kissed him again and tightened her grip around his neck.

Sebastiane loved Heather, and always had. He loved Sarah too and they were all the very best of friends, but Heather was different. The two of them had even dated once, but it ended quickly. Not wanting anything to come between the three of them, like the complications of young love, Heather and Sebastiane mutually broke it off. Fortunately for him they remained friends with an underlying… something. It was a something that just wouldn't go away and frequently led to many a late-night kiss, but never advanced any further.

Heather finally let go and they proceeded into the house to get Sarah. Heather shouted, "Hey, Sis. You ready yet?"

"In a minute," Sarah shouted back, frustratingly.

Heather led Sebastiane into the kitchen. She made her way to the refrigerator and fished inside for some orange juice. She offered him some. He declined. As she shut the door, she asked him, "So, what's the plan for this evening?"

"Whatever you want. But might I suggest Ryan's party. His parents are supplying the drinks, playing chaperon, and his older brother Greg is keymaster." He paused for a second before giving her an option, hating to have to say it. "Besides that, we could always go to the French Quarter."

Sebastiane didn't like going there for one simple reason—he didn't like to dance. The girls loved it, especially Sarah. And any anonymous group of guys in town for a party night in downtown New Orleans usually liked the view when twin sisters danced together. The girls loved the attention.

"Ryan's is fine…. Sarah? You good for Ryan's tonight?" she shouted again, so as to be heard over the distraction of the hairdryer.

"Yep," came the return shout.

Sarah looked into the mirror as she continued her arduous beautification process, trying as quickly as possible to complete her tasks. She was still doing her hair and wasn't fully dressed yet. She wanted to look perfect. High school was over, finally, and college was beckoning, loudly. She couldn't wait for the fall semester to start so she could move up to Baton Rouge, find an apartment, decorate it just so, get a job, and start classes at Louisiana State University. Heather and Sebastiane had the same feelings and ideas about college, the apartment, and everything else. Life was going to be just that—life. No more hiding. And no more living in fear of what was.

It had taken four long years to get over her disenchanted childhood, a process started by her 'big brother' in the other room. Sarah was thankful for that. She had always wanted a brother, maybe a younger one to dote over, but life had played a cruel trick on her and her sister so a big brother was what she got. It was definitely what she'd needed. She continued with her eyeliner, half staring at her eyes and half staring into her thoughts.

When today is over, tomorrow will become a new beginning; and besides, Baton Rouge is only ninety minutes away. It is far enough to start anew but still close to Mom.

Sarah picked up her silver watch from the vanity and realized she was now really late... again. And she still wasn't anywhere near finished either.

"Damn it!" Sarah instinctively jerked her arm backward after accidentally touching her wrist on the hot curling iron sitting precariously on the counter. It was nothing major, but a small welt was forming. She needed ice. She made her way to the kitchen.

As she entered, she saw Sebastiane and Heather standing together by the kitchen sink talking—as usual. Sarah had always noticed his eternal burning flame for her sister; it was a constant twinkle in the corner of his eye when he stared at her. Sarah never quite understood why they didn't just get a hotel room and get it over with already.

Maybe Heather thinks it would ruin things. Maybe things might get awkward at the new apartment. Maybe they think I might be offended!

Sarah didn't think of Sebastiane that way. She thought of him as her big brother, with a definitive sappy side. He'd always been a complete mystery to her. From when they were younger to even now, she just couldn't quite figure him out. Boys were generally easy to understand; they liked tits and ass and sexual tension. She had command of the first two, and definitely loved playing with boys' emotions by using the third. But with him... he was just, well, strange—not in a bad way of course. Just, strange.

So many times she'd thought she had it. The most logical theory being that he was a hopeless romantic and that Heather craved the same thing, only living vicariously through him. It made sense. Sarah's proof for this theory was four-fold.

First was Sebastiane's passion for movies, accompanied by constant requests to watch either eighties' romantic comedies, sci-fi movies—that inevitably revolved around two people trying to survive alien hordes while finding time to have sex—or anything James Bond-ish.

Second was his annoying ability to not like one particular kind of music. He was very eclectic and had several mixed CDs for the stereo in his truck, which included everything from NewWave to Grunge to Classical, yet not in any civilized order.

Third was his ability to read as many books as possible, as if it were a contest; he was always finishing his history, math, or English literature homework first. Actually, this one turned out to be beneficially compensating to her utter inability to ever finish her own homework on time, so she let this one go. Then he would move on to some stuffy political book of the day, or something else typically classical in nature.

Fourth was his love of that damn game of soccer. *Sorry, football*, she told herself—he was always correcting her just so. However, it was this last proof that made him look damn good though. His muscular tone and constant presence always helped to make other boys jealous when she needed it.

The first three proofs made him who he was on the inside, and that was just fine—all the makings of a good big brother in her eyes. For Heather, Sarah hoped, they would all combine to make a really good boyfriend. Or maybe even a husband?

Yikes!

Sarah continued to stare at the two of them; they hadn't noticed her yet. She shook her head, foregoing all further attempts at understanding whatever it was that made him tick or understanding the mutual, unrealized attraction between her sister and him. Then she remembered the one thing that really made her comically nauseated—it was that damn poem. She began a fake and over-theatrical retching motion, with sound, and finally caught their attention. Hopefully they would get together soon, she thought, because this puppy love crap was starting to get a tad boring. She headed for the freezer, and upon opening it grabbed an ice cube from the tray to rub on her arm. She teased them, "Is he quoting more poetry to you, Sis?" It was a playful jest that completed her thought process behind the suggestive theatrics.

Quickly remembering what she was referring to, Sebastiane began his retort with a mockingly quaint, and hopelessly lost, English accent, *"To every captive soul and gentle heart, Unto whose sight may come the present word..."*

"Oh, God. Please stop. That stuff works on her, not me." Sarah glanced in Heather's direction, getting a smirk back in response. She continued, "Guys, I'm not ready yet. I'll take Mom's car and be right behind you."

Sebastiane immediately protested, "Hell no. We'll wait." He noticed the red welt on her arm and approached to assist with first aid. "What happened?"

"Curling iron. But really, don't wait for me. I won't be long. Just save me a seat—OUCH." Sarah winced as Sebastiane applied the ice to the burned area. As the pain began to subside, she giggled, "Really, don't wait. Besides, you can hang all over each other in the truck without me having to watch." Sarah stuck her tongue out at her sister and reached up on her tiptoes to plant a kiss on Sebastiane's cheek, solidifying her victory in the quick discussion.

Sebastiane glanced over at Heather, and with a shoulder shrug and a nod said, "Fine." Looking back to Sarah, he said, "You'd be late for your own funeral. You know that, right?" He kissed her cheek in return and reached inside his pants pocket, took out his Nokia flip phone, and placed in on the table for her.

Heather was already heading for the door, satisfied with the realization that this was ultimately the only outcome of the morning's preparations. Sarah was perpetually late for every damn thing, and it annoyed Heather only long enough for her to thank the Almighty for the one and only true difference between them. Heather found the keys to their mother's car and brought them back into the kitchen, jingled them in Sarah's direction, then set them down on the table next to the flip phone.

"Right behind ya." Sarah smiled as she headed back into the bathroom to finish getting ready.

Heather and Sebastiane exited the Prescott home. He opened the passenger door to his truck for her, made sure her gown wasn't hanging out after she got comfortable, and shut the door. Walking around the front of the truck, Sebastiane paused.

Seeing him standing there, motionless, Heather rolled down the passenger window and asked, "Hey! What's wrong? Did you forget something inside?"

He looked back at the front door to the Prescott home and then turned to look at Heather. He didn't know what it was, but he suddenly felt... off. Sebastiane took a long, deep breath to clear his head. He stepped towards the Prescott front door but then turned back around just as quickly.

The future starts today. Our future starts today.

He got in his truck, shut the door, started it up, put it into drive, and headed away from the house. He looked over and smiled at Heather as an answer to her question. She smiled back.

Heading in the direction of the Crescent City Connection, the main bridge connecting the Westbank and Eastbank of the Mississippi River in the heart of New Orleans, Heather sat close to Sebastiane on the bench seat. They talked about the day and about their future. They held hands.

CHAPTER 6

After completing her hair and makeup, Sarah was careful not to ruin it all while donning her graduation gown. Mid-donning, she heard the doorbell ring. She finished dressing, grabbed up her watch, placed in on her wrist, and headed to the front door.

She shouted, "It's only been, what, like ten minutes. Please make my day and tell me you forgot something." A giddy feeling of righteousness washed over her. Finally, she thought, it was Heather who would be late from absentmindedness. With a smug look full of that righteousness now smothered with hypocritical glee plastered all over her face, Sarah opened the door. "So, what did you forget?"

"I'd forgotten how good you look."

Sarah's expression quickly changed to an unrecoverable scowl, calcified by visions of days long past. It was an unfortunately dismal amalgam of self-loathing, shame, and self-reproach. As the undeniable smell of fear began to run down her legs, her whole body locked; it wouldn't move fast enough, couldn't move fast enough, away from the door. She could do nothing but stare at the incarnation of an evil long past leaning on the doorframe, hideous as ever, and unknowingly out on early parole.

"It's been way too long, little girl. You are as pretty as ever. Wow, what a woman you've grown up to be." With a satisfied grin and a large inhale, David James Bourgeois sadistically continued his taunt, "You smell wonderful, by the way." He stared at her body with a look of wonderment at what might be hiding under her maroon graduation gown, and his imagination completed the wetting of his appetite. The desire for surprise and the gloating at his success, mixed with his anger and need, made his mouth drool with anticipation. He licked his lips in as menacing a fashion as he could.

The vile persona at the door ate into Sarah's brain like a disease brought on by years of abusive neglect. The only thing she could do was start weeping, beg for mercy, and shuffle her feet backwards to escape his clutches by staying just out of arm's length as he walked into the house. He calmly closed the door behind him as Sarah's feeble attempts to retreat were thwarted when she backed into the coffee table, almost falling over.

He smiled when he realized the table and her fear had trapped her. He slithered towards her, saying, "Your sister and your little friend aren't here to help you, so allow *ME*." He grunted, spitefully, as he backhanded her, catching her flush in the right eye and knocking her over the coffee table and onto the couch.

Shock set in as Sarah heartbreakingly sobbed in fear for her life. Everything she hoped for faded to black as he mounted her. She couldn't struggle fast enough as he ripped at her maroon gown and the white shirt and shorts underneath, tearing them away with his long, unkempt nails that grated at her flesh as he did so. He smacked her again to discourage her from using her arms in self-defense.

Nearly knocking her out, David James Bourgeois paused. He wanted her to be awake for this. He pinned her arms against the top of the couch with his left hand and started undoing his pants with his right to present a manhood already excited by his long-repressed tendencies.

As Sarah's eyes reopened, she flinched. She tried to protect herself by closing her legs in the vain attempt to prevent his unwanted entry.

"Oh no," he protested. "I owe you for all those years in prison, you little bitch. What they did to me in there, you know, I'm going to do to you."

She fought to keep him off, but he was too strong. She did everything she could to stop it, but she was pinned down and half-naked, blood trickling down her arms and chest from defensive wounds caused by his violent disrobing of her.

It was over just as quickly as it had started. Sarah turned her head to stare out the window and saw the sky turn from a beautiful, sun-shining blue to an ominous, dark gray. She tried to scream, but couldn't. Her only thought was that, at least, it was over quickly. But, it was just the beginning.

As he pushed off her, breathing heavily from his exertion, David James Bourgeois looked down upon his niece, reared back, and smacked her in the face again; this time in the jaw, rendering her unconscious.

~

Sebastiane and Heather crossed the Greater New Orleans Bridge, exited at Tchoupitoulas Street, and continued into the Garden District area of New Orleans. The ceremony for their long-awaited graduation from De La Salle High School was to be held at the Holy Name of Jesus Church located on the Campus of Loyola University on St. Charles Avenue, across from Audubon Park. High school would finally be behind them; and thank the heavens for that, they thought, with a shared look while still holding hands. It had been difficult to say the least.

They had wanted to stay together after leaving middle school instead of the twins going to an all-girls school and Sebastiane attending the requisite all-boys school. The only other option was the local public school, but that discussion had been cut off rather quickly by both Nancy Prescott and Edward Bassett, respectively. Things became much easier for them when, rather fortunately, De La Salle High School in Uptown New Orleans converted from an all-boys school to a co-educational institution. So, through a considered and solid argument the three amigos were able to convince their parents to capitulate.

Nancy Prescott had no choice due to her rejection of a public school education for her little girls. She wanted better for them than she'd had and was determined to do what was necessary. She possessed the will to do what was needed for her twin girls, but didn't always have the means. Working overtime at a law firm to make extra money was never an issue, but the late-night invitations to drinks by married men, especially from her boss, bothered her. Nevertheless, she did what was needed to get her girls a better start in life—and those sacrifices were finally paying off. Edward Bassett on the other hand had wanted his son to attend his alma mater, but gave in reluctantly at Elena's request.

After several more minutes, in which traffic played a significant role, Sebastiane finally pulled over and parked just off campus and as close as he could to the church. Heather smiled joyously as he opened the passenger door for her, took her hand, and helped her out. After a short pause, and coordinated exhales, they turned and began to pass through vehicles stalled by that morning traffic and headed towards the church, arm in arm.

~

David James Bourgeois made his way into his sister-in-law's bedroom where he began rummaging through her dresser drawers looking for belts to restrain his conquest. She was stronger than he remembered, and he required something to help confine her aggression if he was to continue his revenge.

Out front, still on the couch, Sarah came to. Looking around, she wondered where her big brother was—wondered where Heather was. She hurt all over. She couldn't think what to do. Sarah knew she had to do something, though, if for nothing else than to save Heather from having to go through this again like she was. She whispered, "Help me."

Of course, they can't help. You told them to leave without you. You're always so late at everything. You deserve this. NO! Not this time. You escaped once before, so do it again. It's up to you. Get up. Get up, damn you!

She mustered as much strength as she could despite the aching she felt from the beating, the scratching, and the violation. She pulled her shirt down and her shorts up, leaving the tattered graduation gown on the floor. Suddenly, she remembered the keys to the car and the cellular phone left for her on the table. A surge of adrenaline, spurred on by the hope of an escape, concentrated her courage. She got up, walked silently into the kitchen, grabbed them up, and headed back to the front door with a purpose.

Opening the front door just wide enough and as quietly as possible, Sarah bolted towards her mother's car. Fumbling with the keys, dropping them once, she smashed the correct one into the door lock, turned it, and grabbed the handle to open it. The klaxon on the car's alarm started belching its noisy repertoire, but she didn't hesitate. She jumped inside, shut the door, and clambered to start the ignition.

Sarah screamed and jumped at the startlingly loud bang of something crashing on the windshield. She didn't look up as he made his way towards the driver's side door and then reach for the handle. She finally looked up and saw him, and screamed again. She pushed the lock down. He fiddled with the door handle. It moved, but the door didn't open. Using the precious seconds she'd gained, Sarah started the car, grabbed the wheel, threw the gearshift into reverse, and slammed down hard on the gas pedal.

The wheels spun wildly trying to gain traction, but the hand brake was engaged. A brick crashed against the doorframe and driver-side window before falling to the ground—shards of glass peppered her face and body. She felt his disgusting hand grab at her hair. She saw the brick swing up high in his other hand. The hand brake gave way under the strain. The tires gripped the concrete driveway and propelled the vehicle backwards twenty or so feet straight into a parked car.

Dazed from the impact, she looked up to see him walking towards her. The car was stalled. She tried the key. She began stomping on the pedal, flooding the engine with gas, and yanking forward on the ignition trying to restart it.

Come on... PLEASE!

She looked up just in time to see the hands of terror reaching in again, grabbing at her hair, again. The car started. She slammed the gearshift into drive and turned hard left.

Having only been able to grab on to the seat belt, David James Bourgeois was now holding on for his life as his feet and legs were being dragged alongside the vehicle as it sped off. He lashed out at her, trying to get a better grip on anything. When she inadvertently cut the angle of her turn too sharply, she side-swiped a parked car which pinned him between the two. The severe pain forced him to release his grip and fall away.

Sarah sped off, steering wheel in one hand and the cell phone in the other. Frantic, she dialed Sebastiane's phone number but didn't get a connection. She side-swiped several more parked cars. She started hyperventilating.

What is wrong with this thing?

Her frustration exploded into pure panic as the car raced faster and faster down the narrow street. She tried the phone again; still no connection. One blown stop sign and another attempted phone call—nothing. Two more stop signs, the second at Huey P. Long Boulevard as cross traffic screeched to a halt, and another phone call—still nothing. She passed the middle school the three of them had attended and remembered how and when her big brother had stopped all of this four years ago. She slammed the phone against the steering wheel, cursing it for its failure to connect.

Her eyes lost focus. In her attempt to put as much distance as she could between herself and a fate she needed so desperately to escape, she glanced up to see the long, narrow street grow hypnotically longer—as if it were stretching itself out and trying to deny her that distance. She stomped harder on the gas pedal, trying to push it through the floor. She blew through the stop sign at Lafayette Street; luckily, there was no cross traffic. All-in-all, her flight from fear lasted one very short mile, five blown stop signs, and four unsuccessful calls. At the sixth stop sign, and during her fifth attempt to make the phone somehow work, she didn't notice a city garbage truck that was completing its next neighborhood of the day.

The driver didn't notice her either until it was too late. He had no clear view of the intersection due to the large, overgrown, and poorly maintained bushes protruding from the house on the southwest corner. Giving him no time to swerve, the garbage truck driver could do nothing but slam on his brakes. He was lucky; the large metal behemoth was able to absorb the tiny car's impact, damaging only the front reinforced bumper. Unfortunately, the truck T-boned the much smaller two-door sedan. The sound was deafening as formed metal collapsed, violently compressing the passenger side and ricocheting Sarah's body throughout the crumpling interior. The impact sent the car flying, two inches off the ground and at the speed of light, until it slammed into a very old and very sturdy oak tree on the northeast corner. The car nearly broke in half.

~

Walking through the oversized wooden doors of the Holy Name of Jesus Church and finding the designated student seating area, Sebastiane set his cap down on the seat next to Heather in order to save it for Sarah as promised. As he sat down, he looked forward and gazed upon the large altar, and then at the stained-glass windows on either side of the pulpit in the cavernous, Gothic-styled House of God.

Sebastiane was not one enamored by religion. He hadn't come to realize anything about church or organized religion that could satisfy his inquiries about life. He just figured that if something was needed of him the man upstairs would let his servant, Sebastiane Maurice Bartholomew

Renault-Bassett, know, personally. He continued to look around, realizing he was sitting in and admiring the beauty of a moment in time that represented the doorway to his future. The past was the past, and the present was ending. But the future, that omnipresent mystery just out of the reach of anyone's hands, was something he was very much looking forward to. The future was bright. Yes, the future had become much, much brighter. From this day forward all would be as it should.

He stared over at Heather and wondered how much things would actually change. Heather and Sarah Prescott, his two best friends in the whole world—as small as their world of Gretna, Louisiana, actually was—would enter adulthood, college, and everything else with him at their side. Sure, new friends would come along, and new boyfriends and girlfriends, pain and joy, triumphs and setbacks. But never again would anyone hurt them like before—he was sure of that.

~

Larry Jackson was a twenty-one-year veteran of the city garbage company and knew the procedures when accidents occurred. "Dispatch, this is Larry." There was a panicked tone in his voice as he spoke into the radio's handheld microphone.

"Come back, Larry. You okay? What you got?" answered the dispatcher.

"Accident. Bad one. Car came out of nowhere. I T-boned it and damn it's messy. We need an ambulance and the police at the corner of Amelia and 9th Street."

"Roger, Larry. Police and ambulance are being sent to your location now. Are you all right, Larry? Larry? Just remember, procedure states not to touch anything. Larry?" The other end of the radio was silent.

Damn the procedures. If someone's hurt, I'm gonna help.

Larry Jackson was out of his truck and jogging over to the destroyed car. He put out his hands to stop oncoming traffic that had arrived at the intersection. His two fellow garbage truck riders looked on in horror, feeling lucky they were not on the back of the truck when the collision occurred. They decided to help divert traffic while the boss went to investigate.

Jackson arrived at the destroyed car and looked into what was left of the passenger side window. Inside, he saw a young girl's mangled body lodged between the seat and the broken steering column. Her wide-open eyes, cloaked in death, stared back at him. He almost vomited at the sight of the carnage. Suddenly ashamed, Larry Jackson felt compelled to drop to his knees and pray. He looked skywards, closed his eyes, and asked God for mercy and forgiveness.

"Lord. Send your angels to watch over and carry this poor young girl to your arms. I tried my best, but I couldn't swerve." A vision of Jackson's own daughter flashed in his mind. He prayed harder, "She's not much younger than my baby girl. And if you'll allow it, please, please show me the path to make things right. Forgive me, Lord."

Larry Jackson solemnly bowed his head, hoping for a sign of forgiveness, hoping his dedication to God throughout his fifty-plus years of life, and all the Sunday morning devotionals he had attended, would light him a path toward that forgiveness.

With sirens quickly approaching, Larry Jackson, as devout as any man could be, opened his eyes. And there, not two feet away from him was a silver watch covered in blood. The glass was smashed and the armband was broken. He picked it up, turned his gaze back toward the heavens, and vowed as part of his penance to return it to the family of the ascending angel before him.

CHAPTER 7

Detective Charles "Chuck" Davis had gained more weight than he'd wanted to in his two years as a detective. Not overly tall, at just under six feet, the added pounds from his time behind a desk began to worry him. His time on the streets while in uniform had kept him lean, and also because he liked to work off the stress from his shifts by hitting the gym. Now, he thought, he would need to stop being so lazy and get back to it. As he began to take the lid off of his morning coffee, his radio beeped. He grabbed the mic. "Go for Davis."

"Davis. Chief Guidry here."

Davis spilled his excruciatingly hot coffee on his fingers and then all over the passenger seat of his car when he tried to place the flimsy cup into the holder that was filled with loose change. In his attempt to answer the call with as little surprise in his voice as possible, fully expecting to get reamed for his latest evidence report—or lack thereof—from his current case, his eyes went wide with awkward relief when he was told to respond to a fatal traffic accident. He exited his unmarked police car six minutes later at the crash scene.

"Detective. Over here."

"Reggie. What's going on?" was the polite reply.

"Why you here, Chuck?"

"When a city vehicle is involved in an accident, the lawyers take over. Remember, us grunts need to make it as clear and clean cut as possible for them and the insurance guys. Didn't they teach you that at the academy?"

"Must have been sleeping that day, sir," replied Dumas.

Officer Reginald Dumas was a proud African American—proud of his city, proud of his heritage, and proud of his job. He was young and fit and stocky—his days of playing linebacker at West Jefferson High School still bulged through his uniform. Dumas continued with his assessment of the scene for the detective, "The fire department is trying to extricate the body from the vehicle. EMTs confirmed her death when they arrived. The coroner is on the way." He pointed at Larry Jackson who was sitting on the curb across the street being questioned by another officer, and said, "That's the city truck driver. Says the young girl blew right through the stop sign and WHAM! Car ends up against the tree over there."

Davis asked, "Big impact. Lots of speed. We know how fast she was going?"

"Truck driver says at least eighty miles per hour. He claims he was only going about twenty. But, maybe, combined speed, side impact…looks about right. I'll make sure we get all the measurements, Chuck. Too bad though, really, good-looking little thing."

It was an unnecessary comment, but Davis would forgive Reggie for it. Davis had seen and heard good things about this rookie. Even with three years on the force, if you were younger than Davis you were a rookie. Officer Dumas had a reputation for accuracy and initiative, and detective grade was on his horizon—Davis was sure of that. Presuming the sit-rep was complete, Davis turned towards the crushed vehicle.

"Just one other thing, Chuck," announced Dumas. "When the ambulance arrived, it had just come from a prior call down the street. EMT's said they were dealing with a half-naked guy in the middle of the road who looked to have been hit by a car. They described him as a white male, short and greasy, with lots of tattoos. No ID on him. When they tried to get him in the back of the ambulance, he just took off. They couldn't catch him even though he was injured, so they came here instead."

"Greasy! What the hell is that supposed to mean?"

"You know, short, stocky white guy... greasy, slicked back hair... lots of tats. Greasy."

"Got it. Might be related, might not be. Maybe a follow-up with the EMT's for a better description, but wait until they're done here." Switching his attention back to something he wished to avoid, Davis moved a little closer to the destroyed vehicle. Before looking inside, he turned and asked, "Any ID on the driver yet?"

"No ID, but the car is registered to a... Nancy Prescott, of Gretna; address is 931 9th Street. That's four to five blocks that way," concluded officer Dumas, as he pointed over his shoulder.

Davis stopped cold in his tracks. His left eye began to flutter violently as his face turned three shades of pale when the name registered to the vehicle exploded in his mind. He quickly fished through his mental library for the file entitled PRESCOTT.

Yes, there!

Then, an unholy fear unleashed a reordering within.

No, don't look there. Wait! What was the other name?

His mind cross-referenced all the bits of information he'd collected over the years and eventually found the one name he hoped to never hear about again.

Bassett. Check for the name Bassett. Damn it!

Detective Charles Davis then lost what remaining color he had in his face, instantly fearing a scenario he didn't want to contemplate. He started barking orders as he turned back towards the mangled car, "Reggie, get a better description from the EMT's about that possible hit-and-run incident. Don't wait, do it right now. Send officers to the address on the car's registration. Tell them to call the crime-techs if they see anything off. Next, call the Bureau of Prisons and ask about the status of a prisoner, one David James Bourgeois. After that, call dispatch and have them contact the owner of the vehicle—Nancy Prescott. If anyone gets in touch with her or finds out where she is, tell her nothing and then lock her down."

Staring into the demolished vehicle he caught a glimpse of the deceased girl. He bowed his head, fearing the possibility of things to come, and exhaled deeply. Slightly more calm, but still trying to regain his composure, Davis continued, "Also, this girl has a twin sister. Find out where she is and do the same—lock her down."

Davis suddenly stopped, thought about it for a second, and then added, "And Reggie, tell the coroner to do a rape kit on the victim. Let me know as soon as you can."

"Victim!" Dumas was surprised and confused. "This isn't an accident?"

"This very well might be," stated Davis as he pointed towards the wrecked vehicle. "But if I'm right, and hope to God I'm not, this may have started elsewhere. So it might end up being something completely different. Until then, *shit…* I want it classified as a homicide."

Still confused, especially about the last statement, Officer Reginald Dumas nevertheless complied quickly. He grabbed up the walkie-talkie from his belt and began repeating Davis's instructions to the Watch Officer on duty at the station.

Davis was already on his way back toward his car. He needed to get any and all information he could on the current whereabouts of a young man named Sebastiane Bassett.

~

Sebastiane felt Heather's hand grip his even tighter. The ceremony had started and Sarah hadn't arrived. She wasn't sitting next to them as promised. He motioned for her to be calm and then turned to face his parents. Elena let him know that Nancy was using his father's cell phone to call Sarah. Heather sobbed, "I can feel it. Something's wrong."

The uneasiness Sebastiane felt earlier while staring at the Prescott house before driving away had returned. He pushed it aside, and said, "Hey, don't think that way. Probably just your mom's old car, right? That thing is always breaking down." He tried to hide his apprehension for Heather's sake because his insides—the uneasy feeling from before—wouldn't leave him alone. His stomach then began to sour wondering where Sarah could be, and why.

"That's not it. Please, I can't be here. I need to go find her."

Heather's desperation grew exponentially as her mind ran wild with fear. Regardless of his comforting actions, which she appreciated but couldn't use at the moment, she could feel the pain of tragedy hovering around her like a blanket of dense fog on a cold morning. For all the talk about the medical experiments and academic papers regarding the interlocking emotions of twin siblings aside, Heather just knew.

Sebastiane looked down the long central church aisle to find Nancy Prescott. He was hoping to get confirmation on Sarah's safe whereabouts. She was pacing just inside the entrance of the church waiting for the call to go through. As the choir started with the second hymn of the proceedings, the large front doors to the church opened. Sebastiane stood up when he saw three uniformed officers entering the church. His heart stopped. He reached down and grabbed Heather's hand, motioning her to rise.

Heather, hoping for the best but fearing the worst, turned to see what he had motioned towards. She collapsed back onto her seat in total shock as she witnessed the distraught, muted screams of her mother when one of the policemen walked towards her while removing his cap.

~

Detective Davis arrived at the church and immediately found his friend and New Orleans police detective Darryl Fuller standing outside in a small courtyard to the right of the main entrance. Davis then saw the distraught mother talking to and surrounded by other Orleans police officers; and phew, there was the other daughter too.

"Where's Bassett?"

Fuller answered by pointing towards a small, wooden bench on the other side of the group of officers situated under a tree. There, guarded by his parents, was Davis's greatest fear on this day—maybe. He had wondered on the car ride over that if he could control the flow of information to the family of Sarah Ann Prescott, and not allow the Bassett kid to know what was going on, he might be able to steer that information in the direction he wanted. It might be unethical, but a few extra hours or days was all Davis hoped for. He needed to find David James Bourgeois; and God willing, he could use that extra time to diffuse a potentially nuclear situation.

Fuller asked Davis, "Your report on the radio was vague. Why the concern?"

"No need to go into details right now. But I'm telling you, Fuller, buddy, you have no idea what that kid is capable of. Do you remember my old partner Anderson? Well, you remember how big and tough he was. It took the two of us and another officer, the same size as Anderson, to keep this kid down. That was"—he used his thumb and fingers to count— "four years ago. I don't want to imagine let alone see what this kid is capable of now." Davis shook hands with his friend and colleague and then walked away, leaving Detective Fuller to grapple with his imagination.

The father, who he recognized, was standing over his wife as she tried to comfort her son. The kid was slumped over on the bench, elbows on his knees, head covered by his arms, and clearly distressed, a far cry from the controlled anger and subdued demeanor Davis remembered from four years ago. Davis motioned for Mr. Bassett to join him just out of earshot from his son. "Mr. Bassett? I don't know if you remember me, but my name is Detective Charles Davis."

"It's Edward. And yes, I remember you. I presume your being here has everything to do with this situation being something other than just an unfortunate car crash?"

Davis explained over the next minute or two what he could, and as delicately as possible. Pleading with Edward Bassett that telling his son any particulars about what the police thought had happened to Sarah would be unwise, Davis promised to do his absolute best for the Prescott family and bring the situation to a quick resolution.

Edward Bassett reluctantly agreed, but informed Davis, "Any further communication between your department and Ms. Prescott, other than for informational purposes about her daughter, can go through my attorney." He handed over a business card and continued, "Because, and if I'm not mistaken, if it was in fact David James Bourgeois who did this, there is a sexual predator database correct? And the police, or, I don't know, maybe the Department of Corrections, or whomever, is supposed to inform the affected family when a person like that animal, someone I know for a fact is on that list, gets released, correct?"

Edward Bassett's ever-increasing voice, retracting only from a full-on shout because he had ended his inquiry, left no doubt in Davis's mind that he had just so long to make things right. Davis's left eye twitched, and for the second time in as many hours. He needed to calm things down and diffuse Edward Bassett's comments, because hearing the terms *lawyers* and *police officers* used in the same conversation usually meant trouble. "I will do so, sir. And thank you."

"Don't patronize me, Detective. My son was affected by that monster too. And even though his name was probably not on the list of contacts, it should have been. But I guess it wouldn't have mattered anyway, right? Hear me, Detective. If that monster is out of prison, I am sure he did this." He pointed toward Nancy Prescott, and said, "Look! Just look at her!"

Davis refused to turn around, thereby accepting the blame for a system that had obviously broken down.

Edward Bassett continued lashing out at Davis, "The system will have to deal with that, and so will the rest of us. I guarantee you the system will hear from me, if for nothing else than to satisfy my need to protect my family. You do realize that if he is out, and until you catch him, no one here is safe." He turned away and walked back toward his grieving son, hoping that one day Sebastiane could watch the switch being flipped on that bastard—if not do it himself.

The implications insinuated by Edward Bassett resonated with Davis. He wasn't sure if the kid's father was talking about another attempted attack by an on-the-run sexual predator or the vengeance of a grieving young man. Neither scenario had an outcome Davis wanted to see, or clean up, so he jogged back towards his car to begin the process of preventing both.

CHAPTER 8

Tampa Bay, Florida

"Gentlemen? I ask that you turn your attention to my right so that we can hear from James Knight," proclaimed the general. He waved his arm, directing everyone's attention towards the window-side center of the table, and then continued, "Mr. Knight, if you please."

"Thank you, sir."

The room fell silent. The only sound was that of a muffled din reverberating through the ceiling from the air-conditioning unit on the roof just above the conference room they were seated in that was keeping them all cool from the higher-than-normal temperatures on this early June evening.

James Knight sat more erect in his chair. He had strategically placed his name tag at the seat in the nine o'clock position for maximum exposure to all those present around the polished, ironwood conference table. Knight took a sip of water in order to calm his dry pallet, and for dramatic effect, before beginning his presentation. He looked around the room and made eye contact with everyone to garner their full attention. He knew what they wanted to hear, and he was more than confident his presentation would kowtow to wanton appetites. It wasn't that the research or the numbers were false or misleading.

I am a lawyer; I don't lie, I convince. I just spiced them up a bit.

The facts really didn't need to be altered in any way, truly, Knight reassured himself. And he knew why; because the financial stability and viability of these men's lucrative business dealings were strong—and only getting stronger. But spice was what he was ordered to add, so he did just that. Knight stood to show proper respect to the men in the room.

Without looking at the first page, going on memory alone, he began, "After a complete and thorough review of recent international treaties, maritime and international law, statutory regulations, and the original company charter and bylaws, we are assured of solid legal foundations for any future expansion in the Middle East, Eurasia, Southeast Asia, and South America. Balanced by an independent audit of the accounts covering the first three years of the company, 1993, 1994, and last year, 1995, including estimates of employee benefits and contracts, employee retention and expansion going forward, we are also assured of a continually increasing and rock-steady trend upwards in net profits. Furthermore, assessments on equity investments, property holdings, the company's stock portfolio, estimated growth in market share, as well as continued sector growth, we are also assured of progressive and stable liquidity levels allowing for further corporate expansion when necessary. In conclusion, an assessment of current and in-process contractual agreements leads us to the following…." Knight paused, making sure all eyes were wide with anticipation as if they were children waiting at the top of the stairs on Christmas Day. "It is the recommendation of Skips, Ruston, Strong & Knight that we should proceed as intended." He gently cleared his throat, signaling Rebecca to begin her task.

His assistant, Rebecca, with her tight black miniskirt and even tighter white blouse, was right on cue as she began handing out the exquisitely expensive, leather-bound folders for the board member's respective signatures. The desired effect of her pleasing figure, and her skimpy outfit, distracted these powerful men just enough, but also helped to psychologically reinforce compliance and destroy any lingering doubts. Each man around the table looked up to thank Rebecca, and then watched as she continued to walk by.

Damn, I'm good.

As the distribution continued, Knight took the time to contemplate his rather fortuitous and immediate past as well as his potentially very powerful and prominent future before continuing with his grand finale.

James Buford Knight, the middle child in a family of nine, including three brothers and three sisters, of Mr. Dennis and Priscilla Knight, of Bremerton, Washington, had had to fight for almost everything he could get his hands on—both at the dinner table and at the toy box. It was a hard upbringing, one that taught him to take advantage of every opportunity—whether presented to him by someone or presented for him by happenstance—and eventually afforded him the requisite ability to recognize both instantly. That, coupled with an overly studious work ethic, made him tops in his class at every level.

Actually, he wasn't really amazed by his rise up the ranks of Skips, Ruston, Strong, and now, Knight, LLP. He was a damn good attorney, not overly ambitious or aggressive, and yet he still made partner after only three years. He didn't have a massive client list. He wasn't the proverbial rainmaker usually so desired by law firms. Nor did he feel he worked extremely long hours. He just kept making the firm lots and lots of money with the very sturdy and wildly expanding interests of his only client. Usually having only one client was a hangman's noose in his line of work, but not when that client was very quickly becoming the new sheriff in town in the burgeoning field of global security. So here he was, sitting at this table, part of a company poised to be the leader if not the totally dominant player, maybe in a decade or so, of an industry requiring a mutual respect for someone with his skills combined with its ideals. He loved his job, and he worked hard on behalf of a shared commitment and respective ethos. Also, he had to remind himself, it was rather fortunate timing.

His relationship with the men in this room was distant but familiar. As a former member of the United States Navy's Judge Advocate General Corps, Knight knew of these men's reputations. His military background had been the main reason Mr. Skips, the Big Boss, had originally hired him. It was an attempt to guarantee the signing of a new client, this client, whose offices were coincidentally situated near the Skips, Ruston & Strong main offices in Tampa, Florida. Being so close to retirement, the Big Boss didn't really care all that much for this potential new client's meager portfolio, but he was smart enough to realize that there was strong growth in this sector of the economy. So Martin Skips took a chance, something he hadn't done in many years, and hired Knight.

Knight had just left active-duty service after nine years and joined the Reserves. Having given up on a promising naval career, but still wanting to serve his country, Knight was looking for a place that could fill in the other three weekends of the month. He found it almost instantly. And now, Lt. James B. Knight, USNR, was reaping the benefits as a named partner and newly appointed in-house counsel to The Slater Group, Inc.

His presentation, culminating with its acceptance by all those present, would bolster another ten percent of market share at a minimum, solidify his advancement, and allow him to continue his rise up the gold-plated ladder of success. He could also go out and purchase that hot little Italian sports car he'd always dreamed of—he was assured Rebecca would love it too.

Knight looked around the table one more time to make sure everyone was paying attention although they were respectfully flipping through their folders. His eyes then fell upon the chairman. Remembering his first meeting with the chairman of the board of directors of The Slater Group, Inc., Knight had been awestruck.

Every member of the Slater Group is like kin, both by blood and of blood.

General Sykes was a legend. Tennessee born and bred, General Randall Sykes, USMC (ret.), was the original brain trust behind The Slater

Group, Inc. An experienced, well-respected career military man forced to retire in the early nineties, and thinking he would quickly decline towards death without his beloved Marine Corps, decided to cheat the Grim Reaper. And so, with his closest friends, like-minded colleagues, and trusted subordinates, he used his professional contacts within the Pentagon, and at MacDill Air Force Base, as his own private scythe in opening a path for the creation of the newest player in the world of PMC's—Privatized Military Corporations.

Cashing in initially as a subcontractor to bigger companies like Brown & Root, DynCorp, and BDM International, the Slater Group started slowly; first with logistical, mechanical, and engineering support, then branched quickly into security, security training, and tactical support. Having been beaten to the punch one too many times in the last year, it didn't take Sykes long to realize where the true money lay within the industry. Therefore, with timing being everything, and with the second iteration of the congressionally approved United States Army Logistics Civil Augmentation Program, or LOGCAP II, forming on the horizon, a potential two-and-a-half-billion-dollar windfall for companies in the game, it was time to play ball with the big boys and become a major player within the industry. This they did; and The Slater Group was now in prime position to split the contract fifty-fifty with one of its former prime contractors, DynCorp.

The future was bright and about to get a whole lot brighter for all those seated at this table. And as for James Knight, who now knew he finally had them right where he wanted them, it was time to conclude his presentation, "Again, it is our legal recommendation that we proceed. So, if you will please turn to the last page in your folders, sirs, and affix your signatures at the appropriate places." They did so, eagerly. "Thank you."

Knight quietly cleared his throat again before continuing, "With your signatures, the new corporate structure will now commence, along with, as you can see"—he pointed to a large TV screen on which was projected the image of a schematic of the vast compound that would eventually take up the entire view of the oversized windows of the boardroom—"the completion of the new company offices here in Tampa without the corporate logo, as requested. Also, here you can see the brand new HQ in the Bahamas with the corporate logo, as required." The image on the TV screen changed accordingly. "Continuing, and pursuant to same, all infrastructure costs and pending insurance compliance will allow construction to commence within the week, here and just down the road at the East Bay port facilities. This will include the railroad expansion line down Maritime Boulevard and the aircraft hangars, as well as the storage warehouses. This concludes the summary of the documents within your binders." As their pens stopped scratching on the expensive, bonded white paper, Knight smiled.

Now came the boring part; the legally compliant but wholly unnecessary recitation of the contract in its entirety. Its eventual completion was again followed quickly by all those present affixing further signatures where needed. The binders were then collected. This was the general's cue.

Everyone stood up as the general lifted his tumbler of fifty-year-old Highland scotch—no champagne here—and saluted each man at the table appropriately. There were nine men in total, one representing every branch of the United States military, one former CIA station chief, the recently retired director of the FBI's Anti-Terrorism Task Force, and two former members of Congress, all of whom followed suit and toasted to their good fortune.

Next, a larger than necessary catered dinner was served in an attached office space converted to an executive dining room. The celebration of prosperity continued as elegantly prepared food was served on fine china and expensive wine was delicately consumed from crystal goblets. With non-business discussions dominating dinner and the dessert course, it was back to a little business during coffee and after-dinner drinks.

"Mr. Knight. Well done. Bringing you on board was a good idea, yes?" The statement was a congratulations mixed with a touch of nepotism, reminding Knight of his place.

Knight shook hands and nodded his appreciation, thanking those abilities he had refined over all the years that had put him in the right spot at the right time, "Thank you, Admiral."

Admiral Nathaniel Augustus Westerly had been a career naval officer with his hands in all the right pies. A slender and meek-looking man, a little less than six feet tall with a strangely proper London English tone in his voice for a man originally from northern Minnesota, he had always been taken for granted. But Knight knew, no matter what anyone else thought of the admiral, he was always and most definitely the smartest man in the room.

"It is my pleasure, sir. And yes, very fortunate for me. I must thank you again," said Knight, who wasn't just playing along.

His realization that Admiral Westerly was the leader of the minority opinion on the board made Knight careful around him in the beginning. However, once Westerly took him under his confidence, and eventually into his inner circle, things changed. Knight quickly concluded that the admiral was his future within the group not General Sykes, no matter how awestruck Knight had been. It also didn't hurt that Knight's primary goal, his *raison d'etre* for joining the military, a goal that remained today, was the protection of the United States of America at any cost. It was a goal whose central tenant pushed itself away from the general's outdated point-of-view on how to achieve said protection and closer to the admiral's justifications for said protection after the fact. Of course, and in order to maintain his status, Knight needed to march in lockstep with the majority. And now, having performed his tasks as Westerly's Trojan horse so thoroughly, all the while managing his job for the company so effectively, it was only a matter of time before the minority would become the majority.

The admiral continued by repeating a phrase he'd come to admire; it was also a secret request for confirmation of the continuation of his plans. "Just remember, great sacrifice requires great strength of character. To see a task through to the end, no matter how difficult the challenge, or risky the outcome, is what makes you a man, a colleague, and a friend." And with a tip of his glass, a confident smile, and an about-face, Westerly took his leave. "Patterson, there you are. May I have a word?"

Knight responded correctly as the admiral walked away, "Undoubtedly, sir." And with his acknowledgment of, and agreement with, Westerly's quotation, the next stage of the admiral's plan was set in motion.

CHAPTER 9

Gretna, Louisiana

Approximately five-hundred miles to the west-northwest, another ceremony was taking place. This one, however, was far more somber.

"For in as much as it has pleased Almighty God, in his great mercy, to take unto himself the soul of our dearly departed sister, we commit her body to the ground, earth to earth, ashes to ashes, dust to dust, in the sure and certain hope of the resurrection to eternal life, through our Lord Jesus Christ. Amen."

Xavier Masterson, PhD, finished his sermon and sauntered over to the grieving mother and daughter in his one-thousand-dollar suit, placed his hands in theirs, and continued, quietly, so no one else could hear, pausing only to gaze upwards at the heavens with a tear-stained handkerchief clutched against his cheek. Sebastiane simply stared at the prankster.

Is he really a priest? No. He isn't anything close. No one acts like that if they are a true man of God. Priests were dedicated to others, not themselves.

This particularly theatrical charlatan proclaimed himself to be the leader of this small, do-it-yourself, Cajun offshoot of some unheard of mega-church from the Midwest. Calling himself the Anointed Leader of the Congregation of the Holy Enlightenment Church of the Almighty, and in the most bizarre and unrealistic Cajun accent he had ever heard, Sebastiane wondered what this self-proclaimed man of God was truly all about. With nothing more than a piece of paper on his wall, probably from a college in Florida of all places, what could he possibly be saying that could lend any semblance of comfort to the Prescott family?

What is his interpretation of the Good Book that might be different from others, allowing him to actually give comfort? Nothing. Absolutely nothing.

Lost in his own memories of Sarah, fighting to stay poised while hiding his own grief, Sebastiane sat three rows from the front. It was as close as he could get. He wasn't family. His grief stemmed just as much from Sarah's death as it did from his sense of loss and despair at not having seen Heather for over two weeks.

The Jefferson Parish Coroner's Office had kept Sarah's body for all that time, releasing it only four days ago for cremation. The police said they'd needed extra time to process as much evidence as they could. David James Bourgeois was still on the run, and every little scrap, no matter how insignificant, could help bring him to justice—eventually. The thought of it all made Sebastiane sick to his stomach.

Here we are trapped inside a funeral home, this death palace, and he is out there free—hiding, but free.

Sebastiane looked over at his parents and received a head nod in return from his father, silently asking if he was all right. A couple of long talks the night after Sarah's accident, and a few more in the week immediately following it, had convinced Sebastiane that the authorities needed time to do their jobs. He gave a halfhearted smile back; it was all he could muster in response to his father's query. Sebastiane was just too confused and melancholy to find the energy for anything more. He turned and looked forward, hoping to get Heather's attention, trying to see if she needed him. He got nothing, not even a glance.

Nancy and Heather had gone back to Mississippi to see family immediately after the accident, and Sebastiane was not asked to go. He figured it was just something family did when death called—*circle the wagons* someone had once told him. Having never experienced so heavy a loss within his own family, Sebastiane was completely lost as to what he should say or do next—or even could do next. He did want to do whatever he could for Heather, and had offered as much. He was politely thanked. And then, nothing.

Neither Nancy nor Heather had seen their Mississippi family since, whenever. So why go to them?

Nancy needed them, he guessed, and he sort of understood, but the thought of not being needed by Heather left a secondary hole in his heart. Sebastiane had had no choice but to wait, wait until she returned home—wait until she needed him again. He would be there for her. He would do anything she asked.

When they finally returned from Mississippi, he didn't know it. Not until his mother read Sarah's obituary in the local newspaper, informing every one of the place, date, and time of the funeral services, did he understand that Heather and Nancy had returned home. Now, as he walked out of the services, he hoped for the moment she would need him. That moment arrived quickly when Heather approached and requested his help. Without hesitation, Sebastiane complied.

The grieving mother was driven home by a girlfriend from work. Elena and Edward headed home first and then to the wake at 931 9th Street. As the mourners arrived, small talk and fond memories reverberated throughout the house. Questions of police progress were debated as quietly as possible by people who had no idea and no tact. After about two hours, Nancy Prescott realized someone was missing.

"Mr. Bassett, have you seen Heather?"

Edward Bassett turned around to acknowledge Nancy and saw a mother utterly lost in grief and completely unaware of her surroundings. She was wearing a traditional black, below-the-knee dress and black, mid-heel pumps that she seemed to be having trouble maintaining her balance in. Obvious fatigue had set in for Nancy Prescott, he determine, from the emotional rollercoaster of the last few weeks and especially the last several hours, and it showed. Her question was almost inaudible—strained was more like it.

He answered, "It's Edward, please. And no, I haven't.... I'm sorry." He looked around the room quickly and then glanced out the kitchen window at those who had gathered under the covered carport. "I'll ask around and find her for you. Is that all right?"

"Yes, please. That would be great."

Nancy turned and proceeded to walk with a controlled stumble towards the back of the house and into her bathroom. It had only been two hours since her last visit, but she didn't care. She needed another one to take the edge off. Fishing behind the Q-tips for the bottle, she found it, opened it, and shook one out. Staring at the little white pill seemed to be an unfortunate reminder of having only one daughter.

Why? Why are you only one?

She didn't guess, couldn't guess at the answer. Her mind was blurring again under the pressure and the pain and the anxiety. All of the horrible feelings were coming back again, and far more brutally and even more quickly this time. Nancy glanced in the mirror and remembered her heavy involvement with drugs when she was younger, then getting pregnant, and then running as fast as she could to get away from the hell-hole that had become her existence. Having almost overdosed twice by the age of sixteen, she promised herself she would stop, raise her twins better than she had been, and never look back. Now, her reflection was telling her not to care anymore. She felt the cycle of need coming back around. Her body was screaming for the relief. She didn't even try to fight it. The feelings of hopelessness that had plagued her young life, and nearly ended it twice, were back for more. The hopelessness called out to her, trying desperately to reclaim the victim who had twice slipped through its fingers.

The first time Nancy Prescott had courted death she didn't even blink, thinking it almost fun to cheat the inevitable. The second time came and went with the same attitude, until the ER nurse told her she was pregnant. It was at that moment that Nancy Elizabeth Prescott promised herself she would do better. And with an affirmation to God, thanking him for sparing her life, she did exactly that. She accepted the task that lay before her of raising a child, two as it had turned out, with wide-open eyes, as a form of punishment—punishment that would eventually morph into blissful absolution for all of her past transgressions. She took it upon herself to claim her shot at redemption as the chance to pursue a different course in life, one that most young girls from her hometown never got.

Now she had lost a daughter; one of the two, small, precious gifts that had given her the strength to continue through life—gone in the blink of an eye. Heather was still here, but a teenager was vastly different from a small child.

Besides, Heather had Sebastiane now.

Nancy Prescott never paused while shunning aside her feeble attempts at reaffirmation, threw the pill into the back of her throat, and followed it with a handful of tap water. She instantaneously relaxed as the dreamlike state of the intoxicant filled her empty soul, relieving the stress and masking the sadness she felt in her heart. Nancy Prescott escaped her misery by embracing a new hell as she descended slowly down the bathroom wall and crashed quietly and helplessly onto the linoleum floor.

Elena Bassett was in the kitchen playing housekeeper, trying to help with the cleanup as much as she could. Her husband approached her, punching angrily at the buttons on his phone. "What did Nancy want," she asked. "And who are you calling?"

With an exasperated look and strong exhale, knowing full well she would be far more lenient on their son than he was going to be, Edward answered, "Heather isn't here." He waved the phone slightly in his hand and continued, "Nancy was asking for her; and since I can't find Sebco either, well... Sebco? This is your father. Please call me back when you get this. Nancy is looking for Heather." Edward ended the call, fully expecting to hear nothing for some time.

"Don't worry. The kids are probably down the block or around the back of the house," said Elena, trying to assuage him.

"No. They're not." Edward shot back sarcastically, upset at his son for not listening to him. "Wherever they are, it isn't anywhere close to being in the same vicinity as this house."

~

After the funeral service Heather said she needed to feel nostalgia instead of sorrow, so she asked Sebastiane for his help. While everyone was meandering out of the funeral home, Sebastiane stayed behind. When the opportunity presented itself he delicately embraced Sarah's urn, cradling it like a child, and presented it to Heather. They exited through the back of the building and drove off without a hint of trespass to anyone in attendance.

Thirty minutes later, Sebastiane was sitting on the tailgate of his truck; his arms were wrapped around Heather's waist, and his head was on her shoulder as she stood in front of him. Both were staring at the horizon as the rays of the dipping afternoon sun bounced off the waters of Lake Pontchartrain. Sebastiane looked over his shoulder to see Sarah's urn sitting perched up-on-high atop the roof of the truck. Sarah had always liked to stand on the roof of Sebastiane's truck and stare off into the horizon, looking for her future. To them, it was as if she were still here. There had been quite a few Sundays, after the girls returned home from church, that the three of them would drive to the lake. They would pass by Angelo Brocato's Italian Ice Cream Shop in Mid-City, pick out cups of their favorite gelato flavors, and just sit and relax and stare out over the lake. He turned back around and sighed, heavily. Heather didn't react.

As she stared into nothingness Heather realized the gelato wasn't as good as she remembered it, nor was the day as relaxing as it used to be. Instead, the minutes seemed to monotonously and fatefully tick by as she stood there utterly motionless, emotionless, and speechless. She didn't want to be here. She didn't feel like leaving.

Sebastiane wasn't sure what to do, but he knew he didn't want to start a conversation for fear of saying the wrong thing. He had an idea for something to say, but was waiting for the right moment. Now just wasn't the time. All he cared about at that very moment was that Heather needed him again—and that was all he wanted. Besides, mourning the loss of someone, of anything really, had several stages; the most dramatic and confusing of which starts when grief becomes denial and denial becomes anger—or so his father had warned him.

Heather bent over and fished through her purse on the ground at her feet. She pulled out a pack of cigarettes, lit one, and then offered one to him. Sebastiane took it without even flinching. He had tried smoking before, at Sarah's insistence, but had barely tolerated it. Heather picked it back up in Mississippi, obviously, but he hadn't known and didn't ask. He took a light pull. The smoke filled his lungs. His body balked, rejecting the sensation and invasion with a cough.

"What do we do now?" Heather asked the obvious but painful question through a strong exhale of smoke—the thick southern humidity capturing it and forcing it to linger above them like a weighted balloon.

Sebastiane glanced down at his ringing phone, but didn't answer it. "My father has called like six times. I figure he's wondering where we are. Should I call back?" He didn't want to force anything on her. He needed her to want him, to believe in him, and to trust him to do anything for her. Whatever she said and whatever she wanted to do Sebastiane knew he would do it for her. He had to because he needed her too. Problem was, he'd completely misread the question.

"I meant about college. I don't know if I can go to Baton Rouge and be away from Mom. I don't think she could handle it right now." Her statement was matter-of-fact and left no leeway for a rebuttal.

"Sure," he said, with a masked pain that was more confusing to him than it was painful for him. Sebastiane could sense something from her, something he didn't like. She seemed to be giving up on the life they had always talked about. Given what had happened he understood, but felt now more than ever that leaving was the right thing to do. Problem was, he was thinking of a place much farther away than Baton Rouge.

Seven minutes of silence later, she stomped out her cigarette and gestured to him that it was time to leave. Her red, swollen eyes, framed by tears capable of defying gravity as they pooled on top of her cheeks, glanced at him, and then looked away just as fast.

He didn't think it right to interpret whether she was crying at the loss of her sister or at the loss of her future—the latter of which seemed to be fading with the sunlight as dusk gave way to nightfall. The two losses seemed to go hand-in-hand for Heather now, he thought, but that wasn't how he saw it. He thought she was interpreting everything that had happened as the beginning of the end, he was sure of it. He didn't want to see it that way, though, and so chose to ignore it.

Heather got into the truck and shut the door before Sebastiane could do so for her. He walked around the other side, retrieved the urn, got in the truck, put the keys in the ignition, and paused to look at her. Gently, he grabbed her hand and tried to ask her what she wanted to do. Heather just stared straight ahead. He lost his nerve.

As he drove, Heather didn't let go of his outstretched hand on the bench seat, and she didn't know why. She was sitting less than three feet away from him across what seemed like a cavernous hole in the universe posing as the truck's bench seat, and she didn't know why. She didn't look at him, she couldn't. She felt nothing. She just continuously stared out the window and watched as tree after tree or utility pole after utility pole rhythmically passed by like seconds on a doomsday clock.

Sebastiane squeezed her hand gently, hoping for a sign of belonging or a sign of need. He shifted his arm to adjust his grip on her hand, trying anything to get her to respond to him, but he consistently got nothing. She was there, but she wasn't there.

CHAPTER 10

Sebastiane pulled his truck into the Prescott's driveway. Heather exited quickly and approached the front door of her house, urn in hand. Sebastiane followed, not realizing his parents' car was across the street.

They entered the house to one very scathing look from his father, as he stood next to the coffee table, one pitied look from his mother, and one blank stare from Nancy, both of whom were seated on the couch. Nancy's vacant eyes couldn't help her realize what was happening.

Edward asked, "You two all right?"

"Mr. Bassett, I asked Sebco to take me to the lake after the funeral. I just couldn't be in the house with all those people. I'm sorry." Turning to her mother, she said, "Mom? It's me. Don't worry, I'm here now."

"Heather?" The look of recognition, behind a drug-induced haze, preceded her incoherent ramble, "Hi, honey, you missed everyone. They wanted to say hi, but we couldn't find you. I asked Edward to find you and he did. Now you can say hi to everyone that came here to...." Nancy started looking around, and a look of puzzlement furled her eyebrows. "Where did everyone go? Maybe they're outside."

Heather quickly realized the state her mother was in and sat down next to her on the couch, placing her arm around her shoulders. Heather looked up at Sebastiane, smiled a request for help, and then turned to face Mr. Bassett. "Sir. Thanks for watching over my mom. Sebco and I can take it from here. I'll take my mother to her room and get her settled. See you tomorrow. Thanks."

Heather stood her mother up and walked her to her bedroom. Edward and Elena were slightly stunned at the abrupt dismissal, but forgave the child, considering. Instead, they turned to their son for an explanation.

"Well?"

"Dad, look. She wanted to not be here. She asked me to help and I did. Understand, whatever she wants, I'll do it."

"Don't you dare disrespect me, you little shit! I told you that your responsibility to this family in their time of grief is to help around here, not selfishly disappear from the funeral with the urn and leave poor Nancy Prescott to fend for herself."

Elena couldn't see where the conversation was headed but recognized the harsh tone in her husband's voice and felt compelled to protect her son. She tried to mediate, "Edward, please."

He responded curtly towards her, "Somehow I knew you would condone this."

Edward turned to leave, but not before directing his internally building anger toward his son. "Take care of things here and then get your ass home. No later than eleven o'clock, got it?"

Sebastiane was confused. He was, after all, hurting too.

What's the deal? Why is he so angry?

Sebastiane questioned his father without completing his own thoughts—a mistake he wasn't used to making and Edward Bassett wasn't used to hearing. "What's the big deal?"

Edward Bassett stopped dead in his tracks and turned to face his son. Elena knew Sebastiane was in trouble and stood up quickly, but not quickly enough. Edward's anger flared, "Sebastiane, you have no idea what is wrong with this scenario, do you?" He lowered his raised voice quickly due to the echoing nature of the house before continuing more calmly, "All right, look. I'll give you the benefit of the doubt because I realize you're just as upset at Sarah's death as her mother and sister. However, as we discussed the night of the accident, I told you to be strong and do what you could for them. I told you that whatever happens to use your best judgment. And above all else, don't go looking for that asshole."

The reference to *him* was a complete and total blindside to Sebastiane's thought processes. He couldn't understand why he was being told, yet again, not to search for David James Bourgeois when he hadn't done anything of the sort. He tried to defend himself. "We did nothing like that. We were at the lake just sitting and talking; well, not really talking, but we weren't—"

"Edward, please. We shouldn't be doing this here," Elena interjected. She desperately wanted Heather not to come back into the middle of an argument that was quickly escalating.

"And how are we supposed to know that?"

"What!" Sebastiane's own anger began to grow. "Now all of a sudden you don't trust me?"

The retort was so quick, and of such reproach, that Edward was in his son's face instantly. He snarled as he looked his son over. His eyes narrowed as he responded, "I told you, do not disrespect me. Do you remember what you did to him? Do you remember what it took to stop you? Do you? You're eighteen now, and no matter what the cause, you do anything like that again, justified or not, and you'll go to jail—or worse. If you want any kind of future, you'll stop looking for him and let the police do their job."

Sebastiane replied in a surprisingly calm and controlled voice, even though his mind raged with confusion. "I told you, we weren't looking for him."

Edward stared into his son's eyes, hoping not to see any duplicity or deceit. All he saw was confusion, which was exactly the intention of the provocative conversation.

Just one last button to push and I'll be sure.

With a poke to his son's chest, Edward Bassett finalized the test of his son's mental status, "Don't ever defy me again. Elena, it is time to leave—NOW."

That should do it. If he is going to explode, now would be the time.

Sebastiane was thoroughly and completely confused by the verbal sparring match they'd just had—and Dad never yelled at Mom.

What the hell is going on?

Sebastiane slowly shut the door after his mother walked out in a huff, and with his father still glaring at him. He walked back to the couch and slumped deeply into it, trying to fathom his father's attitude. As he kicked off his annoyingly stiff dress shoes, nothing was coming to mind. He closed his eyes and tried to think harder, tried to assess his own confusion and feelings. He could think of no reason for his father's actions—no, his tirade. With his eyes still shut, the unpleasant thoughts of the last few minutes and of the last few weeks were replaced by images of his friend—images of Sarah.

She was about twelve years old, running across the playground trying to catch up to the soccer ball he had kicked at her. She was not very athletic, and never quite understood why he loved the game so much. "*It's a stupid little ball with stupid shapes on it,*" she would say. Frequently reminding him of such, she never questioned his devotion to it, though. It was Heather who had convinced Sarah to come to his games to watch and cheer. "Thank you," he said softly.

"Thank you for what?"

Trying to rub the day's exhaustion from his eyes he answered in a similarly exhausted voice, "Nothing. Just thinking out loud is all. How's your mom?" He looked up at her. His eyes widened when he did. She was wearing nothing save for one of his extra-long soccer jerseys. It was well worn with an extremely comfortable look to it. She'd borrowed it a while back for some reason or another—and at that moment, he couldn't remember why.

"Asleep," she said, as she put out her hand. "I'm going to lie down. Are you coming?"

His compliance was hesitant yet quickly forthcoming. He looked at her in that shirt, wondering if she wore it to bed some nights—or was it just this night?

~

Elena was already in the car, an injured expression on her face from her husband's dismissal of her in front of their son. Edward got in with his nostrils flaring, hoping Sebastiane might still be looking at him through the window. He continued with his angry movements, attempting to start the car. When it started, he over-revved the engine and then drove away. Once out of eyesight, Edward Bassett began to beg for his wife's forgiveness, "Elena, I'm sorry. Forgive me, my love."

Elena's injured look changed to one of confusion, much as her son's probably was right now, she thought. She responded, "Don't ever admonish me in front of others, especially our son. You know I don't like that." She folded her arms and faced the window, not completely accepting his apology.

"Please, forgive me? There was a method to my madness, I swear. I was trying to test him. God I hope Sebastiane can forgive me, but I wanted to show him that he needs to stay in control and not let his anger out. I thought if I could provoke him, his anger would boil over. He'd get upset and then blow up like he did four years ago." Edward finished his apology with an inquiry, hoping to deflect his wife's anger. "Isn't that how it works?"

Elena began to understand Edward's motive for starting the surprise confrontation with Sebastiane, but was unable to offer a satisfying answer with anything more because she didn't fully understand it herself. "I don't know," she replied, finally. Elena knew her son was just like his grandfather—she knew it. But not being privy to the intricacies of the Renault family history, only knowing she herself hadn't acquired the family trait, she could only try to explain it. Since she truly didn't understand any of it, she felt completely hindered in being able to offer any explanations or any comfort. This was the reason why she'd waited so many years to try to tell her son about it, hoping that his age and experience might possibly help him fill in the gaps she couldn't. It was also why she hadn't told him the day he'd saved the girls, thinking that that experience was too traumatic for explanations to help.

No. I couldn't tell him then, and I can't tell him now.

She had convinced herself right then and there that no one, no one besides Maurice, could help Sebastiane understand. She continued, "I don't know how it works. I only saw things my father went through, not what he did or how he did them. He never told me anything. I was never able to fully understand my father, and I don't understand how Sebastiane did what he did that day. I just try to forget about it and hope that it never happens again."

She knew she was being naive, and Edward let her know, gently, "My love. Please don't think that something like four years ago will never happen again. He's only eighteen and he has a long life ahead of him. He's bound to be confronted by something that sets him off, whether he starts it or not, it won't matter. And, even if it is something half as horrible as that day, he could still end up severely hurting someone again—maybe even killing them."

Elena shivered at the thought of Sebastiane going through something as horrific as actually killing someone. She was unsure if at any time in the last four years he had confronted a situation that could have pushed him over the top again. But since he hadn't confided in her about anything remotely close to it, she'd chosen to bury her head in the sand. She now realized she'd lulled herself into a false sense of security. Elena wondered that if she had just gone ahead and told Sebastiane about his grandfather, would it have helped? Could knowing at least some of the truth, at least some of the story, have helped guide her son all those years ago? Could it now?

Edward had continued his analogy of why things could or might happen again, and she hadn't been paying attention to him until she heard the word *college*.

"What was that you said?"

"I said... when he goes to college, and if Heather goes with him, I don't want to think about what could happen."

"You're being pessimistic," she stated, turning her head away from the window and towards her husband. She loved her husband very much, and loved that he cared so much, but his upbringing had made him a pessimist. He was definitely more of a 'glass half-empty' rather than a 'glass half-full' type of person. Edward always liked to call himself a realist, and Elena teased him about it constantly. But there was no room for any of that now. She placed her hand on his cheek and said, "Trust him. Trust our son. Please?"

"I do. Really, I do. At least he will only be in Baton Rouge at school." Edward sighed with some relief.

"Don't be so sure about that," stated Elena, catching him off guard.

"Why?"

Elena almost didn't answer him, but she had let the proverbial cat of the bag. Trying to hide it from him any longer would not please her husband.

Elena had taught her son compassion while her husband had taught him pragmatism. It was an excellent balance that had infused in their son the wherewithal to achieve anything he might want. With these instilled values of understanding, accompanied by a will to do better, Sebastiane, it seemed, had gained another path for himself besides the obvious. Elena finally answered, "I saw an acceptance letter on his desk the other day. It was from Arizona State University."

CHAPTER 11

Sebastiane was lying on the bed in Heather's room, holding her, hopeful that he was being of some comfort to her. He wanted her to feel relaxed and for her to not be thinking about anything at all; nothing, that was, other than what they were doing at that very moment—just being.

~

Heather was as close to him as she could be. Her leg was crossed over his lower body, her arm was across his chest, and her head was cradled in his shoulder. She was comfortable, thinking of nothing except the one thing she desperately wanted. The TV was on, but she paid no attention to it. She said nothing to him. She didn't move.

~

Sebastiane caught himself thinking about their past and how much he'd wanted to be with her but could never quite get over what they had been through. So, not wanting to upset their friendship, but also not wanting to lose her to some random guy, he'd stayed close. Not that he didn't want to be with her, it just never seemed like the right thing to do.

~

Heather had always presumed Sebastiane would never leave her side, that always being around each other would give them plenty of time to get to where they were right now. She thought it cute and gentlemanly that he never approached her in such a way; and sometimes she even welcomed it when the nightmares returned. The one thing she truly understood about their relationship was that his constant presence guaranteed that she hadn't ended up like her mother—very young and very pregnant. She snuggled in tighter.

~

Sebastiane responded cautiously, his hand unconsciously coming to rest on her side. The weight of it ever-so-slightly pulled the loose-fitting soccer jersey up her leg, allowing the curvature of her upper thigh and bare buttocks to be exposed. He noticed she had no underwear on. And perplexing him even further, she didn't object. He wasn't embarrassed, but felt intrusive. Gently, yet quickly, he repositioned his hand on the bed behind her back.

~

The light touch of his hand on her torso and the caressing feel of the long, smooth cotton shirt riding up her thigh teased at Heather's frayed senses. She squeezed him even tighter, letting him know that it was all right. When he didn't place his hand back where she wanted, she nestled her head on his shoulder, moved her arm up to his neck, rubbing his chest on the way up, and moved her leg farther up his body to expose more of her bare skin. She hoped beyond anything that he would respond in kind.

~

Even though he was still in his slacks, dress shirt, and tie, Sebastiane could feel the warmth of Heather's skin radiating into him. His excitement began to grow, but his confusion grew right alongside.

This cannot be happening. Not like this.

~

She could hear his heart starting to race; the blood coursing throughout his body and to all the right places. She began to move her thigh up and down, slowly. Her hand caressed his neck, then glided to his chest, then continued to his belt buckle.

~

His excitement intensified until he was completely ready for what might happen. Her efforts to arouse him had worked so well that she had distracted his ability to think clearly. His confusion was almost completely lost to his desire—almost.

"Wait! Wait! Heather, I don't think this is a good idea," he objected, trying to halt her advances. Sebastiane reached down to grab Heather's arm to make her stop, wanting it not to stop, but trying not to upset her.

~

With his firm grasp on her arm and his untimely words unwantedly delaying her from getting what she wanted from him, but not what she truly needed of him, Heather rolled on top and leaned forward for a kiss. Trying to dissuade his overly protective tone and gentlemanly manners from ruining the moment, she pressed her pelvis down onto his; a breath of anxious desire escaped her lips.

~

The sensation of her flesh penetrated his clothing—fully penetrated him. His back arched, pressing into her, making her inhale deeply in perverse, sensual victory. The eroticism of the moment combined with years of restricted aspirations was almost enough to disintegrate his confusion—almost.

"Please, Heather…," he muttered, feebly, in defense of a fleeting awareness that something seemingly right, but mostly very, very wrong was about to happen.

~

"Don't stop," she interrupted. "I want this."

She looked into his eyes with a begging she hoped he couldn't ignore. She reinforced her dismissal of his intended rebuke by feverishly and somewhat violently undoing his belt, ripping the button off his pants, and breaking open his zipper. Pulling his pants down just enough to expose what she really wanted, she maneuvered back up and pushed her pelvis down again—and much harder this time.

~

Her teeming flesh finally and unequivocally reduced his last whispers of apprehension to nothingness. Sebastiane grabbed Heather's waist with both hands and lifted her up—just enough. She pushed upwards on his chest, raising her hips up—just enough. Her nails dug into him as he pulled her back down. Together, they pushed. Together, they moaned.

~

Her want of something she did not need and could do nothing with, layered with the pain she had endured at the loss of her sister and the torture of a childhood lost through no fault of her own, culminated in a muted, half-crying, shameful apex of pleasure that, once achieved, was not quite what Heather Prescott thought it would be.

~

Sebastiane's youthful virility smiled internally when he realized her satisfaction. Outwardly, his physical exhaustion soon joined her, releasing his long-awaited ambitions inside her.

Unwittingly, the fallen barriers of his compliance quickly reconstructed themselves by returning him to his overly hesitant persona, now dripping in shame, which had almost prevented the last ten minutes from happening in the first place.

~

Morning pierced the window of Heather's bedroom earlier than they'd both wanted. Sebastiane lay behind Heather, his arms around her like a gentle vise. Heather, even though awake, played at continued sleep, cowering inside his embrace and wanting nothing more than to be outside its suffocating shroud. His eyes were open, staring at the light filtering through the shaded, glass portal. He, too, was motionless. For so many reasons he couldn't quite fathom, Sebastiane knew he shouldn't be here.

Sebastiane slowly extricated himself. Trying not to wake her, or so he thought, he got dressed and headed towards the door. Stopping, he turned to see her and took a mental picture of the afterglow of an experience he had wanted for so long. When the emulsion of the Kodak moment finally developed in his brain, all he could see were the after-effects of the life grenade that had just exploded in her room, destroying her bed—and with it, its occupants. Before she could turn and see the terror on his face, he exited.

When she heard him shut the front door a few seconds later, Heather started crying.

CHAPTER 12

Once he got home, Sebastiane couldn't find the shower fast enough. Standing there for as long as he had, unaware of the water beginning to turn cold, he could only wonder what the hell had just happened to him—to them. And why did his confusion about it linger so thoroughly?

"Sebco? You all right in there?" It was his father knocking on the door.

Startled, Sebastiane answered as laboriously uninspired as his mental state would allow, "Yeah. Fine. You need me to come to the warehouse today?"

Understanding the strained tone in his son's voice, even through the door and the noisy downpour, Edward Bassett granted his son's abysmally disguised request, "No, we're good enough for today."

Edward tried to be as understanding as possible by not demanding his son's immediate return to his annual summer duties with the family business. The boy needed time. He needed time to process it all. He needed time to forgive his father for his odd behavior last night at the Prescott home. Regardless, Edward thought his son could use the distraction. Then the thought occurred to him that he could offer up a better choice instead. "How about this? Instead of you working eight-hour days, why not get

Heather to help you out and you guys could work half days and still get things done by the end of summer."

"Yeah. Sounds great. I'll ask her."

"Good. See ya tonight." Edward walked away from the door, believing he was doing the right thing.

Sebastiane thought that having to convert decades of tax documents, receipts, purchasing orders, cargo manifests, and licenses—and everything else that was stored in limitless banker boxes at his father's corporate offices—so that the family's 102 year-old business could enter the digital age was, at its best, tedious. And at its worst, was a total waste of his summer. Converting it all into an integrated computer database was something he could easily do, he sort of just understood computers; not just how to use them, but how they actually worked. Surely the task would be made easier with Heather around—if she accepted the offer.

And if she doesn't hate me.

Toweled off, but only half-dressed for his day, Sebastiane stared into his bedroom mirror still fighting against his own thoughts. His mind was stuck on the events of the night before.

Why did it happen? She was distraught—that had to be it. She wanted control of something for once in her life—that had to be it. And I could give that to her. So she used me. Shit! Stop this. Stop overthinking everything.

Sebastiane's confusion, swallowing him into the quicksand of continued frustration, was abruptly interrupted when the house phone rang. His mother shouted up to him to pick it up. "This is Sebastiane." His mind was distant. He answered the phone on the desk in his room as if at work, even though he hadn't been there in nine months—and wouldn't be today.

"This is Heather," she said, mocking him exactly. "Nice greeting by the way. So. Are you up for a movie? I tried to call you on your cell phone but it didn't pick up."

He was taken aback by her unexpectedly playful jest and giggling response. To him, the strangely timed invite was so nonchalantly delivered that Sebastiane wondered if last night had been some kind of weird dream—or perhaps a nightmare.

She informed him, "That new comedy about the insane TV repair guy is out. We still have time to catch a matinee."

His utter shock was quickly trampled by her need for him. As for his own emotional state, with which he was losing yet another fight, dramatically, it gave in to her request without hesitation, "Great. Um, I'll pick you up in twenty minutes."

"Okay. Bye." And as quickly as that, she hung up.

~

They both thought the movie to be so-so. Afterwards, a quick bite to eat was also coincidingly mundane. A six-pack of stolen beers from the Prescott refrigerator and a cloudy sunset at the lake eventually turned into a silent session of staring at the ground, again. The only thing they actually discussed was Heather's employment opportunity at his family's Emporium. She agreed, and so nonchalantly again that Sebastiane's first inkling of fear about how she was truly feeling settled into the corner of his mind and cataloged itself for a later date. Then, it was back to Heather's house to drop her off. She invited him in, suggesting she needed his company until her mother came home. When she eventually did arrive home, Nancy Prescott very quickly disappeared into her bedroom and never came out. Heather checked on her ten minutes later and found her semi-lucid but ostensibly asleep on the bed, clothes and all.

As another awkward evening turned into an even longer night, Sebastiane found himself, again, in Heather's room lying on the bed, holding on to her, and hoping to comfort her. Trying his best to talk to her about things but never getting any real, direct answers from her, he hadn't realized he was droning on. Growing tired of his talking, Heather turned and kissed him. He returned the kiss because he wanted to.

There were hidden, genuine feelings within their sensual embrace, which irrevocably led to a repeat performance of the sexual conflagrations of the night before. Unfortunately, the next morning was unchanged from the previous as the same disastrous complications clouded their judgments.

Sebastiane awoke just before sunrise and left the room in a state of even greater confusion. Heather cried for the entire three hours it would take Sebastiane to return to her house and pick her up for work. In those three hours, Sebastiane tried to figure out the path he and Heather were on. But no matter how hard he tried, the one thing preventing his understanding was how ultimately finite their path truly was. He tried to make sense of it all by himself and remained utterly silent about the entire matter regarding his, and most likely her, increasingly destructive emotional states. He usually went to his mother or his grandmother when things, or life, didn't make sense. But this! This he couldn't go to either of them with, and that only made things worse.

Every day became a mirror image of the previous one; with confusion or crying upon waking, a mindless workday, or a movie or the lake—or both. Then, at night, came the bedroom. She talked about nothing simply to avoid reality, to avoid talking about Sarah—it was her ideal form of existence at the moment. His ideal existence was trying to talk about something else, anything else—Sarah, work, soccer, college—anything so as to forestall the inevitable. After the cyclical run-around of nothingness chatter, came the sex. Good, bad, indifferent, it was all the same. Heather dominated the situation. He never said no, but also never veered from his role as the submissive plaything he had unwantedly and unintentionally become.

The mind can be a funny thing Sebastiane justified to himself every night, and then again in the morning. It was a phrase repeated to him by his father, constantly. Sebastiane wondered if Heather had received some sort of definitive parental or familial insights during her time away in Mississippi; insights that had somehow led her to believe she needed to be in total control at any cost.

Regardless, it turned out that two minds encircled by the same fears but trapped by different reasoning, and yet both proverbially pulling at a door labeled PUSH, helped to create the cruelest of jokes between them.

The unkindliness of it all, seemingly perpetrated by life itself, continuously divided them throughout their demonstrative, summer-long scenario; both of them hopelessly, unknowingly, and inevitably losing sight of the one thing that truly could have saved their relationship—mutual forgiveness.

CHAPTER 13

Phoenix, Arizona

"Ladies and Gentlemen, this is your captain speaking. As you may have noticed we have started our descent and should be on the ground in about twenty-five minutes. Please obey the 'fasten seatbelt' signs and all instructions from the cabin crew as they make their way down the aisle to conduct their final preparations for landing. The weather for this late August day is beautiful. The temperature is on the lighter side at one-hundred and two degrees, with a rather high percentage of precipitation at just about zero. On behalf of the crew and all of us here at Southwest Airlines, we would like to thank you and welcome you to the Sonoran desert and my hometown of Phoenix, Arizona. Thanks again."

The passengers gasped at the rather unsuccessful comedic announcement by the pilot. His attempts to alleviate their expected suffering fell on deaf ears because most of those onboard knew that as soon as they deplaned they would get a swift kick in the teeth from the hot and extremely dry weather conditions pervading the *Valley of the Sun* this time of year. Along with the pyroclastic kick in the mouth for all who disembarked at Sky Harbor Airport, newbies to the area would feel as if their skin was melting off when they exited the plane.

Preparations by the cabin crew continued as the senior stewardess started her review for any unfastened belts. Mary Lipscomb was as senior as they came for a flight attendant at Southwest Airlines. At fifty-four years of age she wasn't as pretty as the younger ones, but her professionalism, attention to detail, and sincerity meant more to the higher-ups than anything else. Soon she would be training those younger, prettier ones, but for now she had wanted just one more year in the cabin and management had granted it to her for all her years of dedicated service.

As she continued her walk from front to back, Mary's eyes kept floating up to see the young man in seat 34C who never seemed to take his eyes away from the window. He hadn't accepted a complimentary drink or peanuts, or responded to her subtly coaxing attempts to engage him in conversation. He never even looked her way, and just sat there staring out the window the entire trip. She wondered how someone his age could be so depressed. Her experience told her it was probably a girl he was fretting over. Nothing she could do about that, she shrugged, as she continued down the aisle to complete her duties before landing.

~

Sebastiane was staring outwards through the small, oblong-shaped window at the bright blue sky. Its blanket of wispy-white clouds hung effortlessly aloft as if on invisible coat hangers. He could see the beauty of it all, the translucent remarkability of it all, and wondered why? His problem wasn't that he couldn't understand the why, his problem was that he didn't want to think about it anymore.

His mind seemed to be on a rewind and replay loop while it tried to figure out a way that could have changed the outcome of the scenario that had left him all alone on this flight. Deep down he knew; he knew that there was nothing that could have changed Heather's mind no matter what he'd said or what he could have promised her—nothing.

With the rewind and replay loop running continuously for the last four and a half hours, his eyes watered constantly and his breathing was erratic at best. The torment was just enough to make his eyes a harsh, liquid red, but not enough to disturb those around him. His breathing was noticeable, but no one asked. In all that time he could find no other solution that would have changed his state of affairs. He tried but failed—over and over again. So, with the same outcome inevitably presenting itself every time, the only truth he could be assured of was that the people at Webster's Dictionary were currently engraving his picture next to the word *insane*.

He lifted his arms to expose the locked and secured buckle around his waist as the stewardess looked his way. Mary—that was what her name tag said—gave him another courteous smile and moved on. Dropping his arms back down, they landed on top of the box in his lap. The box was something that had been presented to him by Heather. She gave it to him as she sadly and slowly closed the door on him and on their future together. With the end of the summer appearing in the rearview mirror, and the day of this flight only one week away, he had arrived at her house at seven o'clock on the dot with two things in tow. The first was one-way airline tickets for them both; the other was a plan.

It was a good plan, he thought. It was a plan he knew could get their joint futures back on track, but almost immediately he'd realized Heather was missing the point—and maybe even on purpose. She wasn't receptive to the possibility of being somewhere other than in Baton Rouge, like she had originally wanted, or even receptive to being somewhere other than at home, like she obviously wanted to be now. Sebastiane's plan for leaving Louisiana, and his arguments to back it up, had been well rehearsed. In the end, they hadn't work.

After their long talk, in which she'd said next to nothing, Sebastiane came to realize that he had finally lost her. So, he stopped trying and turned to leave. As he walked out the door she handed him a box that had been sitting on the living room table. She kissed him, leaving tears of regret on his cheek and whispers of apologies in his ear, and shut the door. When he got to his car he opened the box, and quickly shut it before driving home.

Even now Sebastiane couldn't open the box again—it was far too painful to see its contents. But as he grasped the box, almost to the point of crushing it, he reminded himself that its contents would be something he could never let go of. Inside the box resided the only physical reminder of his past and the life they all could have had. It was also the only thing he'd brought with him that would anchor him to both—Sarah's silver watch.

CHAPTER 14

Mary Lipscomb finished up her rounds in economy class and then turned back towards the front of the plane to help with the final preparations in business class. As she pulled open and then secured the small curtained partition between the two sections, she leaned down to pick up a stray business card lying in the aisle. After reading it, she quietly announced, "Slater Group?" Sitting in seat 2A was a tallish, rugged, flight-mile weary, professional-looking gentlemen who raised his hand and then offered his gratitude upon its return.

The man in seat 2A looked at the card before returning it to his breast pocket, and then smiled halfheartedly as he yet again questioned his denial of Admiral Westerly's most generous of offers. It was a huge jump in salary, the benefits were great, and the idea of being head of a department was very enticing. But he'd had to say no.

Special Agent William Rutherford Dent, II, of the Federal Bureau of Investigation, was a patriot; dedicated to his country, and to his job. He'd spent his entire adult life working in law enforcement; first with the Tucson Police Department, and then for Uncle Sam. Out of respect he'd traveled to Florida to hear the admiral's pitch. But in the end, Dent didn't quite believe, as Westerly did, that the Slater Group could advance his *Future Intelligence Initiative*—aptly anagrammed FI^2—much farther than his current employer could. The problem always came back to a need to maintain the appropriate checks and balances that in his opinion were most definitely needed with a project this massive and this invasive.

Dent had originally hoped, with some encouragement and a little foresight, that the Bureau would have implemented his plan—or at least run it up the flagpole to another agency. Dent's main concern, and his theory behind creating the FI^2 project, was that somewhere down the road southern United States border security, maybe even all US border security, could become far less porous than it currently was. His narrow-minded colleagues, along with some of the higher-ups, had originally thought it imprudent to suggest tightening security on the southern border. It really wouldn't do anything other than upset certain lobbying groups in DC, they'd said—and it would definitely upset certain minority groups. Besides, border security was not the purview of the FBI; and pissing in someone else's pool, namely the United States Border Patrol and the United States Customs Service, was just about the quickest way to garner a ridiculously large funding cut for the Bureau—and most definitely stall one's career.

In reality Dent knew this, so when his phone rang three days ago, and the caller identification said The Slater Group, Inc., he became instantly intrigued. After he hung up, Dent put in for a few days leave and jumped a red-eye flight to Tampa. No sooner had he arrive at and then entered the Slater Group's offices the following day than was he instantly mesmerized by the scope of the place. Then came the insightful and effective salesman's pitch, which was laid on thick and heavy by the admiral and his lead technical man, Mr. Saunders.

Westerly, of course, said he understood the frustrations of government work and the underfunding of useful systems to protect civilians, doing his best to sell Dent a future in post-governmental corporate contract work. The plans they showed Dent, attempting to incorporate his FI^2 project into a private corporate framework, had almost convinced him to jump the government ship and sign on with the Slater Group that very day. However, Dent was nothing else if not loyal—something Westerly liked immensely in people—so he firmly and very respectfully answered *No, thank you* to their pitch while biting his tongue the entire time. Westerly then shook Dent's hand and sent him on his way.

With that firm, respectful, yet semi-confident dismissal, Dent was now returning home to pick up right where he left off, hoping somehow or someway that someone else in the Bureau would at least listen to him as Westerly had. And if not, Dent only had three years left before retirement anyway, so maybe then he could revisit the Slater Group and Admiral Westerly's generous offer.

Wait! Westerly wouldn't try to implement this project on his own, would he? No. Westerly isn't in charge at the Slater Group, General Sykes is; and everyone knows the general would never put up with some pseudo-secret surveillance project that could be used, or might look as if it could be used, within the United States.

The general had rejected any and all domestic security contracts sent his way to date. It was an oddity for a private security firm, Dent reminded himself. *Go to where the money takes you* was a traditional business acumen, and was absolutely the modus operandi of any firm like the Slater Group. But Sykes was different—*Keep it out of the USA and on foreign soil and we'll be friends*. It was something Dent had read in some business magazine who'd interviewed and quoted Sykes directly. The man was a legend in the military, and Dent was sure he was the man in charge of everything at the Slater Group.

Besides, Dent's FI^2 plan was ambitious. It called for a seven-year-implementation schedule—from design and construction of the satellites, to testing and systems confirmation, then launch, and then activation. With government funds, seven years was easy. The bureaucracy of government would obviously delay things a while, but that was to be expected. Westerly didn't have the bureaucracy to deal with, but certainly lacked the funds to begin let alone complete such an immense project. Dent decided to play devil's advocate with his own argument.

Could it be that neither I nor anyone else for that matter might comprehend the fact that a lack of funding could stop Westerly's obvious ambitions when it came to a project like this? Not even the technical application of his theories is impossible. The software is already being developed. The only thing he needed now is hardware.

Hardware systems, or more to the point satellites, are expensive yet relatively available. But my plan called for designing the satellites for a specific requirement. What if Westerly were going to modify existing satellites so he could initiate the system more quickly?

Satellites. All Westerly needed were satellites and the system would be a fully functional, integrated intelligence-gathering platform. Where would he get the satellites, though?

Dent put aside the academic argument for now, relaxed back into his seat, and took another sip of his drink. He really needed to stop drinking so much cola. His wife nagged him all the time about it, so he drank it only at work. It wasn't as bad as smoking, something he also used to do, but the bureaucrats at the Bureau had really started cracking down on poor fitness performance evaluations—and he wasn't getting any younger. Dent reached for the seat pocket in front of him to grab the in-flight magazine to try to pass the time, but stopped. Instead, he closed his eyes and tried to sum up for himself the differences between his original proposal on FI^2 to the Bureau and what it was that Westerly had pitched to him about Slater's version of the project.

The Slater project, as Admiral Westerly called it, was eerily similar to his own and yet far more elegantly simplistic. The system, or satellite platforms, would combine sophisticated cameras like those currently on-board military KEYHOLE satellites, cell phone towers—down here as well as up there—a double-redundant, encrypted, ground-based communications center, and a multi-tiered server farm. And there you have it, signals intelligence *(SIGINT)* for the next century.

Not much to it actually, thought Dent. But Westerly had also asked him about the current state of human intelligence *(HUMINT)*, a topic the admiral seemed overly interested in. Dent's curiosity had spiked at that. His answers to Westerly's continuously poignant questions unwittingly confirmed for Dent what Westerly probably already understood to be the Bureau's, the CIA's, and the rest of the government's positions on the subject.

Post-Cold War government *HUMINT* had been on a serious decline. With the collapse of the Berlin Wall came a severe reduction in human intelligence resources—spies, analysts, and their support structures—that had concentrated solely on the former Soviet state including its Eastern European allies. There simply wasn't any need for these groups to be so big anymore. America had won the war, and by virtue of that victory had made these structured intelligence apparatuses completely obsolete. But then, instead of simply re-tasking these extremely important, very expensive, highly educated, and highly trained collectives, which would have allowed them to learn all new regions of the globe and investigate any new potential or previously undetermined threats to the United States, all its components had been individually reassigned. The hope was to spread the wealth, so to speak.

Instead, the system drastically deteriorated and almost collapsed in on itself. Most other regions of the world—China, Southeast Asia, South America, Africa, the Middle East—had competent groups that were already underfunded and lacked the penetrative human assets required to run consistent and successful operations. Simply divvying up and interjecting the former Soviet experts into these *divisions*, or *desks*, as they were referred to, couldn't recreate the successes human intelligence agents had had in Europe; nor did it help to carry over the successes achieved in winning the Cold War. With a continued lack of funding by the government in the years shortly thereafter, the system never quite recovered.

Now, *HUMINT* was practically nonexistent across the globe and would take decades to build back up. Consequently, the only way to stay effective in the fight against its enemies, whomever they might be, had forced the United States to begin investing massively in *SIGINT*, and thus diverted the funding required to rebuild its human intelligence assets. Admiral Westerly, Dent presumed, had seen this coming from a long ways off, and getting ahead of it seemed to be a good business decision on his part. Most of those in and around Washington, DC knew how government intelligence worked these days, and Dent didn't need to presume that Westerly wasn't somehow aware of the problem. Dent began to focus in on his misgivings about his job at the Bureau, and then began to correlate that with how bad he thought the government was becoming at protecting the United States.

After the failure of the World Trade Center truck bombing in 1993, things started getting dicey around the world while the United States government was trying its best to stick its head deep into the sands of complacency. To pull themselves back out drastic measures were needed, and Dent was sure his FI^2 project was a means for doing just that. But no one was biting yet due to a complete lack of will, understanding, and the inability for forward thinking. The *SIGINT* the government was using was good, but without his FI^2 initiative, to put it on steroids, Dent knew *SIGINT* itself wasn't good enough.

For the big boys at the top of the CIA, the NSA, and the like, their version of signals intelligence had become easy. Just give the politicians what they wanted, and not what they needed, and then those same politicians looked good when things went right and couldn't look bad if things went wrong.

Private military outsource companies probably did the same thing to try to win their over-inflated contacts from the government. Then, by applying the appropriate pressure on the right people at certain agencies, these companies could guarantee future profitability by providing what was deemed 'good' intelligence but was actually 'directed' intelligence.

The argument was that if you could deliver 'directed' intelligence disguised as 'good' intelligence, at a cost-effective yet disambiguate price, then by virtue of same, you could control part of the government's intelligence budget. Why? Because directed intelligence, good or otherwise, usually begets directed outcomes. And with directed outcomes, good or otherwise, everything always came out roses. And with the sweet smell of their directed successes, agencies and PMCs with intelligence divisions, like Slater, were given major infusions of future funding. Inevitably, that higher funding could then establish a slush fund for creating more directed intelligence; and voila, a vicious circle that continually manufactured directed outcomes and instant profits. Of course, all this directed intelligence actually hindered and obfuscated the good intelligence needed to actually be effective in preventing bad outcomes.

Nobody seemed to care about that fact anymore.

Dent came back to reality when the plane struck the tarmac a little too hard. One problem with desert climates, Dent knew, was rising air from an overheated earth generated pockets of unstable currents that forced aircraft to buck and wobble and then slam the runway hard as the pilot had trouble maintaining an even glide path. After the aircraft finally came to a complete stop, it turned right to begin its long taxi to the gate.

This gave Dent time for one last thought: that the key aspect of his FI^2 system was to present the back end production of accurate and polished 'good' intelligence. Not just supply the raw data but manage the data, sift through it, analyze it, and present detailed and actionable information. This type of analysis was not quite being done on a daily basis by many modern-day intelligence agencies because politicians preferred intelligence that fit a specific ideology—like the proverbial hand that fits perfectly into the proverbial glove.

Intelligence, from the political perspective, required a certain nuanced feel that made it easier to sell to the public. Agencies like the CIA were against supplying what their political masters yearned for—a type of cooperative intelligence that paid less attention to facts than it did outcomes—which could then be easily consumed by the masses. They did it, they just didn't like to.

The major difference between the everyday, governmental-homogenized analysis and Westerly's idea was that he, or more to the point The Slater Group, Inc., was going to infuse the collection of the raw data streams with a fledgling field of mathematics called *Predictive Analytics*. This combined approach could not only help manage the massively growing amounts of data taken in by *SIGINT* assets, it could also assist the human part of the system by helping it compile truly accurate, real-time, actionable intelligence. It would be this type of actionable intelligence that could have a two-fold effect.

One, it could hopefully thwart, if not entirely prevent, some types of military, terrorist, or even commercial actions detrimental to the overall safety of the United States of America—everything the nation's intelligence apparatuses strived to perfect. And two, in deference to those same apparatuses, that the quality of the intelligence would be agreeable to the politicians, and would thereby guarantee its perpetual need. Dent's only worry was that when one and two were combined, it generally led to the inevitability of *Group-Think*. Group-think had become a serious weakness permeating today's intelligence work, making it terrifyingly unusable. But, if the combining thing didn't happen, then the terrifyingly unusable thing couldn't.

Besides, elected officials liked anything that made them look good while also preventing bad things from happening to the United States—right?

Dent realized that he had just answered his own question. Stopping actions detrimental to the safety of the United States only helped bolster a politician's ambitions. Being able to plaster your name all over the news saying *I was on the committee that approved that plan* or *I was the one who voted yes on that* only helped to augment the resumé of those seeking ammunition in the high-profile fight for higher office. This need, this weakness, was always exploitable however, and maybe that was what Westerly had truly identified as the issue at hand, and why he thought the *FI²* project could be so useful in his company's hands and not the government's—and maybe for far more than just border security?

Dent shook his head in disagreement. Westerly was a patriot not a privateer. Besides, politicians truly couldn't be controlled. They were only animals fighting over fame, money, and power. But, throughout that fight for fame, money, and power, they could be maneuvered. Dent's eyes narrowed at the thought that most civilians were blind to the hubris of it all, never realizing that fame, money, power, and even glory were the only real truths in Washington. Worst of all, voters couldn't do anything about it at the ballot box because all politicians were alike. Suddenly, Dent's internal light bulb lit up.

How could it be that after so many years of dedicated service in local law enforcement and the Bureau that one simple little three-hour conversation with a man whose direction and vision was so clear and concise, and was so overwhelmingly impressive, that you didn't even recognize it when it happened? Some policeman you turned out to be!

It was then that William Dent realized that Admiral Nathan Westerly was right about everything; about the future of intelligence and the future of intelligence work. Dent took down a mental note. He would call Westerly, apologize for saying no, and then agree to consult on Slater's intelligence system until such time that the Bureau didn't need him anymore—or when the Bureau didn't want him anymore.

Dent was fourth off the plane yet first into the terminal as he dragged his small carry-on bag behind him as if it were a jet engine. As soon as he cleared the gate, he got on his phone. The reception was terrible in the terminal, but he finally got a good connection at the taxi rank.

"Hello. Could I speak to Admiral Westerly, please?"

~

At the end of yet another long and busy day, Westerly was seated at his desk looking over the resumés of other potential candidates and wondering whom he should try next. Dent had said no, but it was only a small stumbling block in a plan that had started out so efficiently.

First, Westerly had managed to quietly secure, by means of a shell corporation called Ares Equity Investments, LLC, a start-up company in Silicon Valley that had created the computer algorithms he needed. Those algorithms could eventually become the cornerstone of the fledgling Predictive Analytics industry that Westerly knew would become the future of intelligence analysis. The algorithms would help manage the exponentially growing streams of data produced by his *SIGINT* system no matter how big those streams became.

Second, Westerly had wanted to hire a strong and effective manager to not only run the department but to also create the infrastructure required to use the data proficiently. Westerly had tried to convince William Dent that he was that man, but he would have to find someone else now that Dent had declined.

Lastly, the project needed satellites. The overall design of the satellites was actually very simple. Mount very expensive, very good cameras to very good, very cheap, multi-frequency intercept antennae on soon-to-be deployed communications satellites. The only problem was the initial cost outlays. Unfortunately, satellites didn't grow on trees. Governments and the private sector had hundreds if not thousands of satellites roaming the heavens every second of every day, but to create an entire constellation so quickly was a whole other story. You had to pay for launch facilities and then you had to pay to launch all those satellites—it was just too cost prohibitive. Westerly needed to find a company who already had the satellites, and had those satellites racked and ready to go. Then, with only slight modifications, get them prepared for immediate launch. Luckily, during his research into William Dent, Special Agent for the Federal Bureau of Investigation, Phoenix Field offices, Westerly stumbled across just such a company.

"Admiral? A call on line one."

~

Sebastiane eventually made it off the plane and found his way to the baggage claim area. Standing there for a while, waiting for his four large bags and still in a mental fog from the last 168 hours, he hoped he wouldn't regret his decision to come here. His parents thought it was a good idea for him to leave Louisiana. He knew it was too, but it hurt. He saw three of his bags come through the flaps in the wall on the moving carousel.

While Sebastiane waited for the fourth, an elderly man approached him and asked if he could retrieve a newspaper from the plastic upright dispenser behind him. Sebastiane moved off the little blue kiosk apologetically. When the man departed, Sebastiane looked at it himself and noticed it was for a local newspaper—the *Chandler Sun Times*. The headline on the front page, siting slightly askew within the visual display, read: *Bankrupt Local Satellite Company Bought by International Equity Firm. Luckily, Jobs to Remain.*

CHAPTER 15

Tempe, Arizona, 1997

Sebastiane shook his cup at the waitress, the one who always seemed to be on duty at their favorite little food joint, and she nodded her approval. He grabbed both cups, got up, and went to the soda fountain to get two free refills of Sprite. When he arrived back at the table, Kenny Dominguez, his roommate, grabbed his cup, gulped down half of it, and then slammed it on the table almost cracking the Styrofoam. When Kenny wiped his mouth clear like a drunkard at the bar on his tenth scotch, Sebastiane realized he'd been right—something was up.

"What's the deal?"

"I told Maria," said Kenny obstinately.

"Holy shit!" It had only taken seven months for Kenny to get around to it, and it looked as if Sebastiane had been correct in his assumptions about her reaction to his advances. Women really weren't all that difficult to read, thought Sebastiane; they just kept flipping the book of life to another chapter and then kept going while guys had to start over every time they did something wrong—or right. And with the look on his roommate's face, it wasn't hard to tell what her answer had been. "I take it by your attitude she didn't reciprocate."

"Oh, dude. She totally reciprocated all right. She kissed me, quite passionately actually, then pushed me down on the bed, grabbed at my hair, and then tried to take off my shirt. But then she stopped and said, 'If things were different, I wouldn't hesitate.'"

"Let me guess. She left and went back to what's-his-name?" Sebastiane knew his name, he just didn't like saying it. The guy was a total asshole and didn't deserve anyone's recognition or respect.

"Johnny. Yep. But there was something there. I know it. That kiss meant something to her."

"She's playing you," offered Sebastiane.

"Damn man, you really don't like women do you?"

"Totally not true. I just don't... I can't trust... I really don't know," responded Sebastiane haltingly.

"You need to get laid, buddy, seriously."

Sebastiane disagreed wholeheartedly with his friend's suggestion that a meaningless sexual encounter was all he needed to alleviate his distrust of women. He didn't hate them, not at all, it was just that his only experience with a girl had left him trying to come to terms with the reality that love was something he might not be able to handle. He'd been to parties and he'd partied with girls, but nothing seemed to click with any of them. One girl actually asked Kenny if Sebastiane was gay. She'd tried really hard to persuade him to go back to her dorm room, but he'd avoided being cornered just so. And even though he was shocked by his roommate's inactions, Kenny had said no, he wasn't; but like a true friend offered no other excuses as to why his roommate was being so evasive. Sebastiane cleared his head and decided to forget about his own woes with love by reaffirming his position as the *Antichrist* to the subject at hand.

"Look. Did you honestly think she was going to sleep with you? Fall in love with you?" Kenny turned visibly distraught, even more so than usual when the topic of Maria Anita Columbus came up, and Sebastiane knew his roommate didn't like it when he played this card—and it seemed especially so now.

Kenny lashed out uncharacteristically, "How long have we known each other?"

"Seven months," answered Sebastiane affirmatively.

"And how long have I known Maria?"

"That would be one day longer than you've known me, if I remember correctly."

"Exactly. So don't tell me you know her better than I do because I've known her longer. And that makes me the expert, GOT IT?"

Sebastiane bit his tongue, trying his best not to laugh. Kenny smiled, embarrassingly, shook his head, tauntingly, and then began laughing, hysterically. Both of them laughed for a time, but Sebastiane understood Kenny's true feelings towards her.

"Christ, I need a drink," stated Kenny.

"You want another Sprite?"

"No, dumbass. I think it's time for the three amigos to get together and have some fun."

"I am not drinking anymore of that repulsive liquid licorice. No third amigo tonight, bro, please."

Kenny laughed louder. "You can't even say its name! Or is it that you just don't remember the last time we drank the darkened, succulent Ambrosia of the Gods?"

"I wouldn't want to remember even if I could." Sebastiane shook his head violently at the prospect of having to remember anything about that night. The last time they'd drank it, he had woken up on the card table with his face lying next to a pool of regurgitated chicken wings. Mortified by his lack of tolerance, Sebastiane could only fall over and pretend he was still alive. His justification was that it was his roommate's fault. And thanks to Kenny, who was passed out in the closet, they'd missed their first two classes that day.

"I'll go to the store. You go back to the dorm and keep the RA busy for when I arrive."

Sebastiane balked, "Really?"

"Yes, really." Kenny shot up from his chair and ran to the register to pay the bill, thinking that springing for dinner would rally his roomie to action.

Sebastiane moaned because Kenny was extremely hard to say no to. Besides, he probably needed to drown his sorrows. Fine, he thought, as he stood up and headed for the door Kenny was now holding open with great anticipation.

"Question," stated Sebastiane.

"Answer," stated Kenny.

"Was the kiss all you'd hoped it would be, seeing as how it's probably all you're ever going to get?"

"I wouldn't say it's the last time I'll get a kiss from her. There was something in her eyes when she said no. And besides, she tasted like black licorice, so…."

Sebastiane winced at the comparison, and then completely understood why it was that Kenny wanted to celebrate his pseudo-triumph with a bottle of Jägermeister.

"I'll meet you at the room in twenty," said Kenny as he fast-walked towards the liquor store.

Sebastiane waved his agreement as he headed in the opposite direction on Rural Road towards East University Drive. It wasn't far to the Manzanita student dormitory from the little Chinese Bistro they loved to eat at. The food was good, and cheap too. And besides, they never went to the liquor store together because two college students, both with fake IDs, usually prevented either from illegally purchasing alcohol. So Kenny, who looked older, would retrieve the liquid supplies while Sebastiane set up the card table and got the poker chips out back in their dorm room.

When he arrived at Manzanita, the door to the elevator in the lobby was already open. Sebastiane got in and pushed the button for the eleventh floor. As it started moving upwards, he began to formulate a plan on how not to drink as much as Kenny would want him to. The thought of reliving their epic chicken wing devouring, alcohol engorging, waking up late for class extravaganza was something Sebastiane really didn't want to do. But Kenny was Kenny; therefore, Sebastiane decided, his roommate needed his friendship tonight.

Little Kenny Dominguez, little because he was five foot four, at best, was truly a good roommate; and as it turned out, a good friend as well. Hailing from Goodyear, Arizona, where his family managed several acres of farmland—and for quite a few generations now—he'd always wanted something different for himself. His parents made sure he was able to follow his dreams. He was the first in his family to go to college and had grown up a dedicated *Sun Devil* fan after his father had taken him to his first sporting event, a football game, when he was only nine. Kenny didn't play football, but fell in love with the school and with the idea that he could go to college and stay close to home. Arizona State was the only application he sent out. The day he got the acceptance letter, he fainted. That was his mother's favorite story, and it amused her greatly to retell it for her son's roommate from Louisiana every time he came to Sunday dinner.

Kenny was also a devotee, and not too shabby of a player himself, of the greatest game on earth, as he described it, soccer. Kenny could be friends with anyone, anywhere, and anytime, and was generally the life of all the dormitory parties—and even the classroom. But when he found out his assigned roommate at the Manzanita high-rise student dorms could play the game he loved so much, the two young men became instant friends and quickly spent every waking moment, besides their classes, training and playing.

The door to the elevator opened on the designated floor. As he exited, Sebastiane was surprised to see that the door to the resident assistant's room was shut. Normally the door was open at all times before nine o'clock just to make sure no funny business was going on. It was a mandatory drawback of the job—the responsibility for all aspects of student welfare on each floor—and Sebastiane valued his privacy too much to ever consider applying for the position. You get free room and board when you get the job, but those drawbacks, of which the heightened responsibility for other students was the most important, seemed not to be worth it. Sebastiane was tired of being responsible for others, enjoyed being self-indulgent in his chosen activities, and wondered if he could be that responsible ever again.

As he continued down the hall, he stopped and looked back. The door to room #1101, the resident assistant's room, was open slightly, but then shut again just as quickly. So much for responsibility, thought Sebastiane, as he continued walking down the corridor. At his door, he inserted his key and turned the handle. Sebastiane walked into a darkened room and turned to flip on the light switch while shutting the door. Before he could turn back around, something struck him on the back of the head and knocked him out cold.

CHAPTER 16

As he came to, Sebastiane's sight was obscured by the clear plastic of the contoured oxygen mask covering his nose and mouth. He removed it slowly because his hands and arms wouldn't cooperate as instructed. Only then did he realize it was his brain that wasn't cooperating.

When his focus returned, he was greeted by the white, metallic ceiling of the inside of an ambulance. He glanced right and left to see the shelves and cabinets containing all the equipment needed to render assistance to someone who occupied the gurney he was currently strapped to. He tried to sit up.

"Whoa there, buddy. Take it easy." The EMT placed his hand over his patient's chest so he wouldn't rush it.

Sebastiane groggily asked, "What happened?"

The EMT leaned out the door and motioned for someone to come over. "He's awake."

"Sebastiane Bassett. My name is Officer Smallings. I'm with Campus Police. I have some questions for you, if you're up to it?" Smallings stepped up on the tailgate of the ambulance and made his way inside. He then took a seat next to the gurney as the EMT continued to check on the health of his patient.

Micah 'Tuari' Smallings was once a police officer for his tribe under the auspices of the Bureau of Indian Affairs on a small Reservation near Albuquerque. He had always made it quite clear to his fellow officers that he wanted to leave New Mexico and work for a metropolitan police force. He eventually ended up in Phoenix and found a comfortable place to land—minus the metropolitan part.

"What happened?" Sebastiane was asking again, and a little more forcefully than the officer was ready for.

"Take it easy. We were hoping you could tell us."

"Where is Kenny?"

Officer Smallings stayed silent just long enough while contemplating his answer that Sebastiane became visibly angry, slightly aggressive, and something else entirely, all at the same time.

Smallings noticed and tried to catch up, "He's on his way to the hospital. He was pretty messed up."

Sebastiane removed the arm band the EMT was using to check his blood pressure, and then began to unstrap himself from the gurney.

Smallings said the only thing he could think of, "We're going to take you to the same hospital to get you checked out. You can see your friend then, okay?"

Sebastiane stopped, and then laid back down. His head was pounding and the pain was one of the two things preventing him from turning his presumptions about what had happened to him, and to Kenny, into unsubstantiated fact. The other was his reluctance to inhabit a persona he'd been negligent of for many years now—and for good reason. He nodded, and Officer Smallings exited the ambulance and closed the doors as the EMT signaled for the driver to take off. As the vehicle's lights and sirens announced his departure from the scene, Sebastiane closed his eyes. And then suddenly, something flashed at him from his subconscious. He'd missed it then, but now he knew it meant something—the quickly closing door to room #1101!

~

"Son, are you all right? What happened?"

The urgency in Edward Bassett's voice led Sebastiane to the conclusion that his father seemed more concerned about what his son had done, or might have done, or might do, rather than how he was actually feeling.

Irritated, Sebastiane rolled his eyes and rubbed his forehead before answering matter-of-factly, "My roommate and I were attacked in our dorm room last night. I have no idea who it was and the police aren't telling me anything either. I don't think they know what happened, but Kenny might. They are still waiting to talk to him."

"How is he doing?"

"I don't know. I haven't seen him yet. I think his parents are with him. I'm going to go talk to them when the doctor lets me." The next thing he heard was the sound of his mother's tears cascading through the phone line. He calmed her nerves, "Mom, I'm all right. I promise. The doctor said the blow wasn't really strong enough to cause any serious damage. He says it just caught me in the right spot. He also said my x-rays were negative and that they are going to release me soon."

His mother could barely speak, "Good... good. We were worried... worried that...."

He answered abruptly, "I don't know what happened or who did it, and so neither of you needs to worry."

His obstinate voice portrayed an eerie, prophetic tone, and Edward Bassett jumped back on the line, "Sebastiane, get a grip. You do anything like before and it will be the end of you at that school. You realize that, right? You need to let the police do their job."

Sebastiane wanted to leap through the electronic circuitry and stuff his father's words right back in his mouth. His anger was palpable, and he was having trouble drawing a line between a concerned father's warnings and the necessities of revenge for what had happened to him.

His mother came back on the line, the purest of referee's. "Sebastiane, get some rest. And please let the doctors know they can contact us at any time."

"Yes, ma'am."

Sebastiane returned the phone to its cradle with a frustrated forcefulness that shocked the nurse as she came into the room. She informed him, "Your friend's parents are asking for you."

An hour or so later, Sebastiane was staring down at Kenny. He was covered in tubes extruding from several machines that ended inside his arms, nose, and mouth. Sebastiane saw his friend open his eyes. They weren't Kenny's eyes, though, usually so bright and full of his mischievous pretenses. Instead, they harbored something different. It was a look Sebastiane recognized all too well.

The doctors wouldn't tell anyone other than family what it was that had happened exactly, and Kenneth Dominguez, Sr. hadn't said anything to Sebastiane yet. He was a proud man, and the embarrassment of the situation prevented him from doing so. The look in Kenny's eyes confirmed it.

Sebastiane didn't show it, but he recognized the look on his friend's face as the same look from five years ago when he finally noticed it for what it was, in Heather and Sarah's eyes, during that horrific afternoon. The look didn't come from the multitude of violations they'd endured, it sprang from a sense of worthlessness brought on by an inability to protect oneself from what had occurred—at least, that is what the research he'd read had indicated. Sebastiane had done plenty of reading, and even though he'd struggled through it, he'd kept going. He hadn't gotten answers from anyone else, and the need to understand what had happened to them, and why, had been overpowering.

The things he had read about the victims of serious crimes, especially sex crimes, had several things in common, one of which was that most victims believed they should have been able to defend themselves from their attacker. Even without some type of formal training, a few karate classes maybe, the belief that one could throw a few haymakers and win, or at least give themselves time to run away, actually made them feel like they had a legitimate chance at survival. Of course it wasn't, statistically speaking, and one dominant trait of those victims afterwards was an almost total lack of self-worth. Another was extremely low self-esteem.

Most of the reading he had done was of no help really. No matter how much he'd read he couldn't understand Heather or Sarah's state of mind before it happened, nor could he dissect his own state of mind afterwards. To be fair, Sebastiane felt as if he were projecting a lack of emotions, which made him seem distant and difficult because of what he had done to protect them. He also didn't know whether or not he should stay close or give them space. In the end, it was actually Heather and Sarah who had prevented him from spiraling, while his parents, especially his mother, had always seemed one step behind in trying to help. As time went on, the twins regained their self-worth; and because of their recovery, Sebastiane regained his self-confidence. He decided he would try to do for Kenny what the girls had done for him—lead the way. He hoped for the same outcome.

After the nurse removed the tube from Kenny's throat, he took a sip of water and was finally able to speak, "Hey, bro. What happened to you?"

Sebastiane rubbed his head and replied, "I think it was a mini-baseball bat to the back of the head. The doctor told me it seemed right for the type of bruising. Turns out whoever hit me only hit me hard enough to knock me out. Maybe the doorway had something to do with limiting the blow. I'm not too sure. Anyway. Besides a small bruise, I have no other injuries. The doctors say I can go."

"A mini-baseball bat you say. Well, at least you got it to the back of your head. Me, I got it straight up the *culo*." He tried to joke about it, that was his way, but Sebastiane could tell the effects of such a traumatic event were already taking their toll on his friend. "I've also got two broken ribs, a fractured eye socket, one broken finger, and one very sore nut sack."

Sebastiane understood Kenny's need to joke about the situation—again, it was his way—but the extent of his injuries was foretelling, and Sebastiane could guess quite confidently as to whom the attacker was now. The personal nature of the attack, the type of attack, meant it could be only one person. What Sebastiane was going to do about it was up to Kenny.

"Don't worry, I'll take care of it," Sebastiane offered.

"You'll do nothing of the sort. You have tryouts in San Diego in a couple of weeks, and you need to do that for me."

Sebastiane couldn't believe what he was hearing. "One thing has nothing to do with the other."

"They have everything to do with each other. Don't let this bullshit get in the way of you possibly playing for a Major League Soccer team, bro. You've got a legit chance at this. Don't blow it."

It was Kenny who had literally forced his new roommate to get involved in playing soccer again, first at some local parks and then with a local club. At one of their games, a scout from a Major League Soccer club gave Sebastiane a card and invited him to a tryout camp in San Diego.

Thinking it crazy that Kenny would be thinking about that at a time like this proved to Sebastiane his friend was a better man than most, so he answered, "You got it, bro," and gently tapped him on the arm.

Kenny winced, and then painfully laughed. And then his eyes brightened slightly when he saw who was at his hospital room door. Sebastiane turned around and saw Maria. Her dark hair, dark eyes, soft complexion, and petite stature seemed smaller in the doorway. Sebastiane immediately discerned the fact that she seemed smaller than normal because she was consumed by regret and apologies—the former for what had happened, the latter for causing it.

Sebastiane nodded to his roommate and turned to leave the room. As he passed her, Maria said nothing to him as she glanced remorsefully towards the floor. Sebastiane whispered to her, "Don't hurt him again."

Sebastiane briefly stopped to talk to the Dominguez family to assure them he was all right, and then also told them that if they needed anything from him, they only need ask. Mr. Dominguez ashamedly shook his hand. Ms. Dominguez kissed him on the cheek. Sebastiane peeked back into the room to see Maria sitting on the bed caressing Kenny's hand, and then reaching down for a kiss. He left without another word.

Having been lost in love and thoroughly confused by its aftermaths, Sebastiane wondered if he would ever come to understand it again—even just a little bit. He loved his parents, he loved his grandmother, but the display he'd just witnessed did nothing more than confound him thoroughly. Girls usually liked bad boys, and good guys always finished last—or so the saying went. Maria's obvious acceptance of a bruised and battered man over the relationship she was in, with the same man Sebastiane was now confident had doled out the beatings, seemed ridiculous. It went completely against everything he understood about that saying. He didn't get it and couldn't figure it out, all the while trying to compare it to his relationship with Heather. It didn't matter that his situation was just as complex, he simply couldn't find an answer that could reconcile either one.

It ate at him. He couldn't figure it out. His demeanor and gait reflected his conundrum as he walked outside and into the parking lot of the hospital before realizing he had no way to get back to the dormitory. He missed Heather, and he missed Sarah. He missed the life he thought he should be having at that moment and he let it fester inside as he aimlessly walked the six or so miles back towards campus.

Before he knew it, he'd passed by the dormitory and had made his way almost all the way across campus. He was exhausted by the situation and his head was still a bit sore, but he wasn't tired from the walk. When he eventually stopped, he found himself sitting on the circular steps of the one place he always knew he could truly think. He came here often to ponder, and to wallow, and to sob. He never did the latter until everyone else was gone, which made it hard to ever do so since this place was so popular.

Practically every student on campus walked past *The Beacon of Knowledge* at some point during their day. Situated atop and slightly askew of the entrance to Hayden Library, it was a fifteen-foot-tall, lighthouse-type structure in the center of a grassy mall. Always so full of students sitting and talking or studying, Sebastiane began contemplating why it was that he had chosen such a public place to be so introspective. No one ever approached him when he sat here nor did anyone already sitting ever ask what or how he was doing, so he'd just presumed everyone else was there to do the same thing. Whatever is was that made him come to this place, he needed it now.

He took out his phone and started to dial home. He needed to talk to someone, desperately, and home was the only thing he could think of at the moment. But before he pushed *SEND*, he realized the dichotomy of his situation.

Why come to such a public place to be a damn recluse? Why want to be alone, and yet at the same time yearn so desperately to talk to someone?

Sebastiane did need to talk to someone, he just couldn't figure out who that person should actually be. Heather didn't call him anymore. She had a few times, but that had stopped—he knew it would eventually. Dad usually didn't help. The only thing he would ever say, no matter how he said it, was *is it something you did?* And Mom? Well, she always seemed to be hiding something. The look in her eyes or the tone in her voice always showed an inward hesitance while the dimples in her cheeks could convince him everything was all right.

He stopped thinking about it and cancelled the call, placed the phone back in his pocket, and confusedly shook away the thoughts of why he had chosen this place. He sighed heavily and lay back on the step to stare at the sky, and got back to his feeble attempts at reconciling a situation he knew he had no hope of actually reconciling.

CHAPTER 17

It was Maria who answered the door to the Dominguez residence, and Sebastiane wasn't all that surprised to see her. Kenny was convalescing at home and she seemed to be helping with his quicker-than-expected recovery. She smiled contritely and then moved aside to let her boyfriend's college roommate inside. Sebastiane ignored her as he had for the last five weeks when he'd come to visit. He found Kenny sitting in his father's designated lounge chair in front of the television.

"Have they called yet?"

"Not yet," answered Sebastiane. "They said it would take a few weeks."

"It's been a few weeks! I thought you said it went well?"

"It did. But like I said before, every player in San Diego was good."

"Don't be so negative, bro. You got invited. You got a shot. Stay positive."

Sebastiane couldn't see that look in Kenny's eyes anymore. Ever since he left the hospital Maria hadn't left his side, except for her classes, and

Kenny was obviously all the better for it. Sebastiane hadn't seen her around campus all that much but he had seen her ex-boyfriend, and every time he did he'd wanted nothing more than to do something vicious. He didn't know what was stopping him; it definitely wasn't his ability to inflict damage, but Sebastiane just couldn't bring himself to act. Maybe the only thing that could possibly be stopping him was Kenny's relationship with Maria.

What if doing something to her ex-boyfriend, Johnny, might make Maria go back to him in the same way she had gone to Kenny when he was hurt?

It was a ridiculous argument. Sebastiane had all but given up on figuring out their relationship—just as he'd given up on figuring out his own.

He hadn't heard from Heather in a long time, until five days ago. He was surprised to see her letter in his dormitory mailbox when he returned from San Diego—it was like she knew somehow. He'd hurriedly opened it too, but only to read an irrelevant two pages of gibberish that left him convinced their relationship was truly gone forever. She said nothing about herself and only seemed to be vaguely interested in him by suggesting she was overly concerned about how his college life was progressing. She asked about classes and friends and girlfriends, but never went as far as to flat-out ask the question—had he moved on? Sebastiane wrote back saying only that he was good and that she knew where to find him if she needed anything.

Kenny slowly extricated himself from the La-Z-Boy, and said, "I think I need some Chinese food. It's too stuffy in here. And besides, I miss driving my car."

"You still can't," said Maria. "We'll take my car."

Sebastiane sheepishly added, "And your car needs gas."

Sebastiane had been using Kenny's car to get back and forth from college to Goodyear to bring Kenny his class assignments. Kenny had been offered the chance to postpone his classes and start fresh again next semester, but the year was almost up and he didn't want to waste time trying to get back into the swing of things. The doctors had said it was a positive mental attitude to have, and that as long as he didn't have any relapses he should be allowed to return—the Academic Dean agreed.

Kenny got into the car, gingerly, his ribs were still sore, and they headed to Tempe for some comfort food. The drive was relatively quiet as Maria and Kenny held hands. Sebastiane sat in the back thinking about Heather, imagining himself in the front seat of his truck while they drove to get something to eat somewhere. He lost his train of thought when he couldn't decide if his waking dream should be taking place in Tempe or Baton Rouge, and before he knew it Maria was pulling into the bistro's parking lot.

Sebastiane went to the counter to place their orders, Maria found them a table, and Kenny went to the bathroom. When Sebastiane made his way to the table after ordering, Maria glanced nervously at him. She needed to say something, he could feel it, but she flinched. He started for her.

"This had better be for real."

Defiantly, she stated, "It is."

"Good. Because he's been through a lot. And whether you knew it or not, it was all for you."

"Are you seriously suggesting this was my fault?" Her riposte dripped with incredulity, and was far too quick for his liking.

"Damn right I am! What did you do? What did you tell Johnny before all this happened? Let me guess, you threw it in his face that you were with someone else but didn't think he would figure out what was going on or who it was you were with and then go after him? Or did you just use Kenny as a means to an end?"

"You're an asshole!"

"Truth hurts, doesn't it?" Maria folded her arms and went silent, so Sebastiane continued, "Have you seen Johnny at all around campus?"

She hesitated slightly. "Yes. And we just talked. And he left when I told him it was over for good."

"Left where? Your dorm room? What, did you have a little going-away party with him? One last fling? Something for him to remember you by before you rode off into the sunset with Kenny? You know, a consolation prize for second place. In my experience you girls are all alike. When you're broken you lash out, and we poor suckers just eat it all up."

Maria shot back, "Kenny was right, you do hate women. And it makes perfect sense now what Connie told me about your prudishness. She said you were scared when she reached into your pants and—"

"Don't change the fucking subject!"

Maria backed away, alarmed by the hideousness of the comment shouted just loud enough for her ears only. The other bistro patrons had been oblivious to what their conversation was about, but started to suspect something was wrong when her chair screeched across the linoleum and away from the reddened, angry-faced young man sitting across from her. When Sebastiane looked in their direction his mannerisms suggested they mind their own business—they did.

Frustrated, Sebastiane got up and headed out the door. He flung the door closed and exhaled strongly to calm down. Not truly knowing why he was so frustrated, he headed straight across the street to the gas station to buy cigarettes. He paid the cashier, cracked open the box as he exited, threw the tear-away wrappers on the ground, broke one while taking it out, and then dropped another before finally lighting up.

The inhalation pulled hard at his chest. He hadn't smoked in almost a year, and all the training he'd done in preparation for San Diego only made the pain in his lungs worse. All that hard work, the hours of running, the weeks of training, the commitment to his one chance at playing the game, was escaping with every exhale and he knew it.

With half of the slender white cylinder full of chemicalized-tobacco leaf gone, his head started swimming from the nicotine intake. He didn't stop, though, forcing himself to suffer through it all—and suffer for a situation he couldn't control no matter how much he wanted to. With every inhale his feelings of remorse and revenge intensified. The nicotine sweats built up on his forehead and started running down his face as he puffed harder. When he started to get the spins, he bent over to steady himself before he fell down.

"SEBASTIANE!"

He looked up to see Maria standing at the door to the bistro, frantically looking right and left. When she saw him, she screamed again, and Sebastiane threw down the last embers of his spiraling psychosis before sprinting across the street while dodging the cars waiting patiently at the traffic light. When he arrived at her side, the tears in Maria's eyes weren't hard to interpret. "What happened?"

Maria sobbed uncontrollably, "He never came back from the bathroom, so I went to check. I found him on the floor. He was just lying there… all curled up in a ball and crying."

Sebastiane ran inside and heard the waitress calling 9-1-1. He made his way to and then entered the bathroom to find Kenny curled up in the fetal position under the sink as another patron was collecting wet paper towels to place on his forehead. When he noticed Sebastiane enter, the portly patron looked up and started shaking his head as if to say *I don't know what's wrong.* When he bent down to try to help, Sebastiane's concern for his friend's welfare grew to a calm rage as Kenny's eyes portrayed only one thing—fear. Sebastiane recognized it for what it was.

CHAPTER 18

"I'm only telling you this because I remember you guys from the last time he was here," said the doctor, knowing full well she was breaking ethical protocols by informing non-family members on the condition of the patient in ER room #2.

Maria asked before Sebastiane could, "Is he going to be okay?"

"Physically he is better, and in that respect he will be. His blood pressure skyrocketed uncontrollably. We had to get that down first before we could evaluate him." The doctor moved the discussion out of the hallway and into an alcove housing vending machines across from the main waiting area before continuing, "Like I said, physically he is fine. I took a look back at his charts from five weeks ago and I think I know what's happening, but I'm going to get an opinion from a colleague of mine before proceeding. I think he might be suffering from post-traumatic stress. It's not my specialty, but I'm pretty sure that whatever you guys were doing tonight, or wherever you were, triggered a memory from his prior incident, maybe, and he basically had a severe anxiety attack. When his parents get here—"

"They're on their way," offered Sebastiane.

"Good. When they get here, I'm going to recommend he see the head of our psychiatry department for a more definitive diagnosis. Other than that, he can be released to his parents when they arrive, okay?"

Both Sebastiane and Maria breathed sighs of relief. Maria asked, "Can we see him?"

"One at a time."

Sebastiane nodded to Maria and she smiled gratefully as she followed the doctor to ER room #2. Sebastiane headed in the opposite direction and made his way outside to the designated smoking area to wait for Kenny's parents. He hoped they would forgive him. It was a silly thought. It had been Kenny's idea to go out for food. But, Sebastiane realized, this was to be the second time Kenny's parents were coming to the hospital, and that both times it was Sebastiane who was not in as bad a shape as their son.

Sebastiane lit a cigarette and puffed on it harder than before. The hot, dry air mixed with the vaporized tobacco and made him feel strange. When the nicotine-induced spinning started again, the strange sensation he was feeling morphed into something else. It wasn't the same as before because the strange feeling wasn't alone. Sebastiane thought it was nausea, but then suddenly developed a flop sweat when he realized it was his emotional state. And, that his emotional state wasn't with him at the hospital; it was somewhere else entirely.

At first he didn't understand. But, when the first inklings of understanding of what it might be began to formulate in his mind, Sebastiane calmed down. Soon thereafter his thoughts became completely clear and absolutely concise. He returned to the present—minus the flop sweat—and then smiled ever so slightly when his recognition of the emotional and physical responses he was currently experiencing, which could be best described as the uneasiness of inevitability, became wantonly familiar. Only one other time in his life had he felt something akin to this. Sebastiane flashed back to the day he was handcuffed on a couch with two police officers on either side of him. As he stared at one of the officers, while the other looked at him conspicuously, Sebastiane fought to understand what had happened and how he'd done it. Just as he'd given up on figuring out what it was that day on the couch, this same type of sensation had started. It wasn't as intense back then as it was now, and Sebastiane realized why.

Back then he was too young to know much about life, let alone what his actions meant in the grand scheme of things. Now, the intensified sensations gripping him in the hospital's designated smoking area, he believed, were simply telling him to try harder.

As he stood there puffing away at one cigarette after the other, and watching as the day gave way to the night, he tried and tried to do what he couldn't do when he was fourteen years old—he tried to understand what he was. But still, there was no conclusion he could come to that made any sense. There was no explanation for why this was happening to him. There was no explanation as to why he was feeling like this. And there was no explanation as to why he so desperately wanted to do the same thing to Kenny's attackers as he had done to David James Bourgeois.

Before he could finish his thoughts, Sebastiane saw the entire Dominguez clan pull into the parking lot outside the emergency room. They exited their cars and hurriedly walked towards the entrance. Sebastiane stamped out the remnants of his third cigarette in twenty minutes and tried to explain to them what had happened as they approached. They all passed him up without a word, or even a glance, and headed straight inside to the front desk. Sebastiane's head sank. Completely deflated by their demeanor towards him, he sat down and lit another cigarette. Feeling suddenly responsible for everything that had happened to his friend, and physically unable to ingest so much nicotine, Sebastiane turned and vomited in the bushes behind him.

CHAPTER 19

Sebastiane decided to make his own way back to his room at the dormitory. When he exited the elevator on the eleventh floor, he turned the corner to find Officer Smallings leaning against the doorframe to his room.

"Can we talk?"

Sebastiane answered, "We'll talk in the hallway. Just give me a minute." He opened and closed the door to his dorm room, leaving Smallings agape with surprise and annoyance at the brush-off.

When Sebastiane reappeared a minute later, Smallings asked, "Is your friend all right, Mr. Bassett? I got a call at my desk from the nursing station at the ER. They told me that he'd been readmitted."

Sebastiane, still standing in the open doorway, answered, "He'll get better."

"Good. I'm here because I wanted to tell you that we are still investigating the incident. But unless either of you can identify your attackers, there isn't much we can do at this point."

Without saying a word, Sebastiane stormed right past Smallings and headed straight for the open door to the resident assistant's room and violently pounded on it. He didn't wait for an invitation and entered the room to the protestations of the young man inside. Smallings arrived a second later and got in-between the two of them before anything happened.

"You know who it was because you let them onto the floor and into our room, didn't you?"

"I didn't know," answered the RA, as he backed away from the uninvited guest.

Smallings turned towards the retreating RA and asked, "Didn't know what?"

Sebastiane answered for him, "That they would beat the shit out of us."

The RA continued, "They pretty much did the same thing you're doing to me right now. They came into my room and threatened me. They said there'd be no trouble if I ignored them. They made me give them the master room key. After I found out about everything that happened that night, I wanted to say something, but I was scared."

Sebastiane moved forward, the anger flaring in his eyes and nostrils, and Smallings put his hand out to stop him. Sebastiane knocked it aside before the officer could react. Smallings stumbled but recovered quickly. When Sebastiane stopped advancing, Smallings turned back to the RA and asked, "Are you willing to testify to that?"

"I didn't see anything. I didn't see them after they left my room. I can't testify to anything. I gave them the master room key, which violates policy. I could get fired. Please don't get me fired."

Smallings turned back to Sebastiane, hoping he wouldn't have to defend the diminutive RA for his reply. Sebastiane was just staring at him with a defeated look. Smallings asked, "What?"

Sebastiane answered, "He's right. It wouldn't matter if he testified. He didn't see anything happen inside the room. It would mean nothing to the investigation and even less towards a possible prosecution. His testimony is simply hearsay."

"You in law school or something?" asked Smallings.

"No," answered Sebastiane.

The RA interrupted, "My girlfriend is in law school. Let me call her and see if she can help. But I can't be part of this, please." Sebastiane headed back to his room while Smallings waited.

Ten minutes later, the RA hung up the phone, put down the pen he was using to scribble down notes, turned to the officer shamefacedly, and said, "Give this to him."

Officer Smallings left the room, walked down the hall, and knocked on Sebastiane's door. When Sebastiane opened it, Smallings said, "Here, he gave me this." Smallings handed over the note and his business card as well. "If you need any help, go ahead and call me."

Sebastiane read the note, looked over the card, and grinned. He could sense the sweet taste of revenge percolating within. Then he began to wonder why his original choice of a violent confrontation, so wanted by him after Kenny's first trip to the hospital, wasn't screaming for the same vengeance through violence anymore? And why, through all the anger, hostility, and self-loathing built up inside of him from last summer, why wasn't he or hadn't he given in to all that anger? Whatever the reason, Sebastiane put it down to his decision to simply try harder. He had a path to revenge without violence, and it was currently staring him right in the face in the form of some scribbled notes on a piece of paper and Smallings business card. "Thanks, I just might."

The wry smile on Bassett's face worried Smallings, so he cautioned, "Don't take matters into your own hands. Let the police… let me do my job, and we'll get something on whoever did this." Smallings sighed, and then gave up when Sebastiane wouldn't stop smiling. "Just don't do anything stupid."

When the closing door almost smacked him in the face, Smallings flinched backwards. He could do nothing at that point but turn and leave. As he waited for the elevator to arrive, Smallings hoped he wouldn't have to come back here to mop up another crime scene.

CHAPTER 20

A few days later, four friends exited an off-campus bar. They had been drinking all night, watching the NBA playoffs, and were talking it up so loudly throughout the entire game that everyone else was glad to see them go. Grab-assing on the way back to the car, one of them asked, "Who's driving?"

"None of you assholes seem fit to drive!"

Startled, all four of them searched for the whereabouts of the insolent quipster.

"Up here, dumbasses."

They looked and saw a figure, featureless in the sparsely lit glow of the singular bulb perched high atop a parking lot stanchion, sitting on the roof of their car, a full-sized baseball bat in hand, and menacingly tapping on its windshield.

"Oh, really. And who the hell are you?" asked John Tuckman—Johnny to his friends.

The featureless figure stood up on the hood of the car and sarcastically stated, "For one thing, you shouldn't drive drunk. Very bad form. It's dangerous and someone could get hurt. And besides, you can't drive because the tires are flat—all four of them. Damn shame, truly. It's as if someone purposely let all the air out one by one."

Johnny glanced down and saw that all four tires were indeed flat. Angry, he looked back up to see if he could catch a glimpse of who it was standing on his car. When he was finally able to recognize who it was, he smiled, and then rhetorically asked, "Did you do this?"

Sebastiane replied, "Nope. I was just sitting here waiting to talk to you and some guy came up out of nowhere and just started letting the air out. I thought, damn, somebody must not like you very much. I didn't stop him, of course, and I laughed the entire time he did it too, even gave him some advice on how to get all the air out. He was doing a good job but this *POS* was probably still drivable, so I told him I saw a movie once where the good guy took a pair of pliers and yanked the nozzle right out of the rim. And then, right on cue, the guy who did this to your car takes out a pair of pliers and starts pulling out the nozzles. I told him that what he was doing was technically called *criminal damage to personal property*, but he seemed not to care too much about that part. And… I laughed some more."

"You're a real smartass," said Tyler, Johnny's friend, who was standing to Sebastiane's left but began moving around to the rear of the vehicle.

"One tries not to be I suppose. Maybe, though, if one were to think he had an advantage over his prey but then comes to find out he is sorely outnumbered does he hide his fear by being said smartass?"

Johnny, Tyler, and the other two smiled at each other, mischievously, and began to form a complete circle around the car. When they finally stopped moving, Sebastiane jumped down, surprising them all, tossed the baseball bat to whomever was on his left, he didn't care, and approached John Tuckman without hesitation. The two stared at each other, intently.

"Well, here I am. You can finish the job now."

"You have no idea how happy this is going to make me," said Tuckman.

Sebastiane added, "As I see it, I owe you for the knock to the back of my head. So you," he said, looking over and pointing at whomever, "hold on to that bat and I'll come get it real soon."

Whomever laughed at the ridiculousness of the statement and then tossed the bat to Tyler as he came around to the front of the car. He placed the bat across his shoulders and draped his arms across it to wait.

As Sebastiane turned back to face John Tuckman he was greeted by a body shot to his gut. He dropped to his knees and gasped for air. Before he could recover fully, Johnny picked him up and hit him again. Sebastiane dropped to the ground a second time.

As the other two moved in to pick him up, so Johnny could administer another body blow, Sebastiane asked through his continued gasps for air, "If this is as hard as you can hit, it's no wonder you wimped out and hit me in the back of the head with a bat. And then it takes the four of you to hold down the littlest guy on campus? What, was he too much for you?"

The two helpers held Sebastiane up a little higher at John Tuckman's hand-waved request. He was getting ready to throw a third punch when Sebastiane interrupted, "Cause the way I see it, if it really took the four of you to beat him that badly, leaving him unconscious and bleeding internally, almost killing him really, it's no wonder Maria left you for him. I mean, if he could take that kind of beating and survive... he's obviously stronger than you are."

Johnny began fuming, but before he could unleash his built-up fury, Sebastiane continued yet again, "Ya know, maybe you did that to Maria too! Or maybe she saw what a limp-dick a-hole you really are, getting your rocks off by beating up people in an unfair fight, and presumed she might be next. Maybe she even thought you would trick her out to your friends here. I mean, after all, that shit in the dorm room, who really knows what you're capable of."

John Tuckman, with rage dripping from every pore, asked for the baseball bat with a snap of his fingers. Grabbing it with his right hand, and twirling it menacingly in the air, he clutched violently at the back of Sebastiane's neck with his left and stated triumphantly, "Maria can have him, or what's left of him anyway. But, and I guarantee you this, what I did to him in your dorm room, when I kicked him in the balls and then tore him a new asshole by shoving that mini-bat straight up his whiny little ass, is nothing compared to what I'm going to do to you with this big... fat... Louisville slugger I got right here."

"Hey! What's going on over there?" A man who had walked out of the bar saw the commotion and started to approach.

John Tuckman looked up to see an American Indian-looking man walking towards them. He pointed the bat to make him stop his approach, and said, "Don't butt into others people's business there, Chief. Just go on back to your bottle of firewater, grab your feather boa, crawl back to the Reservation, and just call it a night why don't you?"

The two helpers dropped Sebastiane where he stood and headed away. Tyler took the bat back from Johnny and followed them. Johnny bent down, still enraged, and said, "Next time, smartass." And then he, too, walked away.

As they disappeared out of sight, Sebastiane was being helped to his feet. "Thanks for the help."

Smallings answered, "That guy is truly an asshole. You're lucky."

Sebastiane interrupted, "No, he is. But not for long."

Smallings asked, "Where to now?"

"I need to file a report with your friends at the Campus Police Department. And, do you know any good prosecutor's?"

Smallings grinned, "Yes. I think I can help you with both of those."

~

The next day, John Tuckman and the others were pulled out of their individual classes and arrested. When they arrived at the campus police station, they learned of the charges against them. By the time the senior Mr. Tuckman arrived with the family attorney, who immediately advised his client not to say another word, it was already too late.

Although he'd said nothing in the interrogation room, Johnny's *admission against interest* statement, recorded the night before by Sebastiane in the parking lot during their altercation, describing in detail what he'd done to Kenny, would be more than enough to convict him and his friend's for the assault on two fellow students. Accompanied by a sworn affidavit signed by Sebastiane as to the authenticity of the recording, it was played for Johnny's three accomplices. When they all started talking, John Tuckman was left holding the bag; eventually, all three coped pleas to save themselves from extended jail time.

The Tuckman family lawyer argued passionately against the digital recording. However, when the Assistant District Attorney for Maricopa County pointed out that his clients *admission against interest* statement was indeed legal, and then began reciting Arizona Revised Statutes 13:3005, and 3012(a), stating that a person could indeed be recorded without their knowledge and that recording could be used as evidence as to their admission of guilt in a crime, the family lawyer sighed in frustration knowing that any further arguments were a lost cause. Then, when Smallings produced three freshly inked plea deals signed by Johnny's cohorts, the lawyer asked to speak to his client alone.

When Officer Smallings and the County Attorney exited the interrogation room, they smiled at each other triumphantly. They had a slam-dunk case on their hands and they knew it. After nearly thirty-five minutes, they were asked to reenter the room—*slam dunk!*

As they sat down, Smallings could sense the fear in the room. When he saw the dried tears and red, swollen eyes on the face of John Tuckman, Smallings resigned himself to the fact that those tears, and those broken eyes, would have to be enough to soothe his slighted ego. But he wanted more, and he wanted John Tuckman to know who it was sitting across from him. Smallings stared into John Tuckman's eyes and smiled. When Tuckman looked back and recognized Smallings, the policeman, and proud American Indian, had gotten exactly what he'd wanted.

The xenophobic abuse Smallings had been subjected to in the parking lot the night before from the arrogant little prick sitting in front of him was the potential *coup de grâce* he could use to smear all over the top of this successful prosecution. Smallings had dealt with this kind of crap his entire life, but until now he'd never actually been glad to hear it. His only question at the moment was how he could complain to someone about it. Or maybe he could just note the abusive language in his supplemental report to his commanding officer and stick it to Tuckman officially, and for good measure. Smallings looked down and decided there was no need— the pooling urine on the floor under the chair of John Tuckman would most definitely do.

CHAPTER 21

Flagstaff, Arizona, 1998

It had been almost a year and a half since Sebastiane had crucified John Tuckman and his cohorts on behalf of his friend Kenny Dominguez. He took a long, deep breath to calm his growing anxiousness.

When his first full year at Arizona State had ended, he lost his friend and roommate. Kenny had decided to move back home to continue his education at the community college in Goodyear, Arizona, while he recuperated fully from his injuries. It was what he needed to do, but not what Sebastiane wanted him to do. Kenny then promised Sebastiane that when he did get better, he'd come back, and they'd be roommates again. Sebastiane smiled warmly, realizing it would never happen. Kenny's girlfriend, Maria Columbus, was never that far away, and Sebastiane decided that being a third wheel was not a healthy spot to be in. Watching Kenny drive away that day and then walking back to his dorm room to finish cleaning it out, Sebastiane also realized that he couldn't go home.

The truth was he didn't want to go home. He didn't want to waste his summer working in the office for his father; and yet, he couldn't do nothing. So, he decided he needed to do something else. Sebastiane had felt trapped. He could stay at school and do both summer sessions to get ahead and maybe finish college early. But no, he'd decided that he needed a break from it all. He'd picked up a copy of the student newsletter, looked at the classifieds, and found something that fit his mood. A rancher named Nolan had put in an advertisement looking for a summer ranch hand. When Sebastiane called he'd been happy to hear the position hadn't yet been filled; after the briefest of conversations, he was hired over the phone.

This would now be his second summer working on Old Man Nolan's ranch in the mountains of northern Arizona. Flagstaff was a college town too, but Sebastiane didn't think he could ever transfer to a place where snow closed everything down, except classes, for a few weeks a year. It's not that he minded the snow, he just hadn't grown up with it and didn't want to live in it. But in the summer, the place was stunningly beautiful and had become like a second home to him.

Ranching was always a learning process, and definitely a new experience for him. But Old Man Nolan, who looked more like Charlton Heston than John Wayne, told Sebastiane after only a few weeks that first year that he was a natural rancher and should consider changing professions. Sebastiane found himself smiling and laughing at that comment. And when he realized he hadn't truly smiled and laughed in almost forever, it felt good to do so. Maybe he'd found a place he could just be? And maybe, just maybe, he could sit down at night and rest his weary body after a fulfilling day's work, look up to the heavens and stare deeply into the vastness of space, watch the stars as they reached out in all the directions on the compass, and try to figure out life.

But not tonight.

Sebastiane stood in the light of the full moon, staring at the unlocked barn doors. He was sure he'd locked them before rushing to the hospital to check on his boss. The old man had slipped on melted ice on the kitchen floor and hurt his hip. Sebastiane grabbed at the lock on the barn door to make sure it hadn't been tampered with. It hadn't. And that was good, because having to shoot at another thing prowling on this ranch in back-to-back years was trouble he didn't want or need. He took another deep breath to calm his nerves.

Sebastiane removed the lock, pushed the large barn door open, slowly, and then crept inside. As he paused to listen for sounds of movement, his relative peace began to wane as he pondered why it was that *shit* always happened to him. He paused again when the rafters above him creaked in a way that meant someone or something was in the hayloft.

He made his way along the box stalls. The horses huffed slightly as he passed them. He stopped to assure them nothing was wrong, and then continued towards the workbench at the back wall of the rickety old building. He glanced up to see the Springfield .30-06 rifle hanging above the bench and then down at the drawer where he knew the ammunition was stored, and paused again. He realized that if it was an animal that shouldn't be inside the barn, the horses would have let him know. So he left the gun in its place, unlike the last time, and slowly made his way to the ladder. Sebastiane was glad he wasn't going to need the gun this time; he knew how to use one, he just didn't want a repeat of what had happened last year. The first time he grabbed it, last summer, he'd almost killed Old Man Nolan.

It was three weeks into his first summer. He was bathing Ms. Tildy, the old man's newest-favorite horse inside the barn, when he sensed something. Confirmation came in the sound of the old man's scream. Sebastiane opened the barn door to see Nolan on his other horse about halfway between the barn and the house, a good two-hundred-feet away. The old man was clutching his gashed and bleeding arm. Still on his mount, though, he was backing himself and the horse away from a mountain lion intent on digesting more meat than it had taken with its first attack.

Sebastiane raced back inside the barn, grabbed the rifle, flung open the drawer with the ammo, grabbed two rounds, and ran back to the barn door hoping he wasn't too late. He loaded the bolt-action rifle with one bullet, kept the second between the middle and ring fingers on his trigger hand, rested his cheek on the stock, and then took aim through the scope.

The mountain lion charged. Its advance was halted when the horse reared up to defend itself, its hooves flailing wildly. In the process, the old man fell backwards out of the saddle and onto his backside on the ground. The horse sprinted away. When the hungry cat charged again, Sebastiane pulled the trigger. He missed his bosses head by an inch; the mountain lion went down in a heap.

While at the hospital, not only did Sebastiane have to explain what had happened to an officer from the Department of Wildlife & Fisheries, he'd had to explain everything to Jennifer Nolan—the old man's niece. She was technically his grandniece, daughter of his sister's deceased son, but Nolan had practically raised her himself. Nolan had never married, had only his ranch, and when five-year-old Jennifer took to horse riding and ranch duties like nobody's business, Papa Nolan was as happy as a *Country & Western* song played in reverse. She'd grown up on the ranch and become the son Nolan never had. When Sebastiane's explanation of the incident soothed her nerves, Jennifer Nolan deemed the young city slicker worthy of his residence at the ranch. She called everyone young, even though she was only twenty-six years old herself.

Jennifer Nolan was shorter than Sebastiane, with a rancher's tan covering her pale skin, mid-length auburn hair, dark brown eyes, and features that combined her mother's Peruvian roots with her father's Caucasian ancestry. Her outfits told her true story, though: cowboy boots, a baseball cap, comfortable work jeans, and an appropriate shirt. She was an unmistakable image of western Americana combined with modernism. Sebastiane put it down to her simple upbringings and her dedicated yet misplaced commitment to the lexicons of country music.

While the old man convalesced after the attack, Sebastiane and Jennifer kept the ranch up. The only arguments between them came when she insisted on playing her music while they worked. Sebastiane had always considered himself an eclectic music devotee, all types of songs and artists no matter what the genre, but country music was where he drew the line. Jennifer Nolan had said he just didn't get it.

Sebastiane came back to the present.

Slowly making his way up the ladder to the hayloft, he did so as quietly as possible. Once at the top, he could see a figure standing in front of the half-opened hayloft door. With the cascading brilliance of the full moon flooding through, backlighting everything with a soft, gentle glow, he couldn't tell who it was. When the figure turned at the sound of the last rung of the ladder creaking under his weight, he saw that it was Jennifer Nolan. With a look of utter loss on her face, and what seemed like futility in her heart, she turned away quickly.

As he stepped off, Sebastiane paused before inquiring, "You okay?"

"I'm fine," was her semi-confident reply as she took another sip from the beer bottle in her hand.

"You don't sound fine."

She sniffed at the rebuke, then quickly lowered her proud shoulders when she realized he was right, and said, "I just don't want to lose this place. This is my home. My uncle asked me today if it was a good idea to sell to the Land Development Council. But he asked in such a way… it made me believe he'd already made up his mind. And now, with this latest trip to the hospital for his hip, it wouldn't surprise me if he had already decided."

Sebastiane didn't want the old man to sell the ranch either, but he wasn't getting any younger. The offer was presumably a good one, thought Sebastiane, and the money would probably be more than enough to hand some down to her. Regardless of that fact, the whole area was being converted into a mountainside, gated community, of which the Nolan ranch sat just outside of its southern most edge.

Sebastiane had seen the drawings at the city planner's offices and thought that having ranch land next to a gated community didn't seem to be an optimal lifestyle choice for Nolan. If the place was going to be turned into a gated community, then a mini-mall or maybe even a large shopping center probably wasn't that far behind. No one in the area wanted to sell, especially not Haversham Tiberius Nolan. Some called him H.T., for short, but nobody in their right mind ever called him Haversham. Of course, if he had decided to sell, the other ranchers probably would also. No matter what was going to happen, Sebastiane was convinced that if the old man had agreed to sell, then he'd done so on his own terms.

Sebastiane approached the open hayloft door opposite Jennifer and tried to console her, "At least your uncle isn't the one you're losing. He has a good few years left in him."

"Maybe," she added. "But selling the ranch will probably shorten that. He's worked this place for sixty years. If he stops, he might just lose interest in living too."

Sebastiane agreed with the logic. "True. But he's still got you to keep him grounded. As long as you're still here, I don't think he plans on departing anytime soon. It wouldn't surprise me if he outlives Ms. Tildy."

Jennifer Nolan laughed, softly. Ms. Tildy was just as tough as her owner, and at only three years old, she would easily live another decade or so. She took another sip of her beer and gestured to Sebastiane to help himself to the ice chest. He walked around the red and black, plaid-checkered blanket laying on the hay bales, reached down, and opened the chest to find four beer bottles packed heavily in ice. He grabbed one, opened the non-twist cap with a protruding nail from a beam, came back to the open door, and took a long swig.

"You've really fit in around here, you know. My uncle has liked having you around these last two summers."

"I enjoy my time here. Your uncle is a good man. But maybe it's time for him to do something different."

Jennifer reluctantly agreed, "Maybe you're right." Then, she changed the subject, "I guess if he does sell, you won't be coming up here anymore."

"If he does sell, I'd still come to visit. I have two years left at college. And if he is selling, the paperwork could take a while. I guess that means I'd come up next summer and help pack the house up, get the horses moved to a new stable, and just do what I can."

The thought depressed Sebastiane a little. He enjoyed his summers here and thought he would enjoy all four years of those summers while he decompressed from his studies. That obviously wasn't meant to be, and Sebastiane wondered if he wouldn't just stay on at school and barrel through and do extra classes—maybe even graduate with two degrees instead of just the one.

She agreed, "That would be great if you could come up and help when the time comes. It would make things easier on him, and me."

"Not a problem. It would be my pleasure."

"Can I ask you something?"

"Sure," answered Sebastiane.

Jennifer Nolan inhaled deeply to calm her nerves and then walked over to where he was standing. Without another word, she leaned forward and kissed him.

Surprised, Sebastiane wasn't so much befuddled by her actions as he was upset at the fact that he'd genuinely forgotten how to kiss. As he searched for the reason why, he could only come to the conclusion that the fears of his *first time* were plaguing his thoughts and were therefore preempting his response. He realized he was projecting his past experience with Heather onto Jennifer, thinking she was depressed and needed an outlet. Sebastiane couldn't let the feeling go, though, and hoped she wasn't thinking him a prude. His awkwardness subsided however when she didn't pull away.

He finally let go and kissed her back. And when he did, he felt something different. He felt a comfortable need and a wanting desire to be with her. He didn't understand it. How could he really know the difference between what was happening right now and what had happened to him before with Heather? And, how was he able to distinguish between the two? But he was, and he did. He finally found the courage to thoroughly and completely overcome his inhibitions. He grabbed her waist with his free hand and pulled her in. She responded with a committed passion he had never felt before.

"Come with me."

Sebastiane didn't question it. Instead of trying to fight what he was feeling, and what he wasn't feeling, he simply allowed her to lead him to where she wanted him to be. Kneeling, then lying down on the red and black, tartan-patterned cloth, made all the more comfortable by the loose bundling of straw piled underneath, she put out her hand. He followed her down wantonly.

In the beginning she led the way, and he didn't stop her. Overcoming his past was made easier when he tried to take control of the situation, and she let him. When she wanted it back, he let her. When she became emotional, Sebastiane felt that he should stop. He didn't, though, and she became far more passionate for him in the moment. And in that moment, and with all the moments that burned until the dawn, Sebastiane forgot about who he was and where he'd been. He forgot about his loneliness, his difficulties, and his regrets—and he forgot about his demons.

Sebastiane awoke the next morning to find Jennifer pinned against his back, as close as anatomically possible, with her arms clutched around his waist, her breasts pressed into his shoulder blades, and her cheek resting on his. When he turned to face her, she opened her eyes. He began to speak, but she shook her head and pulled him back on top of her. With this simple gesture, Sebastiane's attitude towards life changed dramatically.

Although not quite the placated paradise of the soul he'd hoped he could find away from his home and his youth, Sebastiane took solace in the fact that the conjoining of his two experiences with a woman—his long-anticipated but hellish intimacy with Heather Prescott, and the passionate, nurturing embraces of Jennifer Nolan—had somehow melded together to become something he hadn't anticipated.

CHAPTER 22

Two days later, Old Man Nolan was sitting on the back deck of his home drinking coffee with his niece when his ranch hand appeared. Sebastiane had his own cup with him and sat down on the open rocker. The five-twenty sunrise over upper Arizona was too good to pass up, and the three of them didn't speak until the sun breached the horizon.

"Nothing quite like it, hey girl?"

Jennifer Nolan always answered her uncle the same way. "Nope, nothing like it."

"Sebco? You're going to miss this too, aren't you?"

"Yes, sir. I will."

"Sebco?" asked Jennifer.

"Nickname my father gave me."

"Oh!" she said, a slight disappointment in her tone at the simplistic answer.

"Boy!" stated the old man. "If there's one thing I've learned in this life, it is to never sleep with a woman before she knows you; always makes things messy when she finds out what you're really like and then doesn't like what she learns. It's one of the reasons I never married."

Jennifer Nolan feigned a look of astonishment that didn't work. Sebastiane's expression didn't give anything away, which actually gave everything away to the senior Nolan. He added, "Time to blush or she'll think it didn't mean anything."

"I'll go make another pot of coffee," stated Jennifer as she snapped up her uncle's cup, frustrated at his omnipotence. As she put out her hand for his, Sebastiane smirked and then raised his eyebrows at her. She snatched his cup and then playfully hip-checked his shoulder as she walked away.

When Sebastiane heard the water faucet in the kitchen sink filling the empty coffeepot, he figured it was time to state his intentions. "Mr. Nolan, I have no plans when it comes to your niece. I figured I'd leave it up to her."

"Good idea. Just don't treat her unfairly."

"Was never my intention."

"And don't let her treat you like shit either." The old man could be feisty when he wanted to be. "Don't get me wrong, I'd shoot you dead if you mistreated my girl. Having said that, she is her mother's daughter and as proud as can be. So watch out."

"Noted," answered Sebastiane demonstratively. He tried to switch the conversation quickly. "I take it you're going to sell?"

"You never beat around the bush do you, except when it comes to discussing yourself." Nolan had never pried into his ranch hand's life, but knew there was something troubling the young man almost to the point of self-imposed reclusiveness—and that constantly worried the Arizonan.

Sebastiane looked over his shoulder to confirm Jennifer was still inside making the coffee before looking back out over a scene he'd grown to admire, would miss greatly, and wouldn't ever forget. He quietly contemplated

Jennifer Nolan's thoughts from the previous evening concerning the health of her uncle and what the loss of this place could do to him. If that meant never seeing the old man again after this summer, Sebastiane suddenly felt the need to unburden himself. "I almost killed a man once."

Old Man Nolan quipped, "With your rifle skills I'm not completely surprised to hear you say something like that."

Sebastiane had been working on the ranch long enough to understand when he was on the receiving end of an offhanded compliment disguised as a derogatory witticism. He smiled internally and continued, "I was fourteen, and didn't know how or that I even could inflict such pain on a person with my bare hands. The police stopped me, but I also think—no, I know—if they hadn't...I wouldn't have stopped before it was too late. A few years later, I lost a good friend and I blamed myself and my girlfriend—her sister—for it instead of blaming the perpetrator, who coincidently just happened to be the same man I almost killed. I ended up losing that girl too, circumstances being what they were and all, and came to Arizona to escape. I think I'm still running away from it all, especially from whatever it was that made me almost kill. If I ever get away from it I wanted you to know that I believe this place helped put me on the correct path."

Nolan didn't react and just kept staring out over the same vista his young friend was. He took a deep breath and offered up some wisdom he'd gained from his long life. "Don't ever regret anything you do, you hear me? Everything happens for a reason, whatever the reason may be. And if you question it or yourself afterwards, you shouldn't have done it in the first place. But if you do end up regretting something, spend the rest of your life making up for it. Got it?"

"Yes, sir."

The door to the house opened. Jennifer came out with a fresh pot of coffee and some toasted bread with butter. She offered each man a piece when she topped off their cups, then sat back down herself. The three of them sat there, quietly, and watched the sunrise complete its chore.

Not long after finishing his toast Old Man Nolan got up and went inside, winking at Sebastiane as he passed by. Jennifer caught the glance but said nothing.

Halfway through her second piece of toast, she got up from her chair, walked over, and sat in Sebastiane's lap. She placed the rest of her piece of toast in his mouth, grabbed his cup, set it on the side table, nestled her head on his shoulder, and spoke softly into his ear, "I enjoyed the other night, but that's all it was. You understand, don't you?"

Sebastiane smiled gracefully while swallowing his pride, and the last of the toast, thought about what the old man had said to him just moments before, and then agreed with her. "I'm good."

"You're going back to school and I have a life. After the ranch is gone, there's no real reason for you to come back up here, is there?"

The comment sounded hopeful and yet finalistic in its delivery, and Sebastiane knew why. No, he more than likely wouldn't come back. Even if she'd said she couldn't be without him, he knew he wouldn't come back. It might be wrong of him to think that way, but it seemed a better idea than moving to Flagstaff permanently or having a long-distance relationship. Besides, he knew those didn't work.

She sat up and looked at him, waiting for his answer. Sebastiane looked straight into her eyes, remembering all of their night together, and said, "I'll probably stay at school over the next two summers and get a minor degree or something like that. So no, I probably won't be back up. But that doesn't mean I'm leaving today. I still have about three weeks left before I have to return. You wouldn't have any ideas on how I could really enjoy those last three weeks do you?"

Jennifer Nolan tilted her head down and put her hand under her chin, mimicking the pose of the famous *Thinking Man* statue, took a few seconds, tauntingly, and then offered, "Well, if you're willing to maintain the ranch to my satisfaction, and avoid the obvious pitfalls of short-timers syndrome, I think I might just be able to accommodate you."

Sebastiane nodded, "Incentive! I like it. Well, I guess it's time to get to work then. First things first; I think Ms. Tildy could use a little workout."

"Get both horses saddled up and I'll join you," she said, smiling.

Sebastiane gulped down the remnants of his coffee and headed for the barn. Jennifer picked up breakfast and took the kettle and cups to the kitchen. As she placed everything in the sink, she stared out the window and watched as the once hopeless city boy went to prepare the horses for their morning walk. She sighed heavily, wondering if she was doing the right thing, but recovered quickly when her uncle asked, "I hope you know what you're doing?"

"I don't think I do. And for some strange reason, it doesn't make me feel bad."

"If you're not ready, then you're not ready. Postponing your engagement to Mr. Turner was the right thing to do. Just make sure you know it was the right thing to do before you call it off completely and end up burning that bridge. Another small bit of advice," he said as he walked over and handed her his cup, "Don't go into town with Sebastiane. I don't think you want him and Henry meeting face-to-face with you in the middle. He is back in town, right?"

"Yes, I've heard he is. He hasn't called, so I'm not sure, though. But why not go into town with Sebco?"

"So… it's Sebco now, is it?" He smiled at his grandniece before continuing, "Just a hunch. Sebastiane seems a real Gemini when it comes to relationships, I think. He's been in love before and lost it, and I don't think he's fully recovered from it. He also has some serious demons and that could make him dangerous. And then, something else entirely tells me he is a damn fine young man and always will be. He's one who would stand in front of a speeding car for someone. He'd also push someone into the street underneath that same car if he felt betrayed. My advice, just don't go into town with him. You understand?"

"Kind of," she offered.

H.T. Nolan walked out of the kitchen and headed upstairs for a morning nap. The drugs the doctor had prescribed for his injured hip made him a little dizzy and a nap was something that seemed to help. Besides, the ranch was currently in good hands; all the work that needed to get done would get done, he was sure of it.

Jennifer finished the dishes, dried her hands, and walked outside. She hesitantly paused on the porch, but only for a brief moment. Remembering the words of her uncle, and then her own words—words that had placed the abrupt stop sign in front of her engagement—she caught herself in a debate. As she hurried through the pros and cons of it all, she focused in on one aspect of her current dilemma: as long as she didn't go into town with Sebastiane, and since Henry never came to the ranch, she needn't worry about burning any bridges. Henry would never know about her fling, and she had no intention of building anything with her uncle's ranch hand. So that was that. She shook her head, realizing the absurdity of it all. She needed to say something to Sebastiane. She proceeded to the barn to help finish the saddling.

When everything was ready, she led Sebastiane out the back gate and into the hills for a two-hour ride. When they returned the horses to the stalls, they spent another twenty minutes finishing their talk. Jennifer asked, "Should I burn that bridge? With Henry?"

"Do you want to?"

She decided she liked the idea that it was her decision. The conversation quickly confirmed for her the fact that she had indeed made the right decision about her engagement—Henry was just too controlling. She smiled maliciously at Sebastiane's next suggestion.

"I am willing to be the fuel and the ignition switch to your inhibitions, though." His thought was that, together, they could be the firestorm that would set the bridges of their unwanted pasts alight—burning them to the ground in all their glory.

She declined, graciously. Then she asked, "What now?"

"I don't know; maybe, work the ranch every day and then eviscerate our emotional inconsistencies every night?"

She lunged forward, grabbed him tightly, and kissed him passionately.

CHAPTER 23

Gretna, Louisiana, 2001

Sebastiane sat next to his grandmother at the front of his parent's living room for all to see. And even though he felt extremely uncomfortable, it didn't matter. He knew that when Grandmother Donah spoke, everyone listened.

His paternal grandmother was a true matriarch. Petite in stature, shrinking was what she liked to call it, with short, silver hair, and a slightly frail body from her advanced years, she was nevertheless the commanding presence in any room—and in the family. She was the personification of wisdom gained through experience. It was a wisdom borne of severe childhood hardship, youthful exuberance, and a mature dedication to her family that had blossomed together into a strong, healthy, and wealthy woman that never looked back. And, since no one had the balls to mention the fact that it had taken five marriages and four divorces, consisted of three children, seven grandchildren, and in another four months or so a ninth great-grandchild to reach its pinnacle, everyone knew she never would.

Donah J. Bassett, nee *Poehl*, was an interesting woman, and had an interesting life. Her own family was not originally from the south. Her people had moved to Louisiana from Oklahoma during the *dirty thirties* when depression and extreme drought forced honest, hard-working farmers to flee in search of greener pastures. Originally relocating to good farmland in south central Louisiana, things didn't quite work out. Eventually, her parents made their way to the city of Gretna—a small community situated on the Westbank of the Mississippi River across from New Orleans.

Forced by circumstance to work from an early age, she did everything from dressmaker to secretary and from factory worker to a playfully raucous bartender in the French Quarter during World War II. After all that, she finally perfected the Norman Rockwell-type lifestyle she'd always planned for with husband number five and his well-to-do business—a now-centuries-old Import/Export company. And ever since her third child, and only son, had taken over, she was able to fully enjoy retirement. She was extremely proud of her accomplishments. She was even more proud today; proud of the fact that at least one of her grandchildren had graduated from college.

In her distinctively raspy voice, aged by drink and the late-night gathering, Grandmother Donah was ending her speech, "Therefore, and in conclusion, to my grandson Sebastiane, well done and congratulations on your graduation from college. And to the rest of your life, may it be full of everything you worked so hard for. Cheers."

She raised her crystal tumbler full of iced vermouth to celebrate his achievement and acknowledge the end of her tribute. With everyone clapping, calls for a speech from the man of the hour echoed throughout the room. Sebastiane raised his hands in humble protest, not really wanting to be in the spotlight and not really wanting to say anything. She eyed him into capitulation. He reluctantly stood.

"Thank you for taking the time out of your busy Saturday night to come help me celebrate this achievement. It's been a long and tumultuous road, but well worth it. And thank you Mom and Dad for affording me the time and the money to attend college out West."

A familiar voice playfully interjected from the back of the room, "Five years is a year too long, bro," offered Ryan.

"Not for three degrees it isn't!" Edward Bassett retorted. Oohs and aahs swept the room.

Sebastiane had stayed in Tempe for three straight summers to do extra classes. In the end, he finished college with concurrent degrees in History, Political Science, and Computer Science. He had his diplomas, but decided not to wait for the end of the summer semester to actually walk in a graduation ceremony. Besides, August temperatures in Phoenix were not something to laugh at. When he'd finished his last summer session, he packed up his dorm room for the last time and flew home only a week ago.

In his growing embarrassment, Sebastiane tried to joke with everyone, "Thanks again, Dad." It worked, slightly, and so he tried again. "Yes, yes. I stayed over the summers and got a couple more degrees. But like I said, Dad was footing the bill so…." He received congenial laughter this time, so he continued quickly, "In closing, I'd just like to say thanks to you all for eating all the food so I don't have to clean up too much." Everyone laughed, as if on cue. "You know me, though, I am not much for words and would hate to push my luck. So again, thank you."

Sebastiane raised his glass in gratitude to all those present, smiled cordially, and then turned to gently kiss the cheek of the Bassett family matriarch. Everyone clapped awkwardly at first, as most realized they didn't know him at all anymore. He had left over five years ago for college and no one had heard from or seen him since. The uncomfortableness eventually decided it was time to leave the room, hurried along to the exit by flowing champagne and other conversation.

"Short and sweet. That's not at all like you. You're usually so verbose," she commented.

"Not anymore," answered Sebastiane, with a solid hint of negativity in his tone.

"Well, you need to get over that shit. You don't have the luxury of any more excuses. It's time you joined the rest of the world in this thing we like to call life. Got it?" She was chastising him but in a lovingly demanding manner, and he knew it

"Yes, ma'am." Sebastiane was sure he'd upset her, but she hadn't smacked him in the face, so he hadn't upset her too much. He needed to apologize. He looked at her, but she stopped him dead in his tracks.

"You're fine, my child. But I think it's about time you realized it too. Snap out of it and go talk to everyone. And get me another drink on your way back over here, would you?" She repositioned herself in her chair to strike up a conversation with others standing nearby.

Sebastiane nodded and took his leave. He knew full well that he needed to get on with life, and get Grandmother another drink. As he made his way through the crowd, trying to get to the kitchen, being stopped by congratulatory claps on the back, he remembered how important she was to him. When the nightmares had come, as often as they had in those early days, Grandmother was the one who talked to him about life. She reassured him constantly that his future would supply him with the fortitude needed to forget. Sometimes she even invited Heather and Sarah to come over so she could specifically talk to all three of them, over nightcaps of iced vermouth and six-packs of beer, to tell them that life was life and that they, not someone else, made it what it could be. Philosophically, she told them she believed that since they had all been through hell to get to their sixteenth birthdays, as she had done, they would be fine the rest of the way—she also reminded the three of them not to tell anyone about the beer.

Mom and Dad had their own versions of life-affirming talks. And yes they did help, but for some reason Grandma Donah's just made a lot more sense. Dad was Dad, and his speeches were practical. Mother seemed to always be holding something back. Individually, their speeches were confusing at first. But combined, and after so many of them, Sebastiane's troubles seemed to meld into a single coherent, commingling enemy that might just be defeated.

Sebastiane finally arrived in the kitchen and found the vermouth. Having done so, he retrieved ice from the freezer. As he shut the refrigerator door, out of the corner of his eye he caught a glimpse of a female figure through the porch windows running away from the front door. Instantly he knew who it was. He dropped the crystal tumbler on the counter, startling those around him, and tried to make his way to the front door. Getting closer, he saw the silhouette of a woman's figure running down the lighted driveway and heading towards a vehicle with its passenger door open and the engine revving with impatience. Too many people were jammed in the house, congratulating him, asking unimportant questions, delaying him needlessly. Finally, he opened the front door and ran towards the street.

All he saw was a car half a block away preparing to turn left. By the time he made it into middle of the street and began waving his arms, he realized it was too late. The car was gone. He looked back at his truck thinking he could catch up. He fished through his pockets for the keys. When he couldn't feel them, he realized he'd have to go back inside the house, through the mass of people, and up to his room to find them. His shoulders slumped and he exhaled deeply, knowing full well he'd missed his chance to see her. Lowering his head, he reflected painfully upon the fact that he hadn't even heard from her in almost three years. A shiver ran down his spine as he tried to justify those three years by convincing himself that he'd treated her so badly that summer.

Or was it the other way around?

After pointlessly waiting for the car to reappear, for what seemed like an hour, Sebastiane gave up and walked slowly back to the house only a minute after he'd ran out.

Stopping short of the front door, not wanting to go back inside, he noticed a white envelope hanging out of the mailbox. He grabbed at it apprehensively. He recognized her writing on the envelope and joy filled his heart as he opened it, hoping the words inside would be an opening. His expression quickly deflated when he read the card. It was nothing more than a miniscule, preformed phrase of meaningless words laser printed on a plain, white Hallmark-like good luck card, with a simple signature in block letters at the bottom. There was nothing else. It was completely devoid of any sense of emotion. It was just a blank white card in a blank white envelope. He folded it instead of crushing it, placed it in his pocket, and walked back into the house as some of the guests started leaving.

~

"You want to stop and get some more beer for the trip back?"

"Yes." He wasn't really asking her; he was telling her, so she just sat in the passenger seat smoking a cigarette and staring blankly into the passing reflections of the city lights as they bounced off the half rolled-down window.

To answer him with a *yes*, as she had done, and to fervently accompany that *yes* with a definitive nod of the head, as she had done, was the correct and compliant way to answer all of his rhetorical questions. And if the yes was not normal or common or had any tinge of attitude or self-determination to it, or if she didn't shake her head affirmatively enough, she knew she would only be subjecting herself to another sarcastic, spiteful retort—or maybe even worse. She didn't really know if she could handle another painful, five-fingered, black-and-blue moniker of his love for her on her forearm. Besides, another one of his beloved monikers of affection would only serve as a continuing and sickening reminder to her of the horrendously deplorable and wantonly forgettable last three years— and of the increasingly regrettable decision she'd made earlier in the day.

The car stopped at a liquor store and he went inside. She did not watch him go. The sight of him had become repugnant and revolting to her. She lifted her hand to take another pull on her cigarette and glanced at the wedding ring on her finger. Her eyes quickly began to tear up.

It was all my fault. Sebastiane, please forgive me.

Quickly, she wiped the tears away as he reemerged from the convenience store. Two of the three paper-bagged, largish beer cans he had purchased were tossed into her lap through the open window along with another pack of cigarettes. He walked around and got back in the driver's seat, opened the beer he hadn't tossed at her, and drank half of it before starting the car.

The car jumped and its tires screeched when he floored the gas pedal to back out of the parking space. They screeched again as he entered the street and headed down the road towards the expressway. He ran the red-light before swerving onto the on-ramp.

After three years of dating, two years in which she had garnered multiple bruises and an ever-increasing volume of virulent, mental abuse, and eight hours of marriage, Heather Prescott-Middleton began to wonder how long it would take to escape from her current disaster.

~

"You sure you don't want to come watch some football tomorrow with me and my brother?" asked Ryan. "It has been way too long and we need to catch up. You need to tell me all about college out West."

Sebastiane had nothing better to do, but didn't feel like it. "I can't. I have to be up early tomorrow to drive my parents and grandmother to the airport."

Ryan Neihaus and his older brother Greg seemed to be the only two friends Sebastiane had left in Gretna, but it would have to be next time. "Next week?" offered Sebastiane.

Ryan wouldn't give up. "The Saints play tomorrow! How about Monday night instead? We go to this bar on Huey P. Long. It's a nice place with lots of pretty girls to look at. Come on!"

Sebastiane reluctantly gave in. "Sure."

About three hours later, Ryan was the last guest out the door. Everyone else in the house was already asleep. Edward had tasked his son with cleanup duties, a task made simpler when Ryan had stayed to help, but Sebastiane was still awake at two in the morning finishing up.

The cleanup had stalled and seemed to go slower and slower the more he thought about seeing Heather again. At one point he found himself practically rubbing the porcelain glaze off the fine china his parents treasured after he realized he'd been using a scouring pad on it instead of a washcloth. Worse off, he had to catch it before it fell on the floor because the soap had so thoroughly covered his hands and lower arms from his absentminded dedication.

Sebastiane took one last look around just to be sure his task was complete. Finally, he thought. He flopped down on the couch, exhausted. He turned on SportsCenter. As he stared blankly at the screen, still lost in his thoughts about seeing and then missing Heather, he wondered what she was doing now. He wondered if she thought about him, or if she thought about them. He wanted to tell her he thought about her all the time. He wanted to apologize to her for that summer. He wanted to say he was sorry about Sarah. He wanted to tell her he missed Sarah, and her, and their times together. He wanted to tell her....

Sebastiane fell asleep while torturing himself about the past.

CHAPTER 24

Tampa Bay, Florida

"You promised me this wouldn't become a domestic issue Nathan, and now it has!" exclaimed General Sykes. He was understandably upset but remarkably reserved, showing nothing on his face that might betray his true feelings while he handed his compatriot a drink.

It had been a long day. The darkness outside the general's office window didn't seem to match up with the hands that ticked marchingly across the face of the wall clock. It was late, and his eyes felt the strain of the day's business far more when he stared at the silver-plated timepiece on the wall. The general was also extremely displeased with having to be at work on a Saturday, especially since it meant missing his grandson's football game—and all because of a telephone call. He hated when it happened and usually dealt with it accordingly when it did, but this had been no ordinary phone call. The call had originated from just south of the Potomac River, near Washington, DC, at the behest of the directors of both the CIA and the NSA, while they were having coffee with the Joint Chiefs of Staff—at the Pentagon no less.

"This situation is not a domestic issue, sir. The CIA, the NSA, the Joint Chiefs, they are the issue not this program," responded Westerly. Feeling cornered unnecessarily yet extremely justified with his explanation, Nathan Westerly was nevertheless very aware of the general's ear being firmly attached to the little blue phone on his desk. It was a private communications line that linked the Slater Group directly to an identical blue phone situated at the top left-hand corner of the communications wall in the Joint Chief's command center. Until recently, it didn't exist. Westerly continued with his rebuke, "They're the ones who wanted this program. And then when it came online and produced as planned, they balked as the realization of their own ineptitude smacked them upside their collective heads. Basically, they came to realize that we are the right man for the job, not them... and certainly not any of their respective agency analysts."

Westerly was trying to control the situation to prevent his plans from blowing up in his face. It was all typical, useless, bureaucratic bullshit and last-minute grandstanding anyway. Those slimy bureaucrats in Washington always wanted nothing to do with anything until that nothing turned into something they could take credit for. Only then would they take control and use everyone and everything to advance their own pathetic careers. Westerly should have known this was going to happen.

Damn it. I'm so close.

It had been five years since Firebird Communications, LLC went belly up. At the time they had been only three months away from completing and then launching their new state-of-the-art, worldwide satellite communications constellation for use by the private sector. When the collapse came, it had been Westerly who'd suggested to several important people in DC that the Slater Group be the one to step in and take over and lift Firebird from the ashes. But instead of just private-sector communications, he proposed a hidden, dual-functioning, and heavily encrypted worldwide communications intercept system. It would become the next generation *SIGINT* platform that could track and then listen in on and read all of the enemies' voice and data communications.

These important people, namely CIA and NSA, bought into the plan and helped fund the project through a few undisclosed business entities. What Westerly hadn't realized, and was only now kicking himself for, was the fact that the CIA and the NSA had played him. They thought Westerly too naive and greedy; how could anyone other than themselves, the government, be the ones to review the raw intelligence data this system would spit out? They convinced General Sykes, for better or worse, that it always had been and always would be the government's purview to *spy* on people from their level, not private industry from theirs. By not telling Westerly, the CIA, NSA, and eventually the DIA, the Defense Intelligence Agency at the Department of Defense, had the time to talk the general into turning the whole project over to them. Figuring it out now, and not then, truly infuriated Westerly because he had no leverage to use against them at this point.

How did I get caught out? No matter. If those are the games they want to play, so be it. All they did was play games anyway.

Westerly knew government agencies were consumed by pitiful little turf wars, and then would insulate themselves from the blowback when those same little turf wars made them vulnerable. They always lost focus on what really mattered. While they played pathetic games of *we don't have the assets to cover that,* or *that is not your jurisdiction, it's ours,* they never could realize what potentially destructive and irrevocable harm was lurking out in the world while they did. Because of those inept, petulant, sibling rivalries between the alphabet soup agencies within the United States Government Intelligence apparatus, all of them were no longer at the forefront of risk-taking. They couldn't protect the country the way it needed to be, and everything was going to hell in a hand basket. Westerly knew that, and it was time to do something about it.

Fool me once, shame on me. Fool me twice, not gonna happen cause payback is a bitch.

Westerly knew his planned schedule would be thrown off by this unwanted, late-afternoon phone call. So what if he wasn't quite ready. But if his complaints about the government and the safety of the country were not to be bathed in hypocrisy, he needed to finally put his own neck on the line and get things moving. No more hiding. No more planning. It was time. He would just advance his timeline a little. It was time to initiate the final phase of his takeover of The Slater Group, Inc.

One year off, not too bad actually.

The general could see that his company vice president was stewing a little and tried to calm him down, "Nate, look... I understand this was your baby, and I know you had big plans for it. And I know you believe this project could propel this company to the forefront of the industry, but damn it if this whole thing doesn't just smack of some domestic surveillance conspiracy hullabaloo."

Westerly grew angrier at the repetitive nature of Sykes's complaints. He could not only sense the palpable inevitability in his superior's tone, but the whole conversation seemed to be leading down a rather unfortunate path in his eyes. Westerly needed to avoid that path at all costs. His mind raced as he quickly ran through several options while taking another hefty swig from his glass. Once he decided on his tactics, he tried to create an opening for the general to step into.

"I assure you that that is *not* the case. Sir...." Westerly softened his tone before continuing, "Sir, you gave me seven years to get this project up and running, and I did it in four. Now here we are one year removed from initiation, and they all finally realize we have them by the balls—financially speaking, of course. And that is it. No more, no less. They're deflecting the argument by advertising this as some sort of private entity overstepping its bounds and jumping into the government's private pool. It's not. They know as well as I do that domestic surveillance is not the primary function of this system. In fact, it isn't even a function of this system at all."

"Quite the analogy, Nathaniel. But you do realize that to them it looks like you're pissing in their private pool, and they are not impressed by your bravado."

"General, I've done nothing of the sort. Surely you can see that. With them bitching at us now, only after the system has gone online! Basically, they blinked. We called their bluff and they blinked. The sophistication of the system accompanied by the ability to interpret the data and then sell it, that's what this is about. It's about the money, pure and simple."

"Hell of a game of poker you play, Nate." Both men loved the game and were good at it, but Sykes was starting to understand why he lost most times to this Navy puke. It was not an endearing term, not at all, but it was a respectful one coming from this particular jarhead. "Another scotch, Nate?" offered the general.

Westerly accepted. He'd had a long day too, and the plush leather couch in Sykes's office and the good scotch were going a long way towards soothing his frustrations. Westerly continued after receiving his refill. "Sir, by keeping the analysis contract within we could have given them exactly what they had asked for—true, actionable, real-time, solid intelligence. The back-end contracts to supply that information so the agencies don't have to incorporate a new cog into their bureaucratic system, for lack of a better phrase, would make things simpler for them and make this whole endeavor worth the investment. For us, without those contracts we only break even on the deal."

Westerly decided to interject some much-needed and far stronger rational into the conversation, trying to justify his point of view but also trying to paint the general into a corner. "Besides, even if this project had been completely integrated with their bureaucratic, non-sensical, outdated abilities, do you honestly think they could have realized its full potential and used it to prevent Tanzania and Kenya from happening? Surely they had enough information without the system to prevent the attack on the USS Cole. In the end, for me, I don't think they could have. But I know in my heart that we would have."

The general lowered his head in deep contemplation. Remembering the carnage of Beirut during his own military career, and all the other aforementioned instances of attacks on United States military personnel around the world since the Slater Group had been founded, was what had convinced Sykes that Westerly's satellite gambit was a solid move when initially proposed. But now it seemed as if Westerly was alluding to something far more disturbing. The general asked, "Are you trying to tell me that we could have prevented all of those incidents if we'd had the system back then?"

Westerly did his best to hide his growing confidence, and said, "We can't know about Africa, but surely we would have learned from our mistakes and done a better job before the USS Cole incident. We have a good intelligence division. The open-source material our shop put together before the Africa incident might, and I stress might, might have led us down the correct path to prevention. We just didn't have enough closed-source information, in-house or otherwise, to make that call."

Westerly took a sip of his scotch before continuing, "I do believe, however, that the information our system—sorry, the system—could have provided, if it was available, would have been more than enough to prevent the attack on the USS Cole. But since the CIA wasn't playing nice then and isn't playing nice now, I don't think we are ever going to get a look at the raw intelligence data or the after-action reports to see if we would have been right on either. The only way we are ever going to prevent something from happening again is if we control the system—all of it, from beginning to end." Westerly swirled the drink in his glass. The scotch was good, as usual. The first one had gone down rough. The second was getting much smoother.

"Sir, the only thing I do know is this," Westerly continued, hesitating slightly. He needed to guard against betraying his thoughts. He needed to carefully word his next phrase. If he did so, perfectly, his carefully laid plans would come to fruition and he could plop a delicious Maraschino cherry smack dab right on the top of his two-fold endgame. Part one would be sealing the upright coffin he'd just opened for the general to walk straight into. And part two was making sure Admiral Nathaniel Westerly, (ret.), came out on top when the corporate dust settled. "General, if something like Tanzania and Kenya or the USS Cole happened again, and we are not in control of the system, we'll have no one to blame but ourselves." Westerly wanted to add *you'll have no one to blame but yourself,* but didn't. He was just hoping the general would take the last step without the extra push.

And he did, right on cue.

"If anything like Africa or the USS Cole happens again, I'll quit right on the spot, regardless of whether we have control of the system or not," Sykes said confidently.

Westerly smiled internally, but feigned caution externally. "Sir! That's crazy talk. If we are not in control, how could you possibly blame yourself?"

"Because, Admiral, it would mean that I'm getting too old for this shit. It would mean that I should've listened to you in the first place and not let myself get talked into or pressured into relinquishing the analysis contracts. Stupidity breeds inefficiency, and I will not abide by anyone's stupidity being the cause of any more incidents like West Africa or the Cole—especially if they are my own. But I had to agree. And I am sorry to have to say it again, but you will have to comply with the Government and their agencies handling of the analysis from the system. Affirmative?"

"Sir. Yes, sir," said Westerly, in as courteous a tone as he could muster. Inside Westerly felt overwhelmed with the success of his maneuverings and began to feel pity towards the general. Westerly finished his scotch. It now tasted exquisitely good.

General Sykes was done. "All right. Since that seems to be it, I'm leaving. Tomorrow we'll start anew. Sound good, Nate?"

CHAPTER 25

Westerly accompanied the general to the lobby and then returned to his office while contemplating the outcome of his win/lose conversation with the boss. He was happy about the win—helping to plant the seed of retirement in Sykes's mind—but he feared that the loss of the analysis contract would definitely sting the company's bottom line.

We need those analysis contracts back. That's where the money is. All we really need is another incident like the USS Cole to seal the deal.

STOP! That was unprofessional and disconcerting to say the least. To hope for the death of American servicemen or United States citizens only to advance my own financial gains is not why I am here.

"That is not why I am here," he repeated out loud.

I am here to prevent any harm to my country, its servicemen and women, and its citizens. Should I make a profit as well? Why not? It's not a conflict of interest as long as the money comes in later, right?

"Right!"

After the First Gulf War, Westerly had watched as his beloved United States Navy suffered at the hands of Orwellian downsizing and Machiavellian-style cutbacks. Even after his retirement, his honor couldn't justify why things kept getting worse. He imagined a still beating heart ripped from the chest of a living body, spewing blood, and smothering the country he swore to protect and defend. Then came Somalia. Then came the Balkans. And that was the last straw. Enough was enough. His decision to join the Slater Group had given him the opportunity and the means to do what he thought was right to help restore the country to what he remembered. Now, he was at the cusp of doing exactly that. Damn the afterthoughts of profiteering. He had seen too much and lived through too much. He had endured far too many years of apathetic, anemic, debilitating, governmental pedestrianism while he watched, worried, and then grieved as his beloved United States declined towards mediocrity. And now he most certainly was not going to start entertaining thoughts of profiteering. Westerly nodded his head in agreement with his own capitulation.

As he pushed aside all the last-minute doubts and fears within, a mental projection of an angel on one shoulder and the devil on the other popped into his head. He stared at both of them in the reflection of his office window. The angel on his right unsheathed its sword, jumped across his morality, and decapitated its brother-in-arms. But, he thought belatedly, on which side of this cerebral dilemma did the angel represent? Only time would tell as Nathaniel Westerly was startled back to reality by the phone ringing on his desk. He picked it up.

"Admiral. We did it! The system conversion is complete," announced Dr. Theodore "Ted" Saunders, Director of *R&D*, the Research and Development Department, at The Slater Group, Inc.

"Really! That fast? I knew we hired the right man for the job, Saunders. Good work." The phone call brought a confident smile back to Westerly's face. This was an unexpected bit of good news and Westerly could feel the scales of chance tipping in his favor. The ethical dilemma he had just watched in his office window was quickly forgotten.

No more arguments, and never again question your decisions—ever.

Saunders responded, "Yes sir, Admiral. However, we do have some things to discuss regarding activation. If you'd like me to come up and explain?"

"It's Saturday night, Mr. Saunders, and very, very late. Don't you have a game to prepare for tomorrow?"

With week one of the NFL season just a few hours away, most of upper management was already gone. Westerly admired Saunders dedication, but also liked his staff to be family people too. Saunders explained, "Denver doesn't play until Monday night. I have the time if you do, sir."

Five minutes later, at almost a quarter past eleven, Saunders entered the admiral's office with several binders of technical manuals and one rather large, backpack-sized computer that looked more like a circa 1940s military radio. It was equipped with a handset-type telephone and an *LCD*, liquid-crystal display, monitor on the front. After about twenty-five minutes of technical explanation, the admiral finally asked, "And that is the only drawback to this version?"

"Yes," replied Saunders.

"And we can eventually fix it when the next generation hardware becomes commercially available?"

Saunders quizzically asked, "Sir? Commercially?"

Westerly explained himself. "I know, I know. The CIA has it, but they don't know we also have it. If we go online with the new hardware, they'll know we copied everything before handing it over. That wouldn't go over very well with *Big Brother*, so we'll just have to wait."

Saunders nodded immediately, realizing the correlation—potential blowback from the China operation. Not being privy to the ins-and-outs of that particular operation, all he'd been told at the time was that a little payback was necessary when the Chinese military had intercepted and then detained a US Navy spy plane flying in international airspace. The United

States government couldn't do anything, officially, so the Slater Group was asked to help out. The Slater teams dispatched to the scene were able to destroy most of the captured electronics by setting fire to the facility where the Chinese military was conducting reverse engineering protocols in an attempt to duplicate the technology. Whatever hadn't been destroyed was brought back home, along with some rather interesting bits and pieces of opposition technology as well. It was all handed over to the CIA—after it was copied.

Westerly was an ambitious bastard, thought Saunders. And now it seemed the admiral felt he didn't need to hide those ambitions from him anymore. Dr. Ted Saunders smiled.

Inner circle, here I come.

He was pleased with himself, knowing he had done much to justify his inclusion. Saunders added, "Okay then. Well yes, we can make the fix to this version of the backpack station so it can receive real-time data, images and all, without detection from any other part of the system; or even from whomever is watching a data-stream intercept at that time. Basically, unless someone is really paying attention and knows what to look for, we'll have our own silent and undetectable operational uplink on a backdoor. For now, this pack can do that but only in passive mode. If it is turned to active mode, the operator and his team will be susceptible to detection by the system."

Westerly asked, "To reiterate then; the new version with the new hardware will be clean and clear, but this version won't be until we upgrade?"

"Correct."

Westerly was very pleased. He knew now that regardless of the analysis contract he could fulfill his obligations to protect the United States on his own terms. Without a doubt he wanted the contracts back in his own house to solidify the financial well-being of the company he'd control someday soon, but that would just be icing on the cake. Yes, Westerly was very pleased indeed. Then something else occurred to him, "What about this first generation pack working with the next generation of satellites?"

"That won't be an issue, sir. With or without the conversion to the new hardware, the same rules will apply," Saunders assured him.

"Excellent."

With a firm, congratulatory handshake, and a pat on the back, the admiral welcomed Ted Saunders behind the curtain. He would now be a part of everything that happened from here on out. As Saunders collected his materials and headed for the door, he waved back to Westerly to thank him. The admiral smiled at him.

Damn, I'm going to have to give that man a raise.

CHAPTER 26

Gretna, Louisiana

Sebastiane awoke to the same SportsCenter news story he'd fallen asleep to. Tired from an uneasy rest, as his mind couldn't stop focusing on seeing Heather, he jumped into the shower to wash it all away. Afterwards, he helped pack up the car for the trip to the airport.

The drive was quick, and he was handing the bags over to the curbside check-in steward when his mother approached him. "Sebastiane? Please take care of my plants, especially the tall one in the foyer."

"No problem," he answered.

"I believe the answer you're looking for is *Yes, ma'am*," Edward Bassett corrected his son's manners. As he paid to have the bags taken to the check-in counter, the steward looked at Edward and shook his head in agreement.

"Sorry. Yes, ma'am." Sebastiane's apology was genuine but lacked conviction. He was tired and had a vague look in his eyes that only isolation could cure.

"Listen to me," stated Elena, purposefully garnering his attention so as to make her point understood. She could sense his troubled mindset and wondered if she was doing the right thing after all this time, but she knew she couldn't wait any longer—it was time. "When we return from New York, you and I are going to have a long talk."

Sebastiane began to protest, thinking he was getting an earful for his rather unfortunate choice of words, but she stopped him. "It's about your grandfather."

Sebastiane balked. He had always wanted to hear about her father, but wondered why now?

And why was she being so dramatic about it?

"Sounds good," he said as he kissed her good-bye. He shook his father's hand and waved to his grandmother waiting just inside the air-conditioned terminal in her courtesy wheelchair.

After they disappeared inside, Sebastiane slumped into the car seat and headed away. Driving mindlessly, not knowing what to do with himself, he ended up going straight home, staggered up the stairs, crashed onto his bed, and fell into a depression-like half sleep for the next thirty-six hours. When he rolled out of the bed, Sebastiane remembered Ryan's pleas to come and watch Monday Night Football. So, he got up, splashed some water on his face, forgot to change clothes, and walked to the bar.

As he entered, Sebastiane was greeted by a look of total shock on Ryan's face. His friend was sitting with a group of people Sebastiane didn't recognize. He found his way to a barstool and ordered two beers with a shot of something or other. He downed the first beer and chased it with the shot. Throwing down a twenty-dollar bill, he walked over to the table and was introduced to people he had no interest in meeting and no interest in talking to. As he politely returned their greetings and took his seat, the sound of the game announcer's voice began blaring from the speakers hanging throughout the bar.

"The setting couldn't be any more perfect—sunset over the front range of the Rockies. It's a beautiful night, seventy-five degrees, Invesco field at mile high. Right next door—the old stadium. Moments ago the Bronco legends, led by John Elway, came out onto the field… and the crowd went wild."

Sebastiane spent the rest of the night paying polite attention to Ryan's girlfriend's older sister, Nicole, seeing right through the obvious setup by his friend. When the game ended, he left the bar alone.

~

Without remembering the walk home or opening the front door or even getting undressed, Sebastiane opened his eyes around seven in the morning, stumbled to the bathroom, and proceeded to regurgitate the egregious amounts of alcohol he'd consumed the night before. After finishing, he looked at himself in the mirror and wondered if this was to be his existence from now on. Work for Dad, go out after work, and then drink until whenever. It was only one night, but it felt like a month's worth. What was it Grandmother had said?

Time to get on with life, or something like that….

He shook his head clear, splashed water on his face, rinsed his mouth out, and got dressed for a run.

He closed the front door and turned left, heading towards the Mississippi River levee to do his normal five miles. When he ran at college, he always had to dodge other students on campus. He had craved solitude then and hoped that solitude along the path on the levee would be forthcoming.

About an hour later, at a much slower pace than he was used to, Sebastiane was coming to the end of his return leg. With the growing sensation that solitude can sometimes suck, he nevertheless found himself enjoying the calm of the river as it vigorously flowed past him, meandered through the city, and headed out towards the sea. He was also enjoying a continuous view of downtown New Orleans since there weren't any ships on the river to obscure it.

That's odd!

As he began to process the silent serenity accompanying him all morning, Sebastiane started looking around and realized there weren't many cars on the streets either. He looked over at the Greater New Orleans Bridge, and although far away he could see that it didn't seem that busy— even at this time of the morning. He passed the Gretna-Jefferson ferry landing, and it too seemed quite empty for a workday. He quickly diverted his run into Old Town Gretna.

Again, he noticed cars were not clogging up the streets or lining up to pay for parking on what should be a typical Tuesday morning. He began to sense something was wrong. He looked back toward the courthouse, not knowing why, and finally, deep inside, a cold and unwanted feeling informed him something was indeed very, very wrong. There were far too many police officers milling about at one location for there to be nothing wrong.

He picked up the pace and sprinted the last quarter mile to the house. He bounded up the porch steps, practically crashed through the front door, found the remote, and quickly turned on the television. He stood motionless as he began watching the videotaped replay of the destruction of the Twin Towers in New York City. He remained locked to the floor in the same position for twenty minutes as death was replayed over and over again on every channel he switched to.

Staring unbelievably at the screen for what seemed like an eternity, his heart sank while his body tensed. Nothing allowed him to make his next move. He overcame it all just long enough, though, to reach over and grab the house phone on the small side table next to the couch. He dialed his father's mobile number hoping to hear someone, anyone, on the other end of the line. He was concerned but not surprised when the only thing he heard was a busy signal. He slowly replaced the receiver. The gripping fear immobilized him yet again.

Sebastiane would try the same thing every half hour for the next three days—pick up the receiver, dial the number, get a busy signal, and then hang up. He could hardly eat, couldn't really sleep, and never turned the television off—not once. On the fourth day he was still dialing, and still getting nothing. His mind was numb from the effort while his soul was void from the pain of not knowing. He had just replaced the receiver yet again when it rang back at him. The sound was foreboding and seemed to mock him as he reached for it.

"Hello."

"Sebastiane? This is Jean Francois Bertrand." There was a pause. "I am your mother's uncle and your parents' attorney. Do you remember me?"

The tone of the question hid the unbearable truth of what Sebastiane knew was coming, "Yes, sir. I remember. What can I do for you?" Sebastiane closed his eyes and hung his head in full acknowledgment of the necessity of the next phrase.

"May I come over to the house to see you?"

"Yes," was all Sebastiane could muster as a far more terrible pain— the pain of truth—began tearing him inside out.

He forced his eyes to screw shut, tighter than they already were, trying to block the agony quickly overwhelming him. The tears, breeching the hardened barriers his eyelids had become, started flowing into an emotional abyss that was widening as his heartache grew. They continued trickling down his arm and falling onto the phone handle as he replaced it on its cradle.

The doorbell rang not ten seconds later. Sebastiane walked forward, apprehensively. When he opened the door, he saw Jean Francois Bertrand standing there, stoically. He was an older gentlemen, in his early sixties, and very rotund from years of living on good food and the extravagance of the New Orleans social scene. Although he didn't partake so much anymore because of his advanced age, the years of doing so were etched on his face. It was also a face that bore the excess horror and strain of the past several days. In his hand was a folder of documents.

Jean asked, as he removed his hat in a small gesture of condolence, "I have some information for you. May I come in?" Sebastiane walked away from the open door. Jean followed him inside.

As Jean entered, his emotions overtook him. He thought himself to be an omniscient and ominous presence in regards to the Bassett family. He had taken in Elena when his cousin Maurice had asked and was thus in the unfortunate position of being the letter bearer concerning the death of her mother. And now, this. They were only two events, a small number in comparison to the many he'd dealt with in his line of work, but they were two very significant events that ever-so-slightly undermined his belief in a higher power.

Closing the door, Jean Francois Bertrand, Attorney at Law, cleared his throat and began, "There is no delicate way to put this, so I will be factual. I received a phone call late last night from a Dr. Ramesh of the New York City Coroner's office. Your parents and Ms. Donah were present in the North Tower at the World Trade Center when the first plane struck. It seems that they were able to make it outside just as the tower collapsed. They could not make it to a safe distance, though. They were some of the first bodies to be recovered by NYPD Search & Rescue."

"Stop! I don't think I can handle this," Sebastiane muttered as the shock of what he was hearing truly began to sink in. The tears, emotions, heartache, and rage swelled inside of him. Hearing about how they died was not the memory he wanted of them. The goodbyes at the airport were what he wanted to remember.

"I understand," Jean Francois offered. After a slight pause he continued in as professional a tone as he could, all-the-while fighting back tears of his own. "I have your father's Family Estate Trust Plan with me. Everything regarding the house, the business, everything is taken care of." The young man was doing his best to control his sobbing Jean could see, so there was no need to go into any of the financial details right now.

Jean hesitated to mention the next part, thinking it could wait a day or two, but he thought better of it. Better to get this out in the open and not prolong the inevitable, he decided. "I have your mother's individual Last Will & Testament for you to look over. There are some directions for you to follow—directions concerning her burial rites."

"Individual! Wait, what?" stammered Sebastiane, as he reluctantly yet snipingly snatched the document out of Jean Francois's outstretched hand. Sebastiane stiffened as he read his mother's declarations. What he read had obviously been planned out long ago and never mentioned or hinted at, or revealed, until now. The last paragraph on page one started with her desire not to be buried in the Bassett family crypt at the Hughes Cemetery in Algiers. The first paragraph on page two made him stop reading altogether, "What the hell...? What is this?"

"It is all there, and all the arrangements are being made. As soon as their remains arrive back in New Orleans, you will proceed as instructed. My firm will take care of everything else," he answered, avoiding the question as he was instructed to do.

Sebastiane wasn't fooled. "You didn't answer my question." His rebuttal, backed by an underlying confusion, which grew with every successive word he read on the paper, was sarcastic at best.

Again, Jean avoided Sebastiane's angry, inquisitive question. "Please forgive me. But it is time for me to go. Preparations need to be made. When the bodies are released, they will be flown here. When that happens, I will call you and I will come back and make all the final arrangements with you."

Sebastiane let him leave. Jean Francois Bertrand, his great-uncle, couldn't, or wouldn't, answer his questions about what had happened or what was happening. He walked back towards the couch and tried to come to grips with what he'd just read. After ten more seconds of trying, he crashed into the couch before he collapsed onto the floor. After a few deep breathes, Sebastiane spent the next hour reading his mother's will over and over again just to make sure it said what it was saying. When he couldn't read it anymore, he placed it on the table, stood, and went upstairs to his room.

The walk was long and empty. Instead of sleeping, finally, after four days of hoping against hope, Sebastiane remained at his window, staring outside, continually staring at nothingness while the darkness passed and the sun announced the arrival of another morning.

~

Unfortunate events usually lead to indeterminate situations. Although the death of his family had been confirmed after only four days, it still took over a month and a half for their remains to arrive back home. And so, on a quiet Saturday morning in late October, Sebastiane Maurice Bartholomew Renault-Bassett and his mother's uncle, Jean Francois Bertrand, traveled to the New Orleans International airport to retrieve three caskets. All three were then taken via traditional transportation, under full police escort, to the Northcutt Funeral Home on Teakwood Street where preparations would be made for the next day.

On the next day, Sunday, after a lengthy service and many handshakes, a large procession departed the funeral home and proceeded via convoy to the Hughes Cemetery on Lamarque Street in Algiers. Once there, all walked solemnly behind sixteen pallbearers as they slowly made their way towards the Bassett-family crypt—final resting place of Edward Bartholomew Bassett and Donah June Bassett.

On the next day, Monday, the final casket, his mother's casket, which had been loaded into a large, hermetically sealed, metal container, was driven back to the airport and placed into the cargo hold of a Boeing 737 for the first leg of its long journey home. It was another Monday at the start of another week for most; for Sebastiane, it was the start of a week in his life like no other before it.

CHAPTER 27

Tampa Bay, Florida

"Admiral, please affix your signature here, here, and here," stated Ms. Dietz, as she directed him to three different spots within the pages of the bound document. The admiral did as he was ordered.

"Thank you," said Westerly as he smiled at the most professional, dedicated, and hardest working woman he had ever known—besides his wife, of course.

Marsha Dietz was one hell of a secretary, and the best he'd ever had. Competent, well organized, and not afraid to keep the admiral in his place, she controlled every aspect of his business life. She had only been with him since he'd joined the Slater Group, and in that short time, he had always pondered on the fact that he couldn't do anything without her. He liked to think that if she'd been with him while he was in the Navy, he would have been Chief of Naval Operations (CNO), easy. He joked about it with her, and she insisted he would have made a fine CNO.

"Anything else, ma'am?"

"Yes, sir. Your car is waiting outside for your dinner at The Steak House with Mr. Cummings. Also, Mr. Knight and Mr. Polk are waiting in the lobby."

"Fine. Have a good night then, Ms. Dietz. Say hello to Angelo for me."

As Westerly exited his office, she responded, "I will, sir. Thank you."

Marsha Dietz scrambled to get her task completed. She knew it would only take her a few minutes to electronically transmit the signed documents to the company's Washington, DC offices for inclusion in the contract packet being sent to the Pentagon the next morning. Thank goodness she didn't have to make copies or send the packet out via airmail or anything like that. Angelo had promised her dinner, and she was passed being eager to get home.

Angelo Constantine Di Rossi, they had married but kept separate surnames, had become quite the chef since his early retirement as a plant manager for the local power utility, a job that had allowed him the time to dabble in his boyhood passion—cooking. No more dabbling allowed, though, he'd said recently. Angelo was close to opening up his own restaurant and she was his guinea pig for another possible main course selection for the menu. She couldn't wait.

"Mr. Knight," stated Westerly as he exited the elevator and entered the lobby. He extended his hand to greet his friend and the company's in-house legal counsel. Knight closed his attaché case, stood up, and returned the greeting in kind. "And Mr. Polk." The admiral also greeted the young man who was about to become the next executive accounts manager for The Slater Group, Inc. Polk would be the twenty-third such manager, and the admiral needed him too! He needed him because the size of the Slater Group was growing even more exponentially than his meager knowledge of accounting mathematics could fathom.

When International and Transnational Corporations began signing up in droves with *Consultancy Firms* due to the new global security situation, some of the larger more protection-orientated ones had signed with The Slater Group. It was then that Simon Polk and his expertise were hired to accommodate both a vastly expanding client base and another big contract signing. As it turned out, that big new contract signing was to be Polk's first client. It, or rather he, the Chief Operating Officer of that new client, was to be their dinner guest this evening. What a surprise the admiral had in store for him as they shook hands.

"My pleasure, sir," answered Simon Polk.

His resolute, confident handshake and strong personal presence seemed to assure the admiral that he had again made a very wise choice. Westerly could see that certain something lingering behind Polk's eyes. It was a fierce and competitive motivation that drove the young man through every stage of his life.

Simon Polk had started out at the bottom rung on the ladder of life. Sequestered by a financially strained upbringing in the inner city of Atlanta, it was a situation that had destroyed weaker men. Instead of becoming another victim, though, Polk fought his way out. With an uncanny ferocity for survival, and with the love of a mother who took the time to pray to God while at two jobs—praying her only son would live long enough to make himself into a man—he'd made it through. His tenacity and her devotion worked in concert, and proved to be a winning combination. Salutatorian in high school and ROTC at college were choices he had because he had choices to make. From then on, the sky was the limit for Simon Jefferson Polk.

Westerly was proud of Polk, and proud of himself. He internally patted himself on the back for making such a wise choice, realizing he had made what was now a third such wise choice since he'd been named Chief Executive Officer (CEO) of The Slater Group, Inc. Wise choices always seemed to come in threes, Westerly thought, as he contemplated the evening's event.

Going out to dinner to celebrate may have seemed tactless considering the timing, but Westerly didn't agree. These days he found himself more inline with the poetry of legendary sports broadcaster Jack Buck—and even considered framing his signed copy of *the poem* and hanging it in his office. Dinner may have also seemed overly luxurious, but with General Sykes's promised retirement six weeks ago, only two days after the events of 9/11, Westerly felt he needed a little indulgence to accommodate his recent successes. And although it had taken an ungodly sixteen days for the executive board to meet and confer his new status as CEO, Westerly hadn't stopped to rest on his laurels. His pet project, after some hard negotiations with the White House, was solidly back under his control.

Due to a serious lack of in-house experts it seemed as if the US government was far too busy since 9/11 to confidently and proficiently account for the outrageously critical and obscenely monumental hordes of raw intelligence data pouring out of Slater's satellites. James Knight had considered it rather fortuitous at the time, but Westerly didn't care what it was called. All he knew was that the Slater Group was again back in charge of the raw data. The fortuitous part, of which Mr. Knight had only come to realize after the fact, Westerly had reminded him, was that the government would now be paying double the original contract prices going forward for the analysis. Wise choice number one confirmed, Westerly gloated internally.

Next, Westerly was able to outmaneuver some other firms to get the inside track on a very specific need for the military's new war in Central Asia—alternative logistics supply routes. The need for supply routes through land and air corridors into Afghanistan was essential to the inevitable victorious outcome in the campaign to defeat America's enemies holed up in that land-locked country—a place that had never technically known military defeat. The normal supply routes were precariously cost prohibitive and, as Westerly saw them, completely subject to the mercy of governments and regimes that were, at best, unfriendly to the United States. Alternative routes in that part of the world would be relatively safe and had the potential to be extremely lucrative. Hence, wise choice number two was the recently completed negotiations with the Pentagon placing the *Priority One Logistical Service Contract* into the Slater Group's hands—

the process of which had culminated with the signing of the documents in his office not five minutes ago.

Now, wise choice number three stood in front of him, he was sure of it, and he returned the offered handshake with the same veracity with which it was received. "Gentlemen, shall we?"

Westerly led them out the main door to the waiting limousine. Once seated, the driver headed for the restaurant while the three men enjoyed some light, personal conversation and a before-dinner cocktail. Arriving at the restaurant, they were shown to a private table. Already seated and waiting for them was Johnston Cummings, Chief Operating Officer (COO) of St. Pierre Pharmaceuticals-North America.

"Johnston, good to see you again," greeted Westerly.

"Admiral, it is good to see you too."

"You already know James Knight. This is Simon Polk. He will be your contact man with the Slater Group." Westerly finished the introductions and could see a look of slight surprise in Johnston Cumming's eyes as he shook hands with Polk.

Cummings had never had any dealings with a corporation such as The Slater Group, Inc., and the only types of people he presumed to work for such an organization, at the lower levels anyway, were the ones he'd seen mimicked on TV shows or in movies. Cummings had envisioned being introduced to either some four-eyed, geeky accountant with absolutely no military background and training, or shaking hands with a man who screamed former Special Forces, was covered in a multitude of tattoos, and was wearing a suit bulging with hidden weapons. Polk seemed to be neither and yet both at the same time, and this puzzled Cummings.

"Problem, Johnston?" queried the admiral, just as their appetizers were being served. There was no need to order at this restaurant. The menu was set on the day, and you only came for dinner if you liked what was on offer.

Cummings stated, "No offense to you Mr. Polk, but I was under the impression that my contact man for your company would be, for lack of a better phrase, a more seasoned employee."

"What Mr. Polk lacks as to time in office, I assure you he'll more than make up for in dedication," stated the admiral.

This time it was Polk who flashed a look of surprise at the admiral. Cummings was intrigued by this and turned to his new contact man for an explanation. Simon was speechless. He didn't want to give some boring, standard corporate line about professionalism and work ethic.

At that moment, Westerly let out a chuckle as he swallowed the first bite of his organic arugula leaf salad with lemon-parsley dressing, and then almost choked on his apology, "Gentlemen, I am sorry. The confusion on your faces is too priceless. Forgive me. It is just a little humor to help lighten the mood for the evening. Johnston, you are an old friend and I had to get one over on you. Mr. Polk, just having some fun at the new guy's expense is all." Westerly could see the relief in Polk's face while he continued to grin at the sarcastic finger wagging at him from his old friend.

"Do I get an explanation as to why?" inquired Cummings.

"From me! No, no need," answered Westerly. "Please, Simon, why don't you go ahead and inform Mr. Cummings here how it is that you came to be in our employ. It is a wonderful story Johnston, heartwarming and valiant. I couldn't be more pleased with this young man. His story, in and of itself, should just about explain everything."

Simon Polk began nervously, "Of course, sir. Let's see, the quick and dirty version. I was born and raised inside the Atlanta loop. I am former Army. I served in Desert Storm. I was just a green, twenty-two-year-old lieutenant back then. I had some time in the field and some time with the J-3s planning missions for the aftermath, but that never really happened, did it? When I returned stateside, I accepted a position in Ranger training. I was three weeks out of jump school when I got sick. Wasn't sure what it was until I was diagnosed with testicular cancer. They wouldn't let me continue, and I was separated from the Army. I got lucky, though. I was selected for a new cancer drug trial and ended up beating it. With a new lease on life, I went back to Georgia Tech to get my master's degrees in Economics and International Affairs. I was working on a campaign for a local congressman when the admiral offered me a job.

"And to what do you attribute your success at beating the cancer, Simon?" asked Westerly.

"God of course, at the insistence of my mother who prayed for me every day, and the drug trial."

"And Johnston? Why was it your former company, Skjebne Labs, was purchased by St. Pierre?" Nathan asked his old friend.

The admiral didn't need to explain any farther as to why it would be a mutually beneficial business relationship for Polk, Cummings, and The Slater Group, Inc. Polk's ability to fight off his life-threatening disease, save his mother's insistence on God's intervention doing all the work, turned out to be the very same drug and drug trial Cummings and Skjebne Labs created and then helped fund. Simon Polk had made it through a nightmare he compared only to his experiences in combat, while Johnston Cummings had become a very well-known, well-respected, and extremely wealthy man when St. Pierre Pharmaceuticals stepped in and offered to not only purchase his company for a cool $950 million dollars but also to make him the Chief Operating Officer of their North American Division.

For the rest of the evening the admiral sat back, enjoyed his meal, and smiled while he and James Knight watched as his old friend, Johnston Cummings, and the Slater Group's newest employee, Simon Jefferson Polk, discussed the non-confidential and most important side of any good business partnership—personal relationships.

CHAPTER 28

Marseille, France

"Monsieur, parlez-vous Française?"

Sebastiane dropped his small duffel bag on the floor; he was exhausted. Worse than that, he was stiff from several very uncomfortable airplane seats and had a headache from what seemed like days of traveling and lay-overs. He'd left New Orleans on a domestic flight and had first stopped in Miami to transfer to an international carrier. Then a second stop, this time in Paris, to clear immigration and customs. Then, and finally, he had arrived in Marseille.

Sebastiane stood unevenly, staring out the window of an office attached to a large storage building at the edge of this medium-sized, regional airport. To his right was the runway on which he'd landed about seventy minutes ago; to his left was the Étang de Barre, an inland lagoon on the edge of the airport grounds and twenty-five kilometers northwest of the city of Marseille. The airport staff had been nice enough to drive him here to wait for the delivery of his mother's casket.

"Oui."

"Merci beaucoup, Monsieur. I struggle with your English language I am sorry to say." It seemed too much in the way of explanation, but Tomas Berzac, senior supervisor for cargo at the Aéroport de Marseille Provence, wanted to make things as easy as possible for this young man. Tomas was short and rotund with jet-black hair protruding from the sides of his uniform cap. He continued in his native tongue, "Your package should be arriving any minute. Your documents are in order, and all we need is your signature once the item arrives."

"Thank you," replied Sebastiane, "for all your help." The gracious reply fell short as he couldn't muster enough energy to express any other emotion except sadness.

"Yes, sir. Do you have transport arranged?"

The senior supervisor was trying to do what he could. He could see the distress in the young American's red, puffy eyes, and Tomas understood why. Special paperwork had arrived on his desk a few days back stating that a naturalized United States citizen, who had been killed in New York City, was being brought back home for burial. Tomas took it upon himself to make sure things went as smoothly as possible. He'd pressed his uniform and cleaned up the offices in preparation for this day. He could only hope his efforts weren't wholly inadequate.

"Someone is supposed to come...supposed to be meeting me," offered Sebastiane.

Just then, a white van pulled up to the utility door next to the office and honked its horn. Tomas pushed down on the keypad control button under the counter behind him and the doors began to open. When the doors locked fully open, Berzac directed Sebastiane into the hangar to both inspect the cargo and to wait for his transport.

When they entered the hangar, the driver was standing at the rear door awaiting a signal from his senior supervisor. As they approached, the driver opened the doors and stood aside. Inside the van was a large metallic crate.

It looked like a casket, just much larger at almost twice the size of any typical wooden model. Inside of it, though, Sebastiane had seen, was a beautiful mahogany casket; he was told the insides were lined with egg-white silk panels and pillows. He had only seen the outside of it briefly when the attendants at the New Orleans airport had checked it, for security reasons, and then sealed it up for its long journey—he wasn't able to look at it in the mortuary.

Tomas rechecked the Bill of Lading, verified it, and stated, "S'il vous plaît, Monsieur. Signer ici."

Sebastiane complied, signing where necessary, and sighed for the hundredth time in the last two days. He was on a very long and strange journey, and it showed on his face and in his posture constantly now.

His mother's final request, on the first line of the second page of her last will and testament, had stated that she wanted to be buried in her hometown—in France. It still seemed strange to Sebastiane that his father would have approved of this, but his signature was on her will right alongside hers. So, Sebastiane was now standing in a place he didn't know and didn't want to be in while his thoughts were on one thing and one thing only.

Why? Why here?

He stopped himself from trying in vain, again, to figure it all out. It was then that he sensed the presence of a fourth person inside the hangar.

Sebastiane turned around to see an elderly gentleman standing ten feet behind him. Although pushing seventy-seven years of age, Sebastiane guessed the man didn't look a day over fifty. He was dressed in a simple black suit with a white button-down shirt, a thin black tie, and slightly scuffed black dress shoes. His hair was gray with white streaks. His face was stout yet familiar. It lacked feeling yet was manifest, portraying the same sadness Sebastiane recognized every time he looked in a mirror.

The man raised his hand. A few seconds later, Sebastiane saw another white van, identical to the one holding his mother's casket, just smaller in size, pull forward and enter the hangar building. Letters emblazoned on the side of it in dark maroon, block shapes and arranged in a diamond pattern read: *NVNTY*. Sebastiane had no idea what they meant—and didn't care.

As the newly arriving vehicle came to a stop, a skinnier man, younger than the elderly gentleman standing in front of him, but not by much, with red hair and a pale white face, exited the vehicle and approached Tomas Berzac. He showed the supervisor some type of official-looking credentials and said something in French with an accent Sebastiane thought strange for a native. He couldn't quite understand or make out the words. The attendant obviously could as he motioned for his assistant to transfer the metal container from one van to the other. As the transfer began, Sebastiane and the older man just stood there staring at each other.

Sebastiane felt as if he was being sized up, and didn't like it very much. He was too tired to do the same so he just kept staring and waiting.

Finally, the old man stopped staring, walked forward with his hand out, and in a deep, authoritative yet respectful and softly resonating voice said, "Bienvenue en France, Sebastiane. I am your mother's father. Maurice Renault is my name." He paused, and then asked, "Did your mother tell you about me?"

The greeting and the follow-up inquiry were accompanied by a firm handshake. The coldness of it fell far short of its intended sympathetic intentions. "Sir," answered Sebastiane, as he returned the handshake wearily, "She never got the chance to."

"I understand," Maurice acknowledged. As he stared at his grandson, Maurice could see a youthful version of himself staring right back; a barely perceptible wry smile pierced his lips at the resemblance. Maurice continued to stare into his grandson's eyes and could see nothing except an uneasiness laced with depression and sadness.

Good. Nothing to be concerned about.

Maurice continued, "Fine. Then come with me. We have a long drive ahead." With the loading of his mother's casket complete, Sebastiane got in the van and sat in the second-row seat.

The van proceeded toward the exit of the airport and then headed northwest towards the city of Nimes where they stopped for gas. Once back on the road, they turned southwest onto the A9 dual-carriageway, a road that looked just like any major interstate at home, thought Sebastiane, and continued on until they reached the city of Narbonne. After that, they turned due south.

Accompanying the long journey was a continuous silence. No one spoke or even looked at one another. Sebastiane wasn't concerned enough to mind because his thoughts were falling deeper into an emotionless pit accompanied only by his jet lag. As the day grew into night, Sebastiane's eyes were too heavy to care about anything anymore. He drifted in and out for a while and eventually fell asleep.

Sebastiane was awakened when the van ran across a speed bump. His eyes focused to see that they were finally pulling into a town at the base of some mountains. A signpost at the side of the road said the name of the town was Laroque-des-Albères. A couple of winding streets later, the van stopped at two large, red-stained, wooden doors that looked as if they could have accommodated horse-drawn carriages. The doors were sandwiched between stuccoed walls with no visible alleyways at either side. There were other identical wooden doors, and still other smaller doors, spaced evenly along the front of every building up and down the gently winding street. Above the garage looked to be a duplex-style, three-story villa, dressed in the same clothing as the walls that sheltered the doors directly in front of him.

Sebastiane saw Maurice get out and open the doors one at a time. The van drove through the opening and into the left-side parking space. On the right was a car Sebastiane had never seen before. The paint color looked faded and the body style looked old, and so he presumed it was in fact old. Must be French, he thought. He exited the van and looked around to get his bearings. As the garage doors shut, Sebastiane looked at his watch and realized he'd managed to get ninety minutes of sleep. He didn't feel any better for it; in fact, he felt much worse.

Maurice led him through a doorway. To the left was a door that led back out to the street. To the right was a staircase leading up to the house. They walked upstairs. When they got to the top, Maurice opened another door that led directly to a foyer. Sebastiane followed him through and to the right, and then into the kitchen.

There was some food on the table—bread with cheese and various sliced meats, and a bottle of what looked like Coca-Cola. Sebastiane ignored the food and grabbed the drink. He was hungry, but his stomach was in knots. He hoped the carbonation would help with his travel-induced queasiness. Maurice then led him up two flights of narrow stairs to a small bedroom on the third floor.

"The bathroom is downstairs on the left. Get some rest. The funeral is tomorrow morning."

Maurice shut the door after Sebastiane entered the room, saying nothing more. Sebastiane was left to spend the night in a small, uncomfortable bed in a strange place with his feelings taking a rollercoaster ride from depression to confusion and back again. He was numb all over and was having a hard enough time trying to remember all the little things his parents and grandmother had told him the day they left for New York without having to try and figure out why his grandfather was being so aloof. They had only just met, but even under these unfortunate circumstances his grandfather seemed to be ignoring him to the point of callousness. He couldn't go to sleep and spent the rest of the night staring blankly at the unknown and darkened surroundings. Eventually, Sebastiane's confusion maxed out his capacity for rational thought and he decided it was best that he not even bother trying with his grandfather.

~

The next morning had a peacefully cold start to it. The air was brisk with unexpectedly early, winterish moisture. The ground was starting to harden with the approaching season. Sebastiane wore a three-quarter length black coat, with black gloves, and a black knit cap. The cold seemed to penetrate through the layers, onto his skin and into his heart, as if he were wearing nothing at all. He stood next to Maurice in front of a mausoleum in what was a fairly updated yet strangely art deco and out-of-place looking cemetery on the northern edge of town. The only redeeming quality were the trees—their gentle swaying in the morning wind was oddly soothing to him.

Sebastiane stared at the two names chiseled onto individual marble plates that had been inserted into predesigned slots on the left side of the crypt door; one name on top of the other like stacked name tags on a table. The marble and granite memorial itself looked comparable in size to the Bassett family crypt back home, he noticed, but that one had several generations of names marked on it. This one had only two—his mothers, and someone named Sophia. The name at the top of the crypt was carved precisely in gothic italics, and read: *RENAULT*.

As the casket was pushed into place, the priest began his closing remarks. Sebastiane was listening without paying any particular attention to them. The increasingly odd trip to this part of the world had turned strangely surrealistic to him, and he couldn't understand why his mother had wanted this. It also seemed odd she'd never told him about Maurice. She was going to, he remembered all of a sudden, she just never got the chance.

Why was it she didn't tell me earlier?

Sebastiane resigned himself to the fact that he would never know why, and coincidently would never get to know his grandfather. The man still hadn't said one meaningful word to him, and probably never would. After the priest finished, he walked over to them, blessed them, and then went on his way.

Sebastiane inhaled deeply, forcing the cold air into his lungs in the hope that the painful feelings of loneliness and loss would be exhaled from his body and replaced with memories of all the good times he could remember about his mother. He had tried to do the same thing three days prior when he watched the same scenario play out at the burial of his father and grandmother. It didn't work then, and it wasn't working now. He wanted to cry. He had no tears left.

"Sebastiane, it is time to go," stated Maurice as he began walking away.

Sebastiane followed slowly, not wanting to leave. As he exited the cemetery, he could see Maurice climbing into the passenger door of the van. The same red-haired, pale-skinned man he'd seen the day before was sitting in the driver's seat. Sebastiane climbed into the second-row seat and closed the door. The van took off and immediately began retracing the path it had taken the day before. After a couple of hours, they were back at the airport outside Marseille with Sebastiane still full of confusion now bordering on outright contempt. He opened the door and threw his bag on the curb, and then followed. He looked up as another plane took off— the roar of its jet engines getting quieter as the plane's distance and elevation increased.

"Sebastiane, good luck with the flight back to America," stated Maurice after exiting the van. He stuck out his hand.

Sebastiane stared at his grandfather. He couldn't fully understand what was happening or why it was happening, let alone understand who this man was.

What the hell is going on? And what the hell are you all about? We've never met. My mother, your daughter, dies, and you say no more than ten words to me the whole day and a half I am here. Then, you send me back with nothing more than a handshake!

"Fuck you very much, I don't think I will." Sebastiane bent over, picked up his bag and flung it over his shoulder. Refusing to shake his grandfather's outstretched hand, he turned and walked into the terminal building.

Maurice returned to the passenger seat, closed the door, and motioned for the driver to leave. The van didn't move. "Drive, now," Maurice commanded. When the van still didn't move, Maurice began to chastise the driver, "You red-headed, hard-headed, Irish bastard! If you don't drive this vehicle out of here right now, then so help me..."

Connor McGinty interrupted his friend. "You'll do what? You are wrong, Maurice, and you know it. You need that boy and he needs you. Go inside and invite him to stay. Get to know him. He is the only memory of your daughter you have left. Damn it, he's the only family you have left."

"I can't, old friend," stated Maurice in a more respectful tone. Maurice's emotions were starting to break through his rugged exterior, and the mental strain of hiding his grief had become overwhelming. "My daughter is dead. I...I just can't." His voice trailed off into grief-stricken silence.

"That boy has lost his family," stated McGinty vigorously. His Irish temper calmed slightly as he began to plead with his friend. "Jean Francois kept you apprised of things, but it was never enough and you know it. If you want to know how your daughter lived, then that boy is the only chance you have."

A military policeman patrolling the area, and carrying a rather large weapon, walked directly towards them. He looked around the back of the van and then approached the driver-side door before banging on the window, "Monsieur, you cannot park here—security reasons. Please move on. Merci."

"Oui, oui," said Connor. He put the van in gear and began to drive off. Three seconds later he continued to chastise his friend, "Jean Francois also told you about Sebastiane's past incidents. You cannot ignore them, or him, because if that boy has anywhere near the potential you had! Well, need I say more?"

The van headed out of the airport. After negotiating some traffic, McGinty continued, "He is going to need help to control himself, and you are the only one who can do that." The frustration was building inside the Irishman as the vicious circle of arguing the same point with his bullheaded friend had started up all over again. It was the same conversation they had had almost every night since Jean Francois called to give Maurice the terrible news.

Maurice had both consistently argued with and completely denied his friend's accurate account of the situation due to his own fears—his fears of the past and the realization that his choice to send Elena to America, his choice to never see her again, may have been the wrong one.

Is it too late? A few years ago, maybe things could have been different. But now, it would never happen.

Connor was going to continue his verbal assault, but was cut off.

"Stop! You are right, of course. But what can I do? He is getting on an airplane and going back home. You know I can't leave France, so if I am going to let you win this argument and do things your way, I am going to need a drink."

McGinty shook his head in frustration at his good friend's idiotic sensibilities.

Maurice ignored him and looked at his watch. He knew Sebastiane's flight didn't leave for another four hours, giving him plenty of time to build up the liquid courage needed to ask his grandson to stay for a while. If the young man agreed, then Maurice could learn all he wanted to know about his daughter's life in America over the past forty years. He could also learn of the things Jean Francois could not possibly have known. Then maybe, just maybe, if he was up for it, Maurice would tell Sebastiane all about his legacy—the Renault family legacy.

Connor finally smiled at his friend, but only a little, as he continued his turn around the traffic circle. He bypassed the direction arrow pointing towards the city of Nimes, and back home, and instead found the sign that said *MARSEILLE*. "The old spot, then?"

Maurice nodded in agreement and began to formulate his plan about how to approach Sebastiane. He had four hours. Was it enough time to find that liquid courage? Maurice wasn't sure.

CHAPTER 29

Sebastiane was sitting at the airport bar waiting for his flight, sipping on a beer, and staring into nothingness. His mind was as it had been for the last six weeks, lost. The long trip, the short ceremony, and the even shorter attitude of his grandfather had left him feeling nothing on top of the nothing he was already drowning in. Sebastiane believed he now truly understood why it was that his mother had never told him about Maurice—he was a complete bastard.

The attitude, that had to be it! He wasn't much of a man if he hadn't seen his own daughter in what...how many years? When was the last time she and that minimalistic, emotionless bastard had seen each other? He couldn't even say anything to me about anything. What an asshole! Well, when I get on this plane and go home, I won't have to worry about him anymore.

And then the realization hit Sebastiane square in the jaw. Home was where the real heartache was. Home was where he didn't want to be, nor couldn't fathom being right now. With the airline ticket lying on the bar staring back at him, mocking him, Sebastiane gulped down the rest of his beer, found his way to the airport's information kiosk, and asked about alternative transportation to nowhere in particular.

The information hostess, a lady who obviously meant well but was too outwardly nice to be anything other than tragically annoying, suggested he take the train into Marseille. From there he could go anywhere he wanted.

Sebastiane did as instructed and followed the blue overhead signs which took him out of the terminal building, across the parking lot, and to the train station. He bought a ticket and waited for only a short time before the next train arrived. He grabbed a seat away from the other passengers and rode the train into the city center. After arriving, he decided he should take a walk around before making plans to go anywhere else. He got his coat and gloves out of his bag just in case, and placed the bag in a locker. He deposited the correct amount of change into the slot and removed the key from its lock. He exited the main station doors onto Boulevard Charles Nedelec and just started walking. He didn't know where to go, but anywhere had to be better than another airport. And another plane ride. And back to an empty home.

After a while, he came to a small park at the intersection of several large streets. People scurried about as they finished up the day's business and were heading home, he guessed. Across the park was a plaza and a small bar with simple, white plastic chairs outside. He needed to use the bathroom, and then perhaps maybe have another drink.

After a few drinks, several cigarettes, and what he was told was a ham and cheese sandwich, the sun finally disappeared behind the buildings. He looked around and noticed the streets being emptier than before. Traffic was somewhat lighter too, and those who were still out were walking in one particular direction. Everyone was quiet, with their heads down, and seemed to be forcefully concentrating on not being seen. He turned and noticed the shop he was at also seemed to be closing, with only the proprietor staring out the window and nervously waiting for him to leave. Sebastiane reached into his pocket and placed some money on the table.

Just then, a soft, melodic wave of poetic harmony echoed over the rooftops and swept into the small plaza. The sound of the music washed over the area, bathing it within its serenity, and continued through the air and over to the park across the street. Sebastiane closed his eyes to listen. He turned his head slightly to catch it better in his ear; and when he did, his persona changed without warning.

His ever-present gloominess and slumped shoulders, which had underlined his outward appearance for weeks now, quickly retreated into a deeply dark, blank expression of recognition. His head slowly snapped back to center and his body became rigidly upright, freezing itself in place. He slowly opened his eyes as a once acknowledged and formidable rage awoke within, instantly consuming his inner being.

~

Connor McGinty was finishing another pint of Guinness. Too much alcohol and not enough food was a bad recipe for driving the long distance back home—not that that worried him. He was Irish, and there was nary an Irishman his age who wasn't totally unaccustomed to driving after experiencing the enjoyment of several pints.

Dr. Connor M. McGinty was indeed an Irishman in every sense of the word. With typical red hair and pale skin, a slender frame, and, even at fifty-three years of age, an affinity for large amounts of dark beer, he inevitably stuck out in a crowd. It was an unfortunate image portrayed around the world that undermined the true sense of a people who had far more to offer than that same image allowed. He looked meek, but wasn't. He looked simple, but wasn't. He looked Irish, and didn't mind people's suppositions.

As it turned out, Connor McGinty was the exception that proved the rule. He had been, and still was, a practicing physician, and had been a dedicated relief worker as a younger man who volunteered for what he thought were interesting assignments with the World Health Organization.

He had often traveled to Third-World hotspots helping to contain rampant disease outbreaks or trying to ease the suffering of war-stricken communities. Unfortunately, he had been taken for granted and left for dead at one such stop in North Central Africa in the late 1970s. Were it not for the passionate pleas of a young, French nurse, Connor McGinty would have died in that hellhole. But those passionate pleas had helped to ignite a long-lost sense of utility and faded dignity within the dangerous and mysterious man Serena Brouchaux had run into at a hospital outside Algiers while searching for information about her lover. Fate, it seemed, had intervened on her behalf.

Finding himself trapped in Algeria with no way back to continental Europe, this mysterious man, Maurice, found a new purpose to his life and exchanged his help in finding and freeing Serena's lover, Connor, as reciprocity for her helping him get back home to France.

Connor would never forget his beloved wife, Serena, and so would always lend any assistance he could to the man who had saved his life—payment for twenty glorious years of marriage, two wonderful children, and for saving him from that hellhole.

McGinty refused another pint from the waitress and asked for the bill. The brew was as good as ever, but he needed food, and pub food was not on the menu for this evening. If there were only two good things Maurice had suggested, the other was not eating at the bar but buying food and making dinner at home while trying to talk to his grandson. Connor saw Maurice returning from the local market, load the groceries into the van, and return to their table. McGinty asked as he arrived, "Don't you think it's time we head back to the airport to get Sebastiane?"

Maurice answered with a question of his own, "What was the final score?"

"You and your damned pathetic excuse for a football club," offered the Irishman. And then somewhat jokingly asked, "When are you going to follow a real football team, like Liverpool?"

Although both men were passionate for the game, Connor followed his boyhood favorites from across the Irish Sea while Maurice followed Olympique de Marseille. Both men could remember solemn times when the seriousness of life had been graciously distracted by that passion. They could both see one of those times happening right now, and both were grateful for each other and the game.

"It was a nil-all draw," answered the doctor finally.

"Too bad, I thought Lille was the weaker team."

As Maurice waited, Connor paid the bill. They walked across the street, got into the van, and headed off. As they passed the harbor, they merged onto Route A7 which would take them north out of the city and back to the airport where Maurice would try to make amends with his grandson.

As they turned right off Rue Sainte-Barbe and then began turning left around a small park, Maurice grabbed Connor by the arm. "WAIT! Go around the park and stop on the other side, quickly."

"What?"

Maurice's grip tightened on Connor's arm, and the sudden, commanding sound of his voice prompted the Irishman to immediately comply.

When the van came to a stop, Maurice climbed out. He turned and said, "Stay here."

"Why? What is happening?"

Connor watched as Maurice headed off across the park towards a row of shops on the opposite side. He seemed confused, thought McGinty, as he continuously looked up and down the streets, back across the park, and everywhere else he could like he was trying to find someone. After only a minute, Maurice returned.

Connor asked again, "What is it?"

"Nothing. Leave the van and come with me, quickly."

Maurice led the way back across the park, all the while looking up and down streets and peering into doorways and down alleyways. Connor was hurriedly jog-walking to keep up with him. As they came to a closed shop with white plastic chairs outside, Connor, slightly out of breath, asked again, "What is going on?"

"Sebastiane is not at the airport. I just saw him at this shop and now he is gone. Something is not right, my friend!" stated Maurice.

"Here! Why would he be here?" McGinty asked. Looking around to verify his surroundings, he stated, "This is *not* a neighborhood he should be in."

Maurice asked the question, even though he already knew the answer. "Why not?"

"This is a Muslim neighborhood. At this time of night he might be mistaken for something he is not," offered the doctor, still looking around frantically while trying to figure out how the young American could have possibly gotten here in the first place.

Connor didn't understand what Maurice could already sense; it didn't matter how Sebastiane had gotten here, it only mattered that he was here. "Come my friend, we need to find him—now."

Both men began searching the area. Maurice could blend in with any crowd, he always could, but the Irishman stuck out like the proverbial sore thumb. Together they looked too much out of place for the neighborhood, and people started paying attention. Some looked out through the windows of their shabbily maintained tenement apartments, and then just as quickly closed the curtains. Still others, loitering outside of stairwells, which lead to other smaller buildings, begrudgingly allowed them to pass by without a word.

Maurice's senses were in overdrive. Something wasn't right, and he knew it—he could feel it gnawing at him. As the streets wound around and cut through areas that looked more like back alleys, with graffiti-laced garage doors and unkempt business storefronts, Maurice caught a glimpse of something that didn't belong; it was a figure walking purposefully up the street and staying as close to the walls and out of the glow of the intermittent streetlights as was manageable. Maurice walked faster to catch up. When he got to the top of the street, the figure was gone. "Where are you?" Maurice asked himself quietly, hoping he wasn't going to answer his own question too late for it to matter. After another twenty minutes of continued searching, the streets had taken on a menacing glow as daylight disappeared completely. With its darkened corners illuminated by nothing more than the headlights from the occasional passing vehicle, visibility had dropped to only a few meters.

Suddenly, Maurice and Connor noticed a large group of men exiting a building on Rue Malaval. Most of the men were dressed in jeans and jackets, and all carried a book and what looked like rosary beads. As Maurice continued up the street towards them he looked around and saw a run-down, ten-story apartment complex with clothes hanging on almost every balcony. Directly across the road from the complex, where the men were exiting, was the local mosque. As he continued to survey the scene, looking up and down the narrow street, Maurice realized that there were too many vehicles and far too many people congregating in and amongst those vehicles for anything to happen here. If Sebastiane had plans, and if he was acting like Maurice thought he could, then he probably wasn't here. More people were starting to stare at the two out-of-place men as the streets continued to clog from the flow of worshippers exiting the mosque.

"Let's go, McGinty."

As they walked back down the street, Maurice suggested Connor go and retrieve the van, telling him they would meet up again at this same intersection in another fifteen minutes or so while he continued to look for Sebastiane.

"How can you be sure he's still here? Even if it was him, he could have gone back to the airport. You can't be sure, can you?"

"Yes, I can. He is here…and something bad is coming," professed Maurice, with a calm but predictive tone in his voice that visibly scared his friend.

Even though he was tired from the search, Connor McGinty had plenty of adrenaline coursing through his veins. He made it back to the van and returned to the designated corner within ten minutes. When he couldn't find Maurice, he decided to drive up Rue Malaval—a one-way street. At the top, he turned left, then left again, and came back down Rue Fauchier. As he approached what was the rear entrance of the mosque, the street split in two. The left side continued on as a street and up to the Place Marceau traffic circle. The right, which was becoming lower than the left, ended in a pseudo-parking lane about a hundred feet farther on.

Connor slammed on the brakes as two figures suddenly appeared in front of the van. In the headlights he recognized Maurice, and he was carrying another man by the arm and draped across his shoulder.

"Unlock the doors!" exclaimed Maurice, just barely audible over the sound of the engine.

Connor did as asked, and the side door slid open. Maurice deposited Sebastiane inside. The van's internal light allowed Connor to see blood on Sebastiane's hands and torso, and he became concerned.

"Is he all right? Let me see him," said McGinty, the doctor in him clicking into action immediately.

"No! Drive. The blood isn't his," replied Maurice.

Connor McGinty put the van in gear and quickly departed from the area while Maurice's attention was outside, visually and mentally taking in his surroundings and looking for any signs of danger or potential witnesses.

As the van arrived at the Place Marceau, Maurice directed Connor to head to the central train station. After picking up Sebastiane's bag, Maurice ordered his friend to head back towards the harbor to catch the coast road; and no matter what, he was to stay off the main highways. It would take much longer to get home because of the indirect route Maurice was telling Connor to take, but Maurice could only hope they would make it out of Marseille before the gendarme roadblocks prevented them from doing so.

CHAPTER 30

Sebastiane waited silently, concealed within a darkened, recessed doorway—the vapor from his controlled exhale the only possible sign of his presence. The untethered demon within him watched from across the street as two men, one far younger than the other, both speaking cordially in Arabic-accented French—about what he didn't care—exited a small door encased within a larger, semicircular garage door.

They proceeded directly towards him, and then stopped just above and in front of his position. The younger one perched himself on the protective metal railing that outlined the sub-street level parking area. It was a narrow area paved with black cobblestones with barely enough room for one car to park let alone turn around, and had only a few small steps leading back up to the street.

There was no protection for the two men as the unchecked and unstoppable rage consumed him. Quietly maneuvering, maintaining his stealthy posture, he exited the darkness and crouch-stepped along the small wall just below the two unsuspecting and innocent men.

As he closed to within striking distance, Sebastiane paused when the older man turned around and started walking away while pointing up the street to indicate where his car was parked. The older man continued to walk away as he invited the younger man to come to his house and meet his daughter. The question was hopeful, searching, and accompanied by a raised pitch in his voice. He sounded confident that the younger man would accept his invitation.

Suddenly, the younger man disappeared soundlessly over the railing. With a calculatingly violent maneuver, Sebastiane grabbed on to the young man's shirt collar with his left hand and covered his mouth with his right hand. He then yanked him over the edge, dropping him six feet onto the ground. The young man landed on his back and neck, which knocked the air out of his lungs and paralyzed him with fear. One hundred and ninety pounds of vengeance then dropped onto his chest with a leading knee, breaking three of his ribs and his sternum. A powerful punch directly to the bridge of his nose broke that too, rendering him unconscious from the sudden burst of pain.

Upon turning around, the older man was taken aback by the disappearance of his young friend. As he walked back towards the railing, wondering if his young friend had accidentally fallen over, he himself was greeted by two hands that clutched on to his neck and dragged him over the railing. The ghastly, surprised look on the older man's face faded quickly as the oxygen to his brain was cut off by the powerful grip. His life expired before he could truly understand what was happening to him, or why.

As the younger man started to regain consciousness, he was greeted by another blow to the face. The pain he'd already experienced intensified dramatically. His attempts to scream in pain were destroyed, along with his jaw, as another blow fell upon him. The younger man fell into unconsciousness again, and would never recover. The repeated blows to his face had cracked the back of his skull open on the cobblestone road. The blood raced from his head as if it knew to do so, helping to spare him from a longer, slower, more painful death.

~

Sebastiane surveyed the carnage. The blood, the anger, the rage; it was all projected on the back of his eyelids like a strobe-lit canvas of horror. It became too much, forcing him to wake from his adrenaline-induced blackout.

As the headlights from a passing car illuminated the inside of the van, Sebastiane found himself staring at his grandfather who was staring right back at him.

The look on Maurice's face was comprised of two things—understanding and remorse; understanding of the horrible acts of violence Sebastiane had perpetrated on two unsuspecting and defenseless human beings, and remorse because he had allowed it to happen.

Sebastiane began to notice the pain in his arms. As he lifted them, he noticed blood trickling from his knuckles. The sight of it confirmed for him that it hadn't been a dream, and that it was in fact the undeniable truth of his rage let loose without control. He began to feel sick at the sight of the blood on his hands, and on his arms, and on his pants.

"Pull over," demanded Maurice.

Connor halted the van. Before the vehicle had stopped completely Maurice unlocked and threw open the side door, grabbed Sebastiane by the collar, and led him outside so his grandson could expel his shame and regret.

With the initial wave of nausea lying on the ground at his feet, Sebastiane began to try to scrape the hatefulness of his actions off of his hands with his fingernails thinking this would prevent the nausea from returning. He was wrong. He vomited again, and again. When the waves of putrid bile began to slow, Sebastiane tried to use the soaked dirt to smear the blood away.

"No time for that now," stated Maurice, as he manhandled Sebastiane back into the van.

The long and winding roads back to Laroque-des-Albères were not totally uninhabited by other cars or residences, and Maurice was worried someone might see them. It was safer than the main highway, of course, but it would take much longer. Avoidance of the Gendarmerie was paramount at this point if Maurice was to save the life of his grandson.

Maurice had arrived too late to save the two men lying in the alleyway at Sebastiane's feet. They were just in the wrong place at the wrong time. They couldn't possibly have known what was coming for them, nor could they have stopped it. Meeting such a violent ending, an ending perpetrated by a boy drowning in a swell of unimaginable grief that had remorselessly and temporarily suppressed his ability to determine right from wrong, was simply fate, decided Maurice. It wasn't an excuse. He didn't condone what Sebastiane had done, Maurice just reminded himself of the truth of it—he understood. And with that understanding came the realization that Sebastiane would need to be forced to comprehend his fate so that something this wrong and this horrible could never happen again.

I must tell him why he is what he is.

Maurice then thought about the *how*. How would he tell Sebastiane? How could he tell his grandson what he was in a way that would make sense and not leave him even more confused—or more dangerous? As they continued toward home, and safety, Maurice's only hope was that his grandson could understand.

The van finally arrived back into the town of Laroque-des-Albères. But instead of the villa where he'd stayed the previous night, Sebastiane noticed the van continue south. After several more minutes, the vehicle eventually stopped at a small, secluded farmhouse near the bottom of a hill beneath the old town castle.

Sebastiane was taken around to the far side of the wooden structure where he could use an old well pump to fill a trough with water to clean up. His clothes and his shoes were taken from him and were burned in a hole dug by Maurice. The van had been parked underneath an overhang that formed part of the roof of a carport barely attached to the farmhouse. The doors of the van were shut and locked, and then a large tarp was thrown over it. Once clean, Sebastiane was shown inside the farmhouse. He was shaking from a combination of the wintery night air, the cold water, and the horrors of death and murder constantly flashing before his eyes. He saw his duffel bag sitting on a chair in the corner of the room. He opened it to get fresh clothes.

Maurice started a fire and put on coffee as he watched Sebastiane fumble for a set of warm clothes from his bag, probably not realizing that it could have been the one and only piece of evidence that linked him to his crimes. The train locker key, dropped by Sebastiane during his blinding rage and lying on the ground next to the two slain men, had been notice and recovered by Maurice. He'd cleaned the blood off with a rag and then given it to Connor McGinty to retrieve the bag from inside the train terminal building.

Connor had walked into the station quickly, found the locker immediately, inserted the key forcefully, opened the door cautiously, grabbed up the duffel hesitantly, and returned to the van nervously. He climbed into the driver's seat and drove off, patiently. It had been a calculated risk, staying in the city for the extra time required, but it was necessary.

Once dressed in fresh clothes, Sebastiane zipped up the bag and took a seat at the rickety, linoleum-topped, metal fold-table in the center of the room where a cup of coffee was waiting for him. He didn't want the coffee, but right now it was the only thing offered—and the only thing that could possibly smother the vile taste in his mouth. Sebastiane could see and hear Maurice conversing with the man he recognized from earlier in the day just outside the slightly ajar front door. Maurice was asking him to leave the van so it could be cleaned properly—and he was asking him to leave and return home. The last thing Sebastiane heard before the door fully opened was his grandfather saying that the man couldn't be present for the following conversation. Sebastiane wondered what, besides everything that had just happened, could be so private that it only required the two of them to be present?

Maurice came in and shut the old, squeaky wooden door behind him, walked to the table, sat down, and stared into his grandson's eyes. The look he received in return was one of contemplative confusion residing deep inside a darkened, shallow abyss overflowing with depleted rage and staggering regret. Maurice had been informed that something like this had happened to his grandson before, but it had been stopped by the police before it had gotten as far as tonight had. Maurice looked deeper into Sebastiane's soul and could see, just below the surface of tonight's abhorrent events, a frightened little boy searching for an explanation to one simple question—*If the police hadn't been there to stop me, would I have killed before?*

Sebastiane began to search for an elusive truth within the eyes staring back at him. He searched for anything that might explain the last eight years of his life. His expression changed quickly to one of need, need of an explanation he believed might be forthcoming. He had never been able to figure out how he was able to do certain things; and after tonight, how he was able to kill so easily?

Before Sebastiane could open his mouth to ask the question, Maurice raised his hand, "Stop. I will explain to you the why. From this, you will come to understand the how. You will understand how it is that you killed those men so easily tonight, and how you almost killed the molester from your childhood."

That got a raised eyebrow from Sebastiane, "How did you know about that?" he inquired.

"Jean Francois kept me up to date with your mother as best he could," Maurice answered.

"Okay."

"I only ask three things in return. One is that you tell me all about my daughter when you are able—as much as you can. Agreed?"

With a nod of his head, Sebastiane asked, "And what about number two?"

"We'll get to that," answered Maurice. "But we may need something more than just coffee for that part."

"And the third?"

"Just a side question before we begin. Why is it that your name is spelled with an *e* at the end? The true French spelling of your name has no *e*."

Sebastiane answered his grandfather's odd question matter-of-factly, "The story from my father was that the male nurse who helped with my delivery leaned a little towards the effeminate side and just presumed that every name should have an *e* on the end of it. He was the one who filled out and submitted the paperwork. And by the time everyone signed it, no one had noticed."

Maurice rolled his eyes and grinned slightly at the peculiarity of the explanation before making his way to the small wood-burning stove to put another log inside. The heat radiating from the stumpy, blackened relic, with its exhaust pipe disappearing through the wall, helped to maintain a comfortable balance within the room. Next, Maurice reached into the cabinet to the right of the stove and above the sink and pulled out a bottle of Bushmills Irish Whiskey.

"Put a little in your cup. It will help in covering the taste in your mouth."

Sebastiane grabbed the bottle and twisted the cap off, tilted it, and poured just a touch in his cup. "Is this Irish whiskey?" he asked, speculatively.

"Of course," answered Maurice. He put on his best Irish accent, unsuccessfully mimicking his friend, and stated, "There are only two things I trust in this world—myself, and a damn fine Irish whiskey."

Sebastiane truly wasn't in a mood to laugh, so Maurice's expression became serious. He switched to his native tongue and asked, "Now…how much of our history do you know? How much did your mother tell you?"

Sebastiane understood the question, but apologized for not responding in kind, in French, before continuing in English, "As I said, she never got the chance. I think she was going to tell me after she, they, returned from…." Sebastiane stopped when the lump hit his throat. He took a large swig from his cup before continuing, "…when they returned from New York."

Sebastiane's imagination took flight quickly. He envisioned himself running next to them, fleeing for his life as the debris from the collapsing Towers crashed all around. He tried to reach for them to pull them clear, but they disappeared into the smoke. When the smoke finally dissipated, he could see nothing except for the blood on his hands. He looked down.

And when he did, he saw the wide-eyed faces of two lifeless corpses lying in an unknown street in Marseille—their eyes staring straight into his soul. He ran out the door of the farmhouse to vomit up the coffee and alcohol that had quickly turned to a burning acid in his stomach.

CHAPTER 31

After a few minutes Sebastiane reentered the farmhouse, wiped his mouth off with a towel, and lit a cigarette instead of drinking more whiskey to try to deaden the acrid taste in his throat. He quickly realized nothing was going to drive the horrid bitterness aside and just decided to deal with it. As he sat, he stared at his grandfather and waited—waited for an explanation for everything.

Recognizing the look in his grandson's eyes, and with a large gulp of whiskey straight from the bottle, Maurice began, "You are currently the last descendant of the House of Renault. You are the grandson of Maurice Sebastian Renault," he pointed to himself, "and Sophia Von Furst." Maurice hesitated slightly, remembering his lovely Sophia. He reached into his pocket, pulled out his wallet, and retrieved a faded black-and-white photograph. It was the only one he had left. Handing it to Sebastiane, he continued, "She was the love of my life. She was the only child of Colonel Heinrich Von Furst whose family was originally from the Alsace region. It is in the northeast, on the border with Allemagne—Germany."

"Wow, Mom looks...looked just like her." Staring at the picture, taking in everything he could from the faded image, Sebastiane was amazed at the likeness.

He handed it back as Maurice continued. "My father was Capitaine Michel Renault. He was a company commander in the 33rd Infantry Division, 17th Army Corps, 4th Army Group, and distinguished himself at the Battle of Verdun in the Great War. His father was Lieutenant de vaisseau Jacques Renault. He was a member of the Marine Française. His participation was in the Crimean War, but he spent most of the war in the Baltic Sea Campaign. He led raiding parties on Finnish ports, which helped to destroy facilities necessary for the repair of Russian naval vessels. Next was Louis Renault. He fought under the Emperor Napoleon during the Peninsula Campaigns in the early 1800s."

As Maurice continued, Sebastiane tried to keep up with the history of it all. He tried to remember places and events from the books he'd read; history books that not only described the shape of the world as he knew it, but, as it turned out, helped shape his family's history as well.

Maurice seemed to go on for hours. He discussed the history of war after war, mostly in Europe but sometimes in other places, containing revelations about ancestors of the Renault family as soldiers and sailors, as knights involved in the Crusades, as vassals of Charlemagne, and finally as common men who did nothing more than survive in the harshest of times. Maurice's ability to recall detailed accounts of every individual event, the historical significance behind each event, and the significance of a particular Renault family member's contribution to it mesmerized Sebastiane. He hadn't realized that after several cups of coffee, a half a pack of rather harsh French cigarettes between them, and half a bottle of whiskey, that the dates Maurice was currently citing had become quite ancient.

"Wait!" Sebastiane interrupted. "Who was he fighting for? Because if I'm not mistaken, France wasn't even France at this point. Was it?"

Maurice was visually upset at the lack of understanding from his grandson, but reminded himself that he was, after all, an American and that most Americans became rather uninterested in world events existing before 1776. Maurice's voice increased slightly as he came to the intersection of what he himself could remember at his age and what he had been told by his father, "Arnand of Narbonne did not fight for nor was he incorporated into any regular army. He was just a farmer, nothing more. But he succeeded in preventing the burning of the village, the killing of the livestock, the destruction of the granary and his home, and the killing of his family at the hands of the invaders."

"Who were the invaders? Were they the Moors or someone else?" Sebastiane was trying to remember something from his world history classes at college. Hopefully, he thought, he got it right.

"Very good," applauded Maurice. "As it turned out, the invaders were both. The history of this part of France during the seventh and eighth centuries was fraught with separatist ideals. Far more than not, this area was the borderlands between kingdoms as far back as the Roman Empire. At times it was left completely untouched, or it was left to the idiot sons of noblemen who plundered its riches and then abandoned it as an afterthought. Consequently, these many years of neglect by the powers that be allowed those separatist ideals to fester. Ultimately it created a…how you say…?"

"A disconnect?"

"Merci, yes—*l'élargissement du fossé*—between those who had survived on these lands and those who'd lived comfortably of its riches. After centuries of war and the changing of ownership of the region, we end up with a situation where our ancestors knew many rulers, but had no masters; no king or caliph or duke or viscount truly conquered us, mostly regarded us as allies, and betrayed us at their own peril." Maurice continued after he lit a cigarette, "Of course, most of this is verbal history. It wasn't until the fifteenth century that the Renault family name was established in recorded documents in this area. As it turns out, Renault is a Germanic name in origin from the Lorraine region."

"Isn't that the same region where Colonel Von Furst was from?" Sebastiane was trying his best to keep up.

"Sort of. It is the same area, different *département*—thanks to *les Allemands*. Anyway, as I was trying to say, the name Renault migrated to this region as the constant of war prevailed across the ages. And with the separatist mentality afoot in the region, and no true leader to follow, the past generations of people who were eventually incorporated into the House of Renault had fought for themselves."

Maurice finished his lecture with a head nod and a glimmer of satisfaction in his eyes as to the truth of his recollection of the family history when Sebastiane asked, "So, we go back to when exactly?"

"I have been told that when the Romans ruled this land that it was a Renault, again not by name, but it was a Renault who helped to protect travelers on the road from Faventia, Barcelona, to Narbonne."

Sebastiane had listened and been awed by the story, but interrupted Maurice to question him on relevancy. "As a story it all seems fine-and-dandy. But what does it all mean? And what does all this have to do with you and me?"

"My story I will leave for later. As for you, this story is the answer to how you killed those two men in Marseille. This story is the answer to how you stopped the pedophile, this man named David, in your youth."

"Stop! What are you talking about? How does a history lesson allow me to kill people?" Sebastiane's questions dripped with incredulity.

"Think, my boy. How did you kill those two men? How did you destroy the pedophile?"

"I don't know," offered Sebastiane.

"First of all, tell me what happened when you were young. And then, tell me what happened earlier tonight. Are you up for that?" Maurice prodded.

Without hesitation, hoping to find the answers he had so longed for, Sebastiane recreated in minute detail after minute detail the violent episode from his youth. When he finished, he continued, this time with considerable apprehensiveness, with the details from his actions in Marseille. His confusion about the incident from earlier that night was gone as the whole scenario played itself out in his mind in exact detail before he verbally replayed it for Maurice.

Maurice listened intently. When Sebastiane had finished, his grandfather asked him a simple question, "Now, tell me *how* you were able to do these things?"

"I don't know," offered Sebastiane, a little too quickly this time.

Maurice became visibly angry again. "You listened to me and you heard yourself speak, yes? But somehow you still do not understand! What did I tell you? I told you about the generations of our family, well over a millennia's worth, who have been warriors. Underneath it all, whatever skill they mastered or trade they practiced, whether it was as farmers, blacksmiths, bankers, sailors or soldiers, whether they were Christians, religious monks, Muslim converts or pagan heretics, it doesn't matter— they were all warriors." Maurice paused to let the truth of it all sink in. He could see a lingering disbelief on Sebastiane's face and stood to make his point theatrically.

"These skills you didn't know you possessed, and have unknowingly tapped in to twice in your life, they have been nascent abilities within you all along. You were unfortunately unaware of their presence, and because of a lack of training and foreknowledge, you could not anticipate them. Nor could you anticipate the consequences of your actions. Nor could you possibly fathom an understanding of the acrimonious and unremorseful balance to be obtained, by you, that could allow you to accept your transgressions for what they are." Maurice started pacing around the table. "Let me guess! After the incident in your youth you believed a monster lived inside you, yes? You believed this monster was a burden that you and you alone would have to carry as punishment. You needed to hide it deep inside you, never letting it out."

Sebastiane became wholly unnerved. And then, he became emotionally unhinged.

Maurice could see the look on his grandson's face changing from one of pure confusion to one of unbelievable acceptance. Maurice could also see the wheels turning inside the boy's mind, trying to figure it all out. He needed more, thought Maurice. Maybe just a simple push towards enlightenment, one that he himself had received from his father and something he should have told to Elena—he just never had the time for it. He continued calmly, "After your mauling of the pedophile you tried to look inside yourself to contemplate the reason…not the why, but the how. Am I correct?"

Sebastiane nodded his head. His eyes begged for more insight and he began to sit more erect in his chair. The effects of the late hour, his nicotine intake, and the alcohol were quickly abating. His mind focused, yearning for the completeness of the truth.

"Understand this. The abilities inside you, the ones that have until now plagued you with a sense of internalized regret and festered into an outward mask of loneliness, are an accumulated inheritance…like monetary wealth bequeathed to the next in line. They are a conglomeration of everything experienced and learned and then passed on to the next descendant. This burden, as I know it, and as I can see in your eyes you begin to recognize its face too, is the path of our family history. It is a path created over many generations and built up like large, monolithic stones used to construct the foundations of a dominant fortress. These stones have been shaped by shared memories, traits, choices and actions, passed on through nothing more than genetics, and reinforced by a verbal history that has been repeated down through the centuries from generation to generation."

Maurice sat down before continuing, "In and of itself, the burden we carry is a singular construct of fate if you will. And since you are the ancestral heir and the youngest living male descendant of the House of Renault, this construct, this burden, has fallen upon you Sebastiane. Where once you were its silent keeper, through lack of proper training and because you were ill-informed, for that I blame myself, now you will become its student. Soon, you will be its equal; maybe someday even its master." With his speech finished it was time for Sebastiane to understand what he was without further assistance. If his grandson could understand, might he be amenable to another suggestion? Maurice had just come to a decision that would affect the rest of Sebastiane's life.

"Genetics?" asked Sebastiane, in an awkward and feeble attempt to comprehend what he was hearing. "What do you mean? Genetic manipulation! Are we test-tube babies or Dolly the Sheep or something?"

The boy still couldn't fathom his own history. "Conspiracy theories. What a waste of time," proclaimed Maurice, rolling his eyes. "This is not one of your *X-Files* episodes. It is not some outlandish story about alien manipulation of the human gene pool to facilitate a takeover of planet Earth. We are not a part of some secret government program or Catholic Church-styled secret society with an underhanded agenda to control the world. This isn't a movie and it isn't a video game. Nor is it some poorly written adventure novel from your youth."

Maurice's frustration was building inside of him, trying to take over the conversation—trying to take control of him. Then he remembered something. He, too, had been completely unable to comprehend his father's recitation of the family's history either. He calmed down and decided to present it differently. "Try thinking about it in another way. Some people have a genetic predisposition towards cancer because it runs in their family. You have the same thing, only this is a genetic predisposition for tactical awareness, strategic planning, individual combat, total war, and, albeit contradictory, self-preservation."

The light inside Sebastiane's mind finally clicked on. His raised eyebrows, raised by the sensation of comprehension and understanding, let Maurice know that finally he got it.

Now for the bad news.

"I give you this one warning, though," Maurice cautioned. "These abilities, this burden you suspected all along and will soon become very accustomed to, will from this point forward be the dominant force in your life. It will act like a statistical, systematic, sadistic calculator, charting all your contraventions and all your triumphs, day in and day out, and keep them like totals columns on an economic balance sheet. You must be taught to control them and how to prepare yourself for a life dominated by them. If you don't learn self-control, your life will become a disease riddled by tragedy. Believe me when I say this—your destiny is no longer under your control."

As if anyone ever has control over such a thing.

"Call it what it is or call it what you will, but you are now bound to a fate derived from circumstances that are beyond your ability to comprehend. It started that day, the day you stopped the pedophile, and it will end with…with your death probably. Truly only God knows how it will all end." And with that, Maurice stood and walked out of the kitchen and into a room off the kitchen area, leaving Sebastiane to fully understand the demon inside him.

Maurice returned after a few minutes with a packet of documents in his hand and found Sebastiane staring at the table, holding his coffee cup, and slowly sipping on it. Maurice noticed that the bottle of whiskey was further drained as his grandson had smoked yet another Gauloises cigarette.

Sebastiane acknowledged his return with one final set of questions regarding the family history, "What about you, sir? What happened to you? Why did you abandon my mother?"

The accusation was stinging, but understandable. "Come, we'll talk while we walk. It is time to go." Maurice put out his arm to show Sebastiane to the door. "And please, call me Maurice. You are all I have left." He stopped short of saying that this might be the last time they saw each other, but that was the way it had to be. Sebastiane got up from the table, and together they exited the farmhouse and headed down a dirt road towards Maurice's villa on the other side of town.

As the light from the lantern-style flashlight Maurice was holding illuminated their path through the 3:00 a.m. darkness, so too did Maurice light the way as he began with a recounting of his own life, "I did not abandon your mother, by the way. It had become necessary to protect her. Sending her to America to live with Jean Francois was the only option."

"I take it you're going to tell me why? And can I presume that that *why* has everything to do with what you just told me?"

"Yes, it does," stated Maurice. He took a deep breath. It would be a long walk for his tired, old legs. And talking as well! Well that would be extra strenuous. "I was all set to join the French Army when the Nazis attacked in 1940. After our defeat, the Vichy government was set up as an abomination sent from hell to ruin our lives. It was a government that existed in a vacuum of self-deprecation under the Third Reich…"

Maurice stuttered and then paused, knowing full well he was being apocalyptic. He couldn't really help it, though. Remembering the loss of country and of so many friends, and the purgatory that followed, was permanently etched into his psyche. He used the time to catch his breath and slow his pace. "And so, I found myself fighting alongside my father as a member of *la résistance*. Initially our job was to assist with the movement of weapons and to keep tabs on German military movements, and the like, in the hope that one day help would come. Later, it was our job to help downed allied pilots escape across the Pyrenees. Eventually, we were asked to come north and help devise the plans to sabotage German equipment and reinforcements before the Normandy landings. We were so good at what we had done in the south that our successes had garnered us a reputation which preceded us. Not long after our arrival in the north we were betrayed and my father was captured. I never saw him again." Maurice paused again while his mind recalled the faded but still painful memory.

As they continued along the winding dirt path, Maurice became increasingly slow with his gait. Sebastiane slowed to match it. He finally continued, "I myself was captured and then tortured by the Gestapo. Even with the assistance of an entire company of Wehrmacht it still took four days to find and capture me." He decided to leave out the details of his torture, finding it unnecessary to verbally relive it. "After the war I was asked to join the new French Army by an old family friend, Monsieur Foccart. I almost said no, but that is when I saw your grandmother for the first time." Maurice became a bit livelier as he talked about Sophia. "She helped convince me that life goes on, so I joined and was sent to Algeria to help rebuild the Legion."

Sebastiane interrupted, "Legion? The Foreign Legion?"

"Oui."

"Why Algeria?"

"It was where Sophia was going to be. It is where I wanted to be because I needed her. It was also where the Legion was born, and would be reborn."

The conversation had turned deeply personal, and Maurice was becoming hesitant. Sebastiane could sense it and switched topics. "My mother was born in Algeria, then?"

"She loved Algeria. As a small child she lived in Oran with her mother. As a young lady she spent most of her time here in France at school. But in the summers, she came to Algeria to see us." Maurice smiled when he reflected upon her summer visits, visits that had been like a second childhood for him. It was a far better memory than what Maurice talked about next. "Algeria soon became a very dangerous place, and certain things, unfortunate things, had to be done. One of those things required us to send your mother to America."

"What things?"

Maurice replied, "Insurgency, counter-insurgency, killings, revenge killings, all-out war in the streets—you name it. Sophia was killed. I was blamed."

The curt statement from his grandfather made Sebastiane realize something; that Algeria seemed to affect Maurice just as much as Marseille was affecting him. A greater understanding of things came into focus for Sebastiane, and he decided to leave well enough alone. But with all the histories, stories, and insights Maurice had described over the last few hours to him, Sebastiane was able to use it all to pinpoint the exact moment in his own life that was a mirror image of his grandfather's tribulations. Finally, he was beginning to understand.

But what now?

Instead of asking that question, Sebastiane decided maybe it was his turn to talk. He switched the conversation to his mother, Elena Sophia Renault-Bassett. Sebastiane talked about her, their home, and his life with her for the rest of the walk back into town. His story continued over breakfast at the villa, a breakfast derived from yesterday's leftover croissants and baguettes smothered with butter and honey—and more coffee. Maurice listened intently, not wanting it to stop.

By the time the morning light started to appear, both men were exhausted. Maurice wanted to tell Sebastiane something his own father never could. He wanted to tell Sebastiane that no matter how bad life could get, he was just a man. The decision to be a good man, or something else entirely, despite everything he would endure was up to him. Before he could however, Sebastiane was asleep on the couch.

Maurice watched his grandson for a time, remembering how sleep sometimes made his own nightmares tolerable. He quietly exited the room, made his way to the second-floor balcony via the kitchen to get more coffee, and arrived just as the first rays of sunlight capped the horizon.

Maurice spent what time he had, before Sebastiane awoke, reflecting upon the last time he'd witnessed such an intense, emotional daybreak. He tried valiantly to stop himself from actually reliving his past because the pain simply wasn't worth it. He failed.

CHAPTER 32

Oran, Algeria, 1961

"You! You are responsible for the death of my daughter!" screamed the colonel, as he extended his right arm and pointed his index finger straight at his subordinate officer. The colonel looked as if he was about to have an epileptic fit as he began abusively flailing both his arms, his hands now balled into fists. Quite suddenly, he regained his composure—he was a colonel after all. He was about to blurt out something even more hateful at the officer standing before him when his eyes drifted towards the ground in contemplation. Actually, the colonel's mind was racing—and for good reason.

Colonel Heinrich Von Furst was tall at six and a half feet, and elegantly menacing in stature. With almost white blond hair and light blue eyes, he was the true definition of the Aryan race. French and German by heritage, his family hailed from the Alsace-Lorraine region of France, or Germany, depending on what side of history you placed your family crest in—or what side of that history you supported.

During the war, the colonel was a member of the puppet government at Vichy. He could swing from side to side with any argument as to who he truly supported during the war, exiled France or Nazi Germany. In the process he'd convinced all those around him he was on the correct side—whatever side it was they supported, of course. He always portrayed an outward sense of loyalty to France, but most knew it to be a veil that hid his true Aryan beliefs in the superiority of the German people; and all-the-while waiting for what had to be a German victory. When victory never came, the colonel was forced to survive by lying to all those around him. Saved from the harsh retributions of post-war French citizenry lynch mobs, he was labeled a Vichy sympathizer and allowed to participate in the reconstruction of the French Army. Fifteen years later, he was still just a colonel; a lowly colonel in charge of legionnaires and commander of the city of Oran in French Algeria.

The colonel finally continued, "Her death is on your hands. Had you followed your orders, quite possibly we would be in control of this situation and those animals who killed her would not have had the opportunity to do so."

Maurice Renault stood at attention in front of his superior officer, questioning himself yet again. He quickly searched his conscience to verify his thought process. Finding himself in the unfortunate position of having to choose the lesser of two evils, he needed to make sure one last time. With his thoughts formulated, he gathered himself, looked up, and rebutted, "To follow such orders would be a betrayal of France. You know this as well as I."

"It is de Gaulle who has betrayed France and her people so he does not deserve our loyalty," justified the colonel. "And from your answer I can now understand that your loyalties have been somehow misguided by insane preconceptions of duty, and definitively lay on the opposite side of reality to my own. I now understand that you have betrayed my trust."

Maurice never quite saw eye-to-eye with the colonel on anything. Politically, they differed as to the juxtaposition of de Gaulle as France to

France as her people. Some thought the President of France to be a god while others thought him a demagogue. Personally, Maurice knew that the colonel simply detested him for stealing his only daughter. "I could not prevent her death!" Maurice countered, with a firm yet depressed-laden shout.

Did I make the right decision? Was I to blame for Sophia? Her death was the colonel's fault, wasn't it? Yes, it was.

Maurice could feel the extremely painful hole in his heart widening; the burden of Sophia's loss weighed heavily upon him. His thoughts were usually so precise, so absolute, but not so much now with the events of the last few days. His mind calmed slightly when he reflected upon his last conversation with her.

Sophia had made sure Maurice knew his decision was the correct one before she left him that morning, just two days ago, to confront the colonel about his participation in the twisted plan to keep Algeria in French control. Her soft-spoken words and matter-of-factness, about what Maurice should do or say to her father, was all the justification his mind required to stop his heart from emotionally exploding at that very moment.

Maurice began to realize why the colonel was blaming him for Sophia. It was a futile attempt to extricate his own guilt over the death of his daughter, and by proxy, position himself ahead of the retribution that was to come from his masters for a plan gone totally awry—and from Paris for a coup turning headlong in the same direction. Maurice's guilt was built upon and extended through his confusion within the situation, his love for Sophia, and his love of the Legion. He wanted to confront the colonel about the coup attempt, knowing he should have done so sooner. Maurice needed to be cautious, though. He started to think a little more clearly.

Remove yourself from this room before something happens to you, just like it had happened to Sophia.

She was dead, though; he had waited too long. His confusion began racing out of control again. He collected himself quickly and then continued to dismiss the colonel's justifications with a vicious retort, "If you had not participated in this absurd attempt to subvert Algerian independence, against the wishes of President de Gaulle, and the people of France I might add, Sophia would still be alive. The only reason she was on the streets that day was to come see you. She felt that she had to stop you to keep your family's honor intact. I thought it better coming from her than from me. She was coming to tell you to stop this madness."

The colonel was not a stupid man, and would surely suspect his subterfuge now. Maurice had thought long and hard before drafting and eventually sending the telegram to his friend, Monsieur Foccart, in Paris, outlining the overall plans of the coup.

Maurice had tried to do the right thing. For so many years he had been the colonel's enforcer, attempting to abate Algerian independence at the behest of France, or so he thought, while at the same time trying not to kill every Algerian freedom fighter in sight as the colonel thought prudent. But no longer. No longer would he stand by and let this charlatan command legionnaires, destroy Algeria with the blood of her people, and possibly devastate France as well. He had, through his own lack of conviction, allowed the conniving colonel to deceive and manipulate his legionnaires for far too long by convincing them that Algerian independence was bad for France.

The colonel's idealistic pathology, a version of colonialism with a brutal twist, was his own. It was not the only voice railing against independence for the Algerian people, but it was, however, silently the loudest. Because of his position and influence, his ideology had become the foundation of the plan that had ultimately put the two of them in this room together at this very moment.

Colonel Heinrich Von Furst's only true, redeeming quality was his daughter Sophia. She was his only child and the pride and joy of the Von Furst family. He loved her, that was obvious, but he also despised her for two things—she was not the son he'd always wanted, and for marrying the wrong man. Even though the colonel had raised her to be a strong, independent woman, and it had shown throughout her life, he couldn't help but think his dedication to her had turned against him when she met and married Maurice Sebastian Renault.

For Maurice, the sun rose and set with Sophia. He would miss her for the rest of his days, and those days would be long and unbearable indeed. The colonel may have lost a daughter, but Maurice lost his true love, his wife, and the mother of his only child. He would have to be strong for her now too. Maurice grew angry at that thought, the thought of her crying over her mother. Musings of revenge and retribution stirred within him, but they would have to wait. Maurice regained his wits while holding back his tears of anguish and remorse. His face turned slightly red as he stared across the large oak desk at his father-in-law.

The colonel on the other hand looked as if he was trying to figure out how everything had fallen apart. He was the right man in the right place at the right time. His plans had been so methodical, so exacting, so precise, and so ruthless that they couldn't possibly have failed.

How did it go so wrong? I planned everything for the generals down to the last detail. How did it go so wrong?

Then the colonel paused to remember Maurice's rebuke, just seconds before, and it ignited a coherence of thought and corroboration of evidence that would lead him down a path of enlightenment—it was the path Maurice wanted him to follow.

It was Maurice who betrayed me! Yes, that would work.

The colonel kept plodding along with this train of thought before eventually finding his way out. He saw an escape route from his involvement with the coup, a way to protect his reputation, and a way to keep his undeserved honor intact.

Yes! Maurice planned everything. He planned the coup.

Maurice could sense the colonel's thoughts—it wasn't hard. "Sir, I…"

"Silence!" blurted out the colonel in his thick Franco-German accent.

The beauty of the French language brutalized by the diction of a German. It was a travesty, thought Maurice. A trivial travesty at best, but along with everything else that had happened Maurice couldn't stop himself from tallying up all the things that were wrong with his father-in-law.

Both men continued to stare across the oversized wooden desk at each other. They were both strong men. They were both soldiers. The difference between them was that the colonel was an opportunistic survivor, whereas Maurice was dedicated.

Maurice had come to realize that the colonel had most likely inherited his uncanny ability to stay one step ahead of the game instead of earning it. It was a political savviness that somehow maintained his wholly undeserved military status, all-the-while accompanying an historical-sized ego and misguided belief in his own honor. And now, after everything that had happened, all that Heinrich Von Furst had achieved was for naught. The colonel had been reduced to a lowly minion for *un quarteron de generaux en retraite*—a handful of retired generals—and was left to contemplate his future duties as the bagman for the fall-out. His incredulously, unvarnished military record and dark, shadowy ambitions, accompanied by his fallacious reputation, had landed him square in the middle of a failed coup d'état. His honor on the other hand, always swaying like a dutiful mainsail in a strong wind, was about to be torn asunder.

The colonel was trying to think quickly but couldn't. He was slowed by his intake of overfilled tumblers of cognac. His mind wandered around his daughter. Losing her was not part of the plan. And his son-in-law, whom the colonel truly detested and despised, would have to be the scapegoat. The colonel wanted nothing better than to kill Maurice but couldn't, not now, because a plan had formulated within.

Maurice could see the colonel's blisteringly angry, alcohol-fueled expression of realization growing through his over-tanned, regalian skin— skin that had been perfected by the years he'd spent enriching himself in Algeria. It took everything Maurice had to stop himself from jumping across the desk and choking his father-in-law to death. He would love nothing more than to watch the life drift from the colonel's eyes as the oxygen to his brain was cut off by his strong and vengeful hands.

Maurice stopped himself. He couldn't do it. He couldn't do it because that would mean seeing the same look he'd seen on Sophia's face as she lay dying in his arms. Her expression was that of the realization and understating of the exact timing of her death. She was in his arms, bleeding in the middle of the street. He had just enough time to say good-bye and reaffirm his love for her. He had cried uncontrollably. Then, the look in her eyes changed. The feeling in them, as if every joyous second of her life was passing by at that very moment, that was what he wanted to remember— not killing her father.

Maurice saw the colonel's expression of realization and understanding finally peek through his semi-inebriated state. His plan was working. He only needed one thing more from the colonel. He needed him to see the final piece of the puzzle, and then say the words back to him.

Say it! It was you who drafted the telegram to Foccart. It was you who betrayed my plans. Say it, damn you! Say it so we can be done with this charade.

The colonel was trying to put two-and-two together. With Gagne's information about a late afternoon telegram being sent from Sidi-Bel-Abbès, but not knowing who actually wrote it, and now this early morning confrontation with Maurice, the colonel thought he was close to a complete understanding of the failure of the coup, who was responsible—and coincidently, a way out from this mess.

Maurice sensed it was coming and silently thanked Simon for doing his job. Caporal Simon Gagne was a pitiful, useless little peon. Personal assistant to the colonel for almost a decade, Simon had recently been reassigned to Maurice's command at Sidi-Bel-Abbès. The caporal had unknowingly become the colonel's eyes and ears because his loyalty was childlike—like that of a disadvantaged nephew taken in by a wealthy and manipulative uncle-by-marriage. Small in physical stature and mental acumen due to meager upbringings, Simon was so easily controlled with simple little lies that it constantly exposed his youthful naiveté. It made him the perfect choice for an unwitting spy for both sides.

"She was on the streets, why?" the colonel asked Maurice quizzically. He was hoping his belligerent son-in-law would just simply blurt out the truth and save him the trouble of finding other proof. He probably wouldn't need it because the recording device in his office was running—as it always did.

Maurice thought quickly, taking in all the factors, weighing his options against the only thing he had left—his daughter Elena. Maurice had sent her away, unknowingly to the colonel, to stay with recently emigrated relatives in America when the escalating violence in Algeria became too dangerous. And now, to protect her future, his subtle manipulation of the current conversation would force him to answer the colonel's question with a question, one that would hopefully lay the burden of his father-in-law's betrayal of France, and of the Legion, upon his own shoulders. It was a question that could save his daughter's life, because at this point Maurice wasn't completely convinced his father-in-law was thinking clearly enough not to consider killing him—and maybe even his own granddaughter.

Maurice continued with his verbal redirection of the colonel's thought processes, "If she was on the streets that day to prevent you from disgracing yourself, the Legion, and France, was she not putting your family's honor before me? Surely she was trying to prevent someone, anyone, from linking you to this madness. She tried to stop it. She tried to stop Minister Foccart from linking you to this. And because of it she lost her life. She lost her life trying to save yours."

Colonel Heinrich Von Furst, survivor, was blissful on the inside considering Maurice had just crucified himself with his answer. The Colonel turned and faced the window overlooking the parade grounds within the army compound. Turning his back on Maurice was a show of contempt and bravado on his part—contempt because he thought he was going to win, brave because even the colonel knew as well as anyone how good a soldier Maurice truly was. He continued to stare out the second-story window at the soldiers below, his most loyal legionnaires, men who had been hand-picked, vetted, and then made to swear an oath of allegiance before becoming his personal guard. They were waiting to enter the building to arrest the Capitaine. The colonel smiled, glanced at his wristwatch, and stated, "I will give you two hours to put your personal affairs in order. After that I cannot guarantee your safety." The tone was sadistic, and couldn't be misinterpreted.

This is why you were chosen by the generals to plan the coup, you idiot. You are weak. And because of your weakness you'll never be able to understand why I am doing this now.

Maurice turned without saluting or waiting to be dismissed, opened the door, and exited the office. He left the door ajar.

The colonel turned to see nothing but an empty office and cringed at the final gesture of insubordination.

Well, another excuse not to give Maurice the two hours.

The colonel reached down and flicked the switch under his desk to *Off* to stop the recording device. He returned to the window and tapped on it, signaling to his loyal soldiers below that it was time.

CHAPTER 33

Laroque-des-Albères, France, 2001

Maurice walked back downstairs. He looked in the room to find Sebastiane still completely unconscious on the couch. The boy was dealing with too much, thought Maurice, so he let him sleep. After fetching a fresh pack of cigarettes from a drawer in the kitchen, Maurice walked into the elevated garden at the back of the house and looked for some shade that would hide his tired eyes from the brightness of the morning sun. Reaching down to overturn a fallen, rusted chair, Maurice sat down, lit a cigarette, and closed his eyes. The visualization of his past and the memorialization of the pain that had plagued him for the past forty years continued.

~

Oran, Algeria, 1961

Maurice was now in his own office collecting a few of his personal belongings. There wasn't much, just a picture of his wife and daughter, a packet of important documents, and some small tape recordings of his own. He dropped the documents and tape recordings into a separate envelope, and then placed it next to his satchel.

He paused to take a deep breath. He needed to remember where his friend, Jacques René, was currently stationed. Sophia had always kept that kind of information in her journal which she'd carried everywhere. An image of its pages flashed in his mind. With its soft leather binding soaked red from her blood, clutched in her outstretched hand as she lay in the street dying, the emotions of it all possessed him as if the word horror had taken on a physical form. He felt as lonely as ever, as lonely as she must have felt while lying there in the street as the life drained from her body. He swept the horrifying image away when he suddenly remembered the address.

Maurice wanted to cry, but couldn't afford tears at the moment. He placed the envelope, along with the picture, into his satchel already stuffed with civilian clothing. He hadn't worn such things in a very long time; he would have to get used to doing so from now on. On a small piece of paper he jotted down a quick note and then headed towards the door. The last thing he did was to reach for the coat rack and snatch his side arm from its holster. He might need the weapon from here on out if he was to survive.

Maurice escaped down the back stairs as the colonel's men entered his office. Leaving the building via the side exit, he calmly walked to the rear of the compound. The back gate was relatively small compared to the large elaborate ones at the main entrance of Fort St. Philippe. The two-hundred-year-old citadel had been used for many things in its history, but mostly as a stronghold or seat of power for all who had conquered the area. For years it had been the colonel's little fiefdom. Now, it would be considered by some to be the birthplace of the destruction of the Legion. Maurice hoped *la légion étrangère* could survive this. He knew he wouldn't.

He quietly closed the small gate behind him and headed towards his waiting company car. Opening the door himself he called out, "Simon, drive." His driver did as ordered as soon as the door was closed.

"Where to, Capitaine?"

"To the cemetery," directed Maurice. "I wish to see where my wife will be buried."

Caporal Simon Gagne started driving down Rue Esplanade du Camp St. Philippe before taking a slight turn to the right when he reached Boulevard du Dahomey.

The city was quiet. At almost four in the morning the only sounds breaking the silence were the fishermen and the bakers stirring from uneasy slumber to prepare for the day's activities. Maurice stared regrettably at the ever present, war-torn strife etched into the city's ancient architecture. It seemed as if the exquisiteness of the place had vanished into mediocrity as if painted on by a child's innocence. It could be cleaned and made to look pretty again, but had lost its sense of awe yet again as history took its toll.

Simon continued left onto Boulevard Marechal Joffre, then north past the city center towards the cemetery at the base of the Pic d'Aidour—a massive rock formation dominating the entire western side of the city of Oran. He glanced into the rear-view mirror.

Maurice continually stared out the window, eyeing the bullet-ridden storefronts and trash-strewn streets. The smoke, rubble, blood, tears, and tragedy could be inhaled and categorized for their individual familiarity and then regurgitated as horrific memories of all the things he had done to these people. Maurice was tired of it all; tired of the killing, tired of the destruction, tired of life—tired of death. He glanced up to see his driver looking back to the road from the rearview mirror. As they approached the Hôtel de Ville Simon turned left, crossing Rue de Austerlitz.

"Stop here," demanded Maurice. "I'll get out myself. Keep the car running." Once around the corner, out of eyesight of the young caporal, Maurice walked up to a typical-looking building for the area. With its ancient, Moorish architecture and broken, stuccoed walls, making everything look practically identical, he slipped his handwritten note into the mailbox for the third apartment. The surname on the box read *HADJ*. Maurice returned to the vehicle, entered, and stated as he closed the door, "Continue to the cemetery, please."

"Yes, Capitaine," replied Gagne. The car sped off instantly.

Maurice returned to his thoughts. No longer would he fight against himself. No longer would he suffer the indignity of hypocrisy. No longer would he fight against the belief that freedom for Algeria and Algerians was wrong. The Legion, the *biblical* right hand of French indecision, the sword of repression that had scorned this land for more than a century, was now lost to him. Maurice shook his head in disgust. Algeria had been his home. It was as much a member of his family as any person could be. It would now become his proverbial long-lost father; and he, its prodigal son. To save his beloved Legion, Maurice had to become its betrayer. He had, after all the dedication, all the denial, all the deception, and all the planning, come to realize what needed to be done. He accepted it as his greatest honor. One day, Maurice knew, this honor would require him to make amends in the eyes of his brothers. He promised himself he would. For now, and in memory of all those brothers lost, and for his family, lost, he would become Judas. It was the logical conclusion to all that was happening to Algeria—and to his life.

Maurice looked up as the car came to an uneasy stop outside the gates of the small cemetery. Positioned on the west side of the city and just south of the Casbah at the base of the Pic d'Aidour, this small and delicate piece of land would be the final resting place for his beloved Sophia.

Caporal Gagne exited through the front-hinged, driver-side door of the military command car and immediately turned to pull the handle on the back door. He snapped to attention as his superior officer exited. Gagne closed the doors and watched as his Capitaine walked towards an open plot in the center of a mass of headstones. Gagne lowered his head and held his breath for just a moment, saying a quick prayer for Sophia Renault. Raising his head, he looked back over at the gravesite and couldn't quite see the Capitaine anymore. The young caporal guessed he was down on his knees praying.

Assuming he was out of earshot, Gagne lit a cigarette and relaxed ever so slightly. He was a young man, with dark hair and tanned skin. His extremely boyish features tended to deceive those around him into believing he was not in the military. The characteristic normalcy for soldiers was to have a gritty, albeit lost, and sometimes hollowed-out look that scared most people. His surname was French, but his family had immigrated, escaped really, to Spain to avoid the war with Germany. Instead of returning home to France afterwards they again immigrated, this time to Algeria. The Gagne's worked a small family farm inadvertently ransacked and then burned in the early days of the conflict. With his family dead, Simon Gagne joined the French Army and was taken in by the colonel.

Gagne inhaled deeply on his cigarette, coughing slightly. His smoking habit was an effort to look more manly and fit in with the others, but it still bothered his lungs. He turned and opened the front door of the vehicle, took his seat at the wheel, shut the door, and rolled down the window. As he grabbed the car's radio to inform the colonel's guards where he was, young, naive Simon Gagne found himself torn between his duty to the colonel and his admiration for the capitaine and his wife. But orders were orders. He switched to the appropriate channel, pressed the button on the radio microphone, and spoke softly, "Guard One, this is Caporal Gagne. I am with the capitaine and we are at the...."

His voice cut out. A solid left hook to his chin had come from outside the car. Simon fell into a lump on the front bench seat of the vehicle, lit cigarette and all.

Maurice made sure Simon was unconscious before deciding that a short hike from the cemetery up the Pic d'Aidour to the chapel of the Blessed Virgin, just below Fort de Santa Cruz, would allow him a view of the Mediterranean Sea and the whole of the city of Oran one last time—it was a view Sophia had loved so much. Maurice started up the hill, trying his best to hold back his almost uncontrollable sadness. His beloved wife, savoir of his soul and mother of his only child, was dead.

Sophia Renault, formerly Sophia Von Furst, had been a second chance for Maurice. His bifurcated life, separated by his eighteenth birthday, horrific in all aspects, had slowly become a paradise. And it was all because of Sophia. She was strong-willed and expressively so, but at the same time demure and strikingly beautiful. Classically educated, she could carry any conversation about any subject—and in several languages. She had arrived in Maurice's life just in time to protect him from his emotionally chaotic, suicidal tendencies when they burst out and wrought havoc on all those around him after the war.

Maurice was to join the French Army in 1940 when he was of age. The collapse of the Second French Republic at the hands of the Nazis forced him to become a resistance fighter instead, and he garnered a fearsome and widely known reputation as a warrior. The Gestapo knew him as the one man, a ghost, whom they couldn't catch. It wasn't until nine Gestapo agents and a small detachment of Wehrmacht caught up to Maurice in late 1944 that his life would take a turn towards the unspeakable.

After the war, an old family friend, Monsieur Foccart, tried to convince Maurice to join the new French Army. Foccart was trying to give him a purpose in life and maybe, just maybe, the boy would survive his nightmares. It was then that Maurice met Sophia. She was the only child of a French Army officer who had accompanied Foccart on his mission to recruit officers from the reconstituted, post-war French Army for the Legion.

The Legion at the time was in utter disarray. Split by the war, and split by warring on each other during the Battle of Damascus in 1941, the Legion needed rebuilding. As Foccart and Von Furst began to rebuild the Legion, so too did Sophia begin to rebuild Maurice. Both were difficult tasks; as it would turn out, Foccart and Von Furst had it easy by comparison.

Through her kindness and eventual love for him, Maurice was able to regain some semblance of his shattered life. Slowly he became a man again. Because of her, his loss of self-identify had become tolerable enough that he was able to join the French Army in 1946. Shortly thereafter, they had married. And by the grace of God and their love for each other, she was pregnant before they left for Algeria.

Maurice was stationed to Sidi Bel-Abbès, a small city fort in the *Tell Atlas* of Algeria about forty kilometers south of Oran. It was the spiritual home of the Legion, and it suited his new and reassembled life quite well. And it was here, in Algeria, that Maurice, not the colonel, had become a leader of men—a leader of Legionnaires. This was how it had been throughout the Legion's history, with a French Army officer in charge of foreign men fighting for France. Maurice became not just a good officer, but also a comrade to the legionnaires. To them he was not an officer, but a soldier fighting alongside them. Over the next fifteen years he had become one with the legionnaires under his command—and one with the Legion.

The colonel thought the Algerian command might catapult him to bigger and better things, but it was not the glorious assignment he thought it to be. The colonel tried to downplay Maurice's popularity amongst the men by trying to convince him that he should command them and not assimilate their gruff and unsavory ways. The colonel's attempts were altogether rebuffed. Maurice was a French Army officer, but had become a Legionnaire at heart. From youthful exuberance, to resistance fighter, to knocking at death's door, to rebirth, and finally to belonging, Maurice Renault had found new purpose in life—family, and the Legion.

Maurice gazed upon the city of Oran as it lay in front of him. He peered to his left to see the intense light of daybreak enhance the azure beauty of the Mediterranean Sea. The sight of it all was too personal for him. But before he could collapse to his knees in anguish, his internal demon snapped him back to reality. His analytical processes and warrior instincts quickly took over. Clearing his mind of the happy memories of his rebirth and his new life with Sophia, his daughter Elena, and the Legion, he realized he needed to commit all his strength to his survival.

He had thought of driving his car back into the city and somehow getting to the fisherman's wharf area to steal a boat or hide on one to escape. To do this, he would have had to navigate the city streets and somehow bypass all the army patrols who were most certainly looking for him now. Not too difficult, he thought, but too accommodating for his pursuers, he decided. Maurice turned and looked up the hill, and then a little higher, up towards Fort de Santa Cruz. A wry smile appeared on his face.

Too bad, old man.

It was the first fiendishly, gloating thought he'd had on this day—it was a welcome relief from the mental anguish. Maurice proceeded back down the hill. There was one last thing he needed to do to affect his escape, so first things first. Deception would be the key. His descent down the small path led him back to the command vehicle. Simon Gagne was still lying unconscious on the front seat of the vehicle. Maurice then put his escape plan into action just as a military transport truck arrived on the scene.

CHAPTER 34

Laroque-des-Albères, France, 2001

Maurice slowly got up from the garden chair when he realized he'd been sitting too long. He also knew he was far too old to smoke and drink like he used to. He decided to take a shower and clean up. He made his way inside and into the bathroom, turned on the water, got undressed, got in, and tried to think.

Maurice let the cold water wash across his tired face, down his tired body, and into the tired, old pipes skirting down the interior walls of his tired, old house before flowing underneath the centuries-old streets of his hometown. As the water washed away the effects of the drink and the cloudiness of being awake for so long, his eyes slowly opened to the truth of it all.

Is this right? Can this be the right decision? It has to be.

As the plan to save his grandson solidified, hampered only by his wandering mind, and with the possibility of a manhunt on for a murderer in Marseille, Maurice couldn't help but finish remembering the day his choices had sealed the fate of his daughter's life; and now, maybe his grandson's too.

~

Oran, Algeria, 1961

A quick splash of water from a canteen to the face of the young caporal and he was awake—his jaw was in agony. Simon looked up into the brightening morning sky to see several soldiers from the colonel's private detachment standing above him. They had dragged him out of the car and laid him on the ground. He saw they were armed, and guessed they were looking for the Capitaine. The big one had a radio-phone and was talking to someone, presumably the colonel, but Simon could only hear one side of the conversation.

"Kill him. Yes, sir," replied the soldier. He quickly turned to face the others, and said, "Seek and destroy. Maurice Renault has been designated persona non grata and should be dealt with immediately."

The hulking beast of a soldier then looked down at Simon. "Get up and tell me where he went."

"I don't know," retorted Simon. "He was in the cemetery and then I couldn't see him. I thought he was kneeling down and praying, maybe, so I got in the car to call you, and then I woke up. I got hit, I guess."

The soldiers laughed as he rubbed his jaw again. Another soldier, a rough, seasoned-looking veteran of many things, a bit small when compared to the leader, but still quite large, cautioned, "You're lucky he didn't kill you. The Capitaine is a ruthless bastard." They all laughed again at the diminutive caporal. The same soldier then began propagating falsehoods, devised by the colonel, that everyone needed to hear so as to start believing his version of the story and not Maurice's. This lowly caporal, as the colonel had pointed out, was as good a place to start as any. He started with, "Killing his own wife and trying to blame the colonel! Can you believe it? All of this pathetic subterfuge just to cover his own ass for siding with the generals. For shame."

Simon was shocked. The pain in his jaw and the mocking by the soldiers around him quickly eroded his ability to think or even comprehend the truth.

The lies continued as the soldier bent down to get closer, "The colonel has been informed of the same. He was told to bring Maurice to justice, but the colonel wants blood. Surely *you* can understand that?"

The last portion of the vile and poisoned propaganda was directed at Simon himself. He immediately shouted back, "You're wrong. He would never..."

"Oh, but he did," was the interrupting and penultimate statement from the brute. "Ask the Capitaine when we catch him. If he is an honorable man, he will admit to it wouldn't he?"

The naive caporal thought incorrectly and spoke quickly, "Yes, of course he would. Yes, of course. He is an honorable man. I will ask him." The seeds of deception had been sown. They would continue to grow with all who crossed paths with the colonel, his men, and the naiveté of one Caporal Simon Gagne.

With a wave of the leader's arm, the rest of the soldiers rallied to the transport to head into the city. Their next stop was the port—it was the logical choice. Capitaine Renault needed to leave the country, and a boat was the only way out right now.

Caporal Gagne got to his feet as they drove off. Staggering ever so slightly he got back into his car, started it, and began to make a U-turn out of the cemetery parking area. He was going to head back to the barracks for first aid. It was a struggle to put the car in gear with one hand on his jaw, and when he did the car jumped abruptly. A large thud came from the rear of the vehicle as he completed the 180-degree turn. Puzzled by the noise, Gagne stopped the vehicle. Unsure if he had hit something, an animal maybe, or if something had come loose, the spare tire perhaps, he made his way to the trunk to investigate. As the trunk opened, a leg kicked out and struck him in the right knee. The hit was too much. As the pain from a crushed patella and torn tendons surged through him, Simon fell backwards onto the ground screaming in agony. About to vomit from the pain, Gagne looked up to see his Capitaine climb out of the trunk, lean over, and punch him in the face.

"How could you possibly think I would kill my wife? Mon dieu." Maurice shouted at the unconscious boy as he rubbed his head from the knock it had taken against the frame of the trunk when Gagne forgot how to shift gears. Maurice stared at the pathetic young man lying in front of him, waiting for an answer that wouldn't come—waiting for an answer he knew would be stained with half-thoughts, half-truths, and dripping in suspicion. Hearing the words of the soldiers, and the caporal's replies, Maurice was assured of a violent death if he was caught.

Not today, my friends. Not today.

Maurice dragged Gagne towards the gates of the cemetery and left him on the inward side of the wall and just out of sight of any passersby. Taking the caporal's chapeau and ID, he calmly walked back to the command vehicle, opened the door, reached in, and yanked out the receiver of the radio. He threw the chapeau and ID on the front seat in the hopes someone would think the car was abandoned. Or better yet, that Simon was dead. Or even better, a collaborator. Anything to throw them off.

Next, he took two matches from the cigarette box on the dashboard and lodged them into the exposed tire valves of the driver's side front and rear tires. Both began to deflate slowly. He walked around and grabbed his satchel out of the trunk, removed his sidearm from the front pouch and placed it in his belt, threw the satchel over his shoulder, and started back up the path of the Pic d'Aidour; and this time up a little farther, to Fort de Santa Cruz.

~

The colonel's men were spread out along the Filaoussene Jetty on Quay #1, at the Bassin de Ghazaouet, examining boats of all types and hoping to find their prey. The large brute of a leader was hanging back as the others did the searching. He signaled for the radioman to hasten to his side. He arrived with the radio receiver in his outstretched hand and the call already put through. The leader grabbed it to talk to his boss. "Colonel?"

"Yes, Marcus," came the reply.

"He's not here, sir. My men are continuing to search but nothing yet." Marcus then ventured a suggestion, "We could start boarding some of the smaller domestic fishing vessels and continue searching?"

The answer came immediately, "Yes. But do try to be a little discreet, will you? No sense in alarming the harbor master. If you find…when you find Capitaine Renault, bring him straight to me. Understood?"

"Yes, Colonel," answered Marcus. He handed the receiver back and called the men together to relay his instructions.

As his men continued the search, Marcus turned to his left to see the massive Fort de Santa Cruz on the top of the Pic d'Aidour. Then he turned to look back into the city, wondering where the Capitaine might be.

He has to be here; he just has to be. Where can he go? There's no other way out of Oran. Think, man. What would you do? No, that wasn't the right question. What would the Capitaine do? That is the right question. Might he travel back into the city and hide? Or maybe back to Sidi Bel Abbès? No, that would be suicide.

Capitaine Renault's reputation was well-earned; hard to believe at times, but nevertheless well-earned. If even some of the stories were full of only half-truths then the Capitaine would be ritualistically unorthodox in his method of escape, and exceedingly brutal if anyone got in his way. He was excellent at the former, and couldn't afford the latter. Translation—he wouldn't come down to the port to commandeer a fishing boat.

Marcus stopped thinking because he had been thinking like a common soldier, instantly concluding the only way out of Algeria was by boat from this harbor. The problem was that getting to a boat, any boat, anywhere on the coast, might not be in the Capitaine's calculations after all. Instead of a direct route to the city's port, Marcus belatedly wondered if Maurice would be taking the underground tunnels linking the three ancient forts on the western side of the city—Fort de Santa Cruz, Fort de la Moune, and Fort St. Philippe. With de Santa Cruz on high and de la Moune at the coast below, both at the western edge of the city of Oran and on the eastern edge of the naval port of Mers-El-Kebir, the tunnels would serve him well because they garnered multiple options for escape. Maurice could make his way to the coast and then, by any number of directions, continue out to sea—and freedom.

"Radioman!" he shouted, with a coincidingly loud snap of his fingers. As Marcus grabbed the phone, he looked back up at the Pic d'Aidour.

"Yes, Marcus. What is it?" asked the colonel.

Frustration boiled over into anger with a dash of admiration as Marcus, hesitant to reveal his stupidity outright, informed his master, "He could be in the tunnels." Marcus could sense his superior's anger and fear growing wildly through the radio as if it were stretching out to strangle anything it could.

The colonel's next query was accompanied by a slightly nervous tone, "How long has he been in there?"

"At least ninety minutes." Then, an unbelievable thought occurred to Marcus. The possibility of the Capitaine heading back to…. He shouted into the radio, genuine fear in his voice, "Colonel! He could be heading back towards Fort St. Phillipe. He could be headed for you!"

"Double the guard at the tunnel, quickly!"

The colonel's panic-stricken scream of fear was the last thing Marcus heard before the radio went silent.

CHAPTER 35

Laroque-des-Albères, France, 2001

Maurice smiled as he walked down the street, heading to the shops to purchase the makings of lunch for himself and Sebastiane. His first stop would be the Boulangerie.

Morning was fully awake, and the small town he called home was bustling with activity. Maurice thought he should get out more and enjoy the scenery and the people. He'd isolated himself for far too long—and he wasn't getting any younger. People did know him because he always said hello when said hello too. But besides Conner McGinty and his family, and a select few others, Maurice lived in this town but wasn't a part of the town. That had to change.

Maurice felt refreshed after his cold shower, but after sitting and thinking all night his legs needed a good walk. He would have taken the path into the foothills around town, but that would be isolationist. His decision to change his life had come with his decision to change his grandsons, so isolationism wasn't to be his forte anymore. And, he didn't have time to enjoy today or dillydally around. His grandson needed his future to begin immediately, and only lunch would be the delay of that future. Maurice knew he couldn't very well send the boy off without a proper French meal.

Maurice continued walking, but harkened back to his thoughts regarding his *Plan B* that day in Oran. It was something he wondered about often, but it was harder for him now to understand why he'd even contemplated going backwards through the tunnels to try and kill his father-in-law. It was a moot point. He knew it wouldn't have brought Sophia back to him and he had to protect his daughter, so he'd gone with *Plan A*—escape.

Maurice turned the corner at the bottom of the road and glanced to check for morning traffic on the main thoroughfare. There wasn't any. As he looked across the street toward the Boulangerie, he hesitated slightly when he saw two gendarmes exiting their vehicle and walking towards it.

Damn it!

He crossed the street and entered the shop to hear the Boulangerie owner, Monsieur Fournier, answering the officers' questions.

"Yes. My truck has been here since early this morning, as have I. Before that, it was at my home with me."

"And you did not travel to or near Marseille yesterday? For supplies maybe?"

"No. My supplies are delivered to me. I only use the van for my local deliveries."

"And you didn't loan your van to anyone in the last few days?"

"No one drives my van but me. Why? Can I ask what this is about?"

Fournier was starting to get upset. The gendarmes were putting him behind schedule, and he hated being behind schedule. His large shoulders, raised slightly upwards by his even larger biceps sitting on crossed arms, and his frowning, prominent brow served to disclose his growing displeasure at the continued interrogation.

"Have you ever seen a van like yours around here? Other than yours, of course." The officer pulled a somewhat grainy photograph from his notebook and held it up for Fournier.

Maurice caught a glimpse of the photograph, not enough though to make a determination as to whether or not it was the van now parked under concealment at his farmhouse. But he guessed it probably was.

"No, I have not." Fournier panicked slightly, but feigned nonchalance by motioning towards Maurice, "Monsieur, please excuse me. I'll be with you in a moment."

"Ce n'est pas un problème, Monsieur."

Maurice didn't walk around the shop or ignore what was happening, which should have been a dead giveaway to the officers. Their uniforms designated them as local police, but Maurice didn't recognize them. He wondered where they were from and why they were in his hometown asking questions. As he stood there, thinking, keeping his eyes focused squarely on the two gendarmes, waiting to learn if his supposition was correct about the photograph, the door behind him opened and two stout-looking men entered the small shop.

Maurice kept his gaze forward, trying his best not to look at them as they moved straight past him. The first one that passed him grabbed the photograph from the uniformed gendarme while the other proceeded behind the counter and towards the back of the bakery. Fournier protested—it fell on deaf ears.

As the first man, they were too obviously dressed to be anything other than the *Police Nationale, Officiers de la Paix*—Inspectors—thought Maurice, continued to ask questions while he pointed at the photograph, Fournier continued to answer. Maurice hoped they would show the photograph to him. Only then could he ask some vague sounding yet pertinent questions about what was going on in order to assess the threat he and his grandson might be facing.

"Monsieur, have you seen this van?"

Finally, thought Maurice. He looked at the picture for as long as needed; not too long to attract suspicion, and just long enough to see that the police had almost nothing to go on. It showed no license plate and only a blurry rendition of the diamond-shaped business moniker on the side.

Maurice answered, "Sorry. The only van I know that looks like that is Monsieur Fournier's." Maurice told himself to apologize later for throwing Fournier to the wolves. "Why?"

"An incident in Marseille last night."

"Oh! Should we be worried that you're here in our town and not Marseille asking questions?" Maurice was trying his best to sound worried yet pedestrianly moronic at the same time.

"Nothing to worry about. But if you do see a van like this, please call me." The man handed over a card and then turned to leave. He stopped suddenly.

Maurice saw something in his posture and his mannerisms, something that told him this encounter wasn't yet over.

He turned back to the bakery owner and asked, "Before we leave, if you don't mind, can we check the vehicle's VIN number just to be sure we can delete you and it from our lists?"

The baker stopped breathing before agreeing to the request, and the Inspector saw it. He had something here, he knew it. He kept his own face stone cold neutral so as not to alarm the baker or the customer behind him.

Maurice was right about one thing and horribly wrong about the other. The plainclothes man was exactly who Maurice thought he was because the card he'd handed over read: *Didier Villanueva, Officier de la Paix, Police Nationale-SDAT, Prefecture Office-Perpignan.* Maurice knew *SDAT* stood for *Sous-Direction Anti-Terroriste.* Maurice also now understood that his and Sebastiane's situation was far worse than he'd thought.

The two uniformed officers headed outside to take a better look at the van while Fournier was allowed to serve his customer before locking up his store and joining them out back. Maurice purchased bread and then immediately departed. As Fournier closed and locked the front door in the presence of one of the plainclothes officers, with hands so sweaty they slipped off the lock not once but twice, he began to panic when he saw Maurice heading away—and far more quickly than he should have been able to at his age.

After Maurice crossed the street and turned the corner, he picked up his pace even more. He would have to do something about the van at the farmhouse. It was identical in every aspect to Fournier's, right down to the false VIN number on the dashboard. He would have to do this before he did what was necessary for Sebastiane because Maurice wasn't so sure he could get his grandson to where he needed him to be before the authorities found it. He knew he didn't have that kind of time, though.

What the hell do I do?

Maurice's thoughts and actions became indecisive. He hated feeling like this. It had been too long since this sensation had plagued his efforts to survive; and at his age, it made him feel sick to his stomach. He tried to put everything aside as he arrived at the public phone just outside the local post office. He grabbed the hand receiver and fished in his pocket for some change. Hanging on the wall by the front door, this phone was the only point of contact Maurice allowed between himself and the man who had loaned him the van he'd used in Marseille. Maurice felt his hand trembling around the telephone receiver while his other hand couldn't quite hold onto the change in his pocket. Then, the sickening feeling grew worse. The twisting, turning, and rising consciousness of the acid building in his stomach made his throat burn.

Damned old age.

Maurice tried to stop his body from trembling by placing his forehead on the wall to steady himself. He knew he needed to move quickly, and he needed to stop feeling this way. He took a long, slow, calming breath to clear his mind. He shut his eyes to take in the sensation of his persona switching away from the old-age pensioner he had become back to something else entirely. He smiled ever so slightly when it happened. He stood up proudly, steadied his hand on the receiver, extracted the change from his pocket, placed it in the machine, and dialed.

When the connection was established and the phone began to ring, Maurice began to realize the possibility that the men who had died in Marseille at the hands of his grandson may have been more than just two unlucky passersby. He also wondered how long it would take the police to track down the van he'd borrowed; the van he'd used to transport his daughter to her final resting place; the van he'd used to almost abandon Sebastiane to his fate.

The ringing finally stopped, "Oui?"

"Valentýn. S'il vous plaît?"

Maurice knew this conversation might not go so well. Regardless, he knew his only hope of survival at this point, and the survival of his last remaining heir, would be the fact that the man coming to the phone, Valentýn Novatny, the man who had loaned him the van, still had his wife and young daughter to dote upon.

CHAPTER 36

Tampa Bay, Florida

The S.O.C.C., or Satellite Operations Command Center, at The Slater Group, Inc.'s headquarters was abuzz with activity. William Dent stood in the center of it all and loved it for what it was, not just simply for what it could do.

He loved the adrenaline-fueled, caffeine-induced, rush-of-the-chase feeling he got while hunting bad guys and protecting his country. He never thought he would feel this same type of demonstrative patriotism again after he left the FBI. But now he was starting to get that feeling again—and he'd missed it.

9/11 had changed everything for Dent. He had originally regretted retiring, and regretted being seduced by the admiral. But now, as the hunt for a potential terrorist in the south of France played out on the computer screens and wall displays in front of him, he regretted nothing. He realized he was still protecting America and its citizens. The difference was that he was doing it with his idea, his *FI²* system, and it made him confident they could succeed. No more bureaucracy to deal with. No more supervisors waiting for failure. He only had to answer to the admiral, and the only thing the admiral wanted was his best. Dent had his best, and the adrenaline and the caffeine coursing through his veins at that very moment was proof positive he could get the job done. The phone on the desk to his left rang. "Yes, Admiral. Yes, sir. No problem, I'll be up in five minutes."

Dent hung up and whistled loudly so as to be heard over the beehive-like activity surrounding him, and asked, "The Admiral wants an update in five. What have we got?"

A frantic-looking man, just a boy remembered Dent when he saw who it was, with his shirt covered in coffee-stains, had stood up and was waving his hand vigorously. Obviously hyped up on whatever caffeine he'd been able to ingest instead of spilling on himself, Dent pointed and asked, "Yes, Eek. What is it?"

Eek was the boy's nickname—a pun on his initials, E.K. He began to blurt out what he had discovered as fast as his caffeine intake would allow, "Sir, French police are in a town near the Spanish border hunting down a lead on a van identified at the scene."

"Slow down, Eek."

Eek did so as best he could, and then continued, "We traced a possible route of egress away from Marseille presupposing the terrorists would try to get out of France as quickly as possible. Leaving out the train station because it was too obvious, and forgetting the port because of the strict immigration protocols the French have enacted, the semi-porous and mountainous Spanish border became the clear choice. Using the limited surveillance infrastructure the French have in their southern regions I was still able to capture some blurry images of a van with some kind of emblem or moniker on the side that matched the description from the police. It was seen moving west, and then eventually south and away from Marseille and towards the Pyrenees. I relayed the information back to our established contact with the French *SDAT*, his name is Inspector Villanueva, and he and some men are looking into the possible match as we speak."

"How confident are they this is the van? Have the French identified that emblem on the side yet? And are you sure the Spanish border is the destination?"

"No. There's no positive ID on the emblem, or whatever it is, yet. Villanueva and his men are currently talking to the owner of a similar van right now, a man named Fournier, at a bakery in the town of…Laroque-des-Albères. I'll know more when they call back. As for the Spanish border, not one-hundred percent but it seems the logical choice."

Dent liked Eek. The kid was raw but level headed, and damned smart. "All right, stay on it. And update me when you get anything new."

Dent looked to the others in the room and asked, "Anybody else?" No answers came. "Stellar. I want this van's make and model cross-matched with all existing sales and rental records in France and Spain for the last two years. Look for anything suspicious. Then, whittle the list down to nothing less than a sixty percent probability of a match, either by the whereabouts of the vehicle or the person or company who owns it. After that, shoot the list to our contact in the French police. Also, see if our contact can organize extra security teams at the closest border crossings near the town of," he looked down at his notes, "Laroque-des-Albères. In fact, ask him for extra security on the towns closest to that place as well. If the truck hasn't crossed the Spanish border yet we might get lucky. I want you three," Dent pointed to the other side of the room, "to get me a list of all terrorists suspected of being in the region, but leave out the Basques. And I want a list of all foreign travelers to Marseille within the last two weeks. I want a seventy percent probability gradient for that list. Get on it, I'll be upstairs."

Eek confidently smiled and looked to his colleagues for adulations at a job well done before falling back down into his seat—the caffeine holding him up being conclusively depleted.

William Dent grabbed his report book and his personal notes and then made his way upstairs. When he arrived, he smiled as Ms. Dietz nodded for him to go straight through to the admiral's office. He entered quietly and took a seat to wait while the admiral concluded his phone call. Two more men, unknown to Dent, entered the room and took seats on the sofa across from him. The big one had what looked to be a scotch in his hands while the other one was trying to rub his eyes clear of what had probably been a very long afternoon because of the previous evening's events.

Both men were younger than old, with the big one dressed in casual attire and the *eye-rubber* wearing an expensive suit. Dent figured that the suit was Slater's newly acquired CIA liaison, while the other was a JSOC (Joint Special Operations Command) operator from MacDill—or maybe they were just the newest in-house specialists on all things anti-American. They identified themselves as *Jones and Smith*, respectively. Dent had seen and worked with their types before, and these two were a perfect match to his impressions. Dent gathered himself as the admiral hung up the phone. He hoped the boss liked what he had to say.

"Full report if you please, Mr. Dent," said the admiral.

"Sir, approximately eight o'clock local time last night we received a call from CIA Station Paris via Langley. They requested an immediate assist with an incident. The request was for a dedicated, quick reaction reconnaissance package and also a supplemental resource investigation team to look into the death of one of their undercover operatives. A local police officer, a contact in Marseille, informed Paris Station that he was at a murder scene outside of a mosque in the heart of the city and that he had identified an undercover informant as one of the victims. Also, the case officer in Paris, a Mr. Covington, later reported that the informant had missed his previously scheduled call-in and that most likely his death was the reason he hadn't called in and not something else that would require looking into. We were given access to the police reports, and the reports of their informant, and the psych team is doing a profile as we speak. We immediately initiated the platform and started ingesting all available recorded and live footage in and around the area. We started with the traffic cams and any CCTV footage from the area. Coverage is spotty at best, but we got a hit on a van that was mentioned in the initial police report. The first sighting of the van on CCTV was of it heading away from the area near the crime scene. Then it popped on a harbor camera as it headed south out of the city. The angles didn't allow for an image of the driver or for a license plate capture, but there was some type of business emblem on the side of it. No clear identification yet, but the French police are working on it. In addition, the facial *RECOG* program can't, as of yet, find any statistically significant hits on anyone seen exiting, entering, or inside the van as compared to civilians either in the area or on the streets around the time of the incident. Nothing from the airport, train station, or port facilities either."

Dent flipped over to the next page of his report book and quickly reviewed his notes before continuing. "While part of my team is trying to locate the individual or individuals from the van and then identify them, others decided to concentrate on the van itself." Dent flicked to another page of his notes, "It is a white, Mercedes Sprinter 903 T1N cargo conversion. We are attempting to narrow down the owner and or the rental company. When we get either we will cross-reference that information with all known terrorists in the vicinity, those who might have entered France within the past few weeks, or any other watch-listed foreign nationals who may have entered Europe within the same period. Our best guess, currently, is that whoever did this is more-than-likely heading for the Spanish border. We have contacted the American embassy in Madrid and have also put in a request with French *SDAT* for increased security at all border crossings and other check points in the Pyrénées-Orientales department, especially the towns of Le Boulou, Argelès-Sur-Mer, and finally Laroque-des-Albères. When the system finishes gathering everything, we'll sift through the information and we'll get you answers. Sir."

"Don't you think that'll take too long?" Jones asked. "Cause I think it will."

"Maybe," Dent acknowledged, without turning to face his inquisitor. "But I don't want to miss anything."

"We need something sooner rather than later," added Smith, patronizingly. "I know Covington at Paris Station. He's a good guy. We should get him something quickly no matter what it is. He should be able to take it from there."

Dent tried to hold back his frustrations, but couldn't, "I'd rather be right than quick to the trigger."

In Dent's time with the FBI he'd had quite a few run-ins with hyperactive HRT—Hostage Rescue Team—members, or their over-zealous commanders, who just couldn't wait to breach a house or tear down a crumbling factory door to takedown the bad guys. Dent was always cautious because, regardless of the accuracy of the intelligence that had brought them there in the first place, no one, not even Dent, could ever fully understand or know what was actually inside.

The Admiral cut in before tired tempers could flare, "Maybe we should consider cutting the list down to just European nationals or those from known terrorist-supporting nations, and also only local rental agencies and owners?"

"We could definitely cut out Americans, Canadians, and a host of others," added Smith. Jones agreed. Smith continued, "Or just bump them to the back of the list and then recheck it if no one else pops."

Dent finally turned to address Smith and Jones directly, then shook his head slowly and deliberately like a college professor admonishing his students, "That type of thinking is imprudent at best, and simplistic at its worst. You presume too much with that analysis. If we don't check all possible avenues we could miss something—and maybe even someone. And wouldn't it be a damned shame if the perpetrator or perpetrators we're looking for turned out to be non-Muslim terrorists."

"Save me the bleeding-heart crap," said Jones. "The only reason to kill a CIA asset is because he is a CIA asset. An American, or any other of our allies for that matter, wouldn't do it—nor do it just for kicks neither. So we either have a raghead sympathizer who got lucky, or an informant whose cover got blown and they sent in a professional raghead to end him... end of story."

Dent's face was expressionless from the overtly pompous, illogical stupidity that kept pouring out of Jones's mouth. Dent countered, "Again, you presume too much. And I don't have time for this. Admiral, should I continue with my report or go back to work? I can have a far more detailed and more accurately assessed update of our findings for you in two hours tops."

Admiral Westerly chose the latter, but asked, "Do we have any assets in France at the moment?"

Dent answered immediately, "Mr. Polk just arrived in Paris."

"Good. Give him a call will you. Ask him for some input into how we could stretch this investigation. He might have some insights your team does not. Have him call me directly."

"Of course, sir."

The admiral sent Dent on his way. Once the door closed Smith stood up and went for a glass and the decanter, offering his companion a refill. Westerly swiveled in his chair and said as diplomatically as he could, "I'll get my man to push your considered irrelevant nationalities aside for now, fair enough?"

Both men nodded in the affirmative.

"But gentlemen, can I just say that, well, you just tried to argue the merits of the FI^2 system with its creator. Not a very smart move."

Smith rolled his eyes. "You mean that was the chief lab geek? Makes sense. He sounded like former FBI. All talk, no action." Smith's distaste for his *brother from another agency* was palpable.

Jones chimed in, "With respect Admiral do what you think is right, but we need information and we need it quickly. It's been," he looked at the clock on the wall, "ten hours since we got the call, and twenty-four hours since the incident. Time is not on our side on this."

Not long after Smith began to savor his third glass of whiskey, Ms. Dietz put Simon Polk's call through to the admiral. Westerly put the call on speakerphone for his associates.

"Sir, Mr. Dent asked that I call you."

"Yes, Simon. Just wondering if you had any tactics or strategies to add to our little investigation?" Westerly queried.

"Tactically, I have nothing. Mr. Dent filled me in and I agree with his assessments and procedures."

In unison, Jones and Smith nodded frustratingly.

"And strategically?"

"It may be a long shot, or no shot at all really, but I spent some time in Saudi Arabia working with French Intelligence. It occurs to me that Marseille falls within the French Army's Southern Command, and that Marseille isn't but ten or twenty miles from Aubagne," answered Polk.

"What's in Aubagne?"

"Recruitment center for the French Foreign Legion."

Westerly's eyebrows raised in surprise, but he agreed. "Okay. I'll give our gendarme contact a call and ask him to put in a word for us."

CHAPTER 37

Two hours later Dent walked back into the admiral's office, confidently. Leaving his smug I-told-you-so face at the door, so as not to provoke Smith and Jones because it just wasn't his style, he announced, "Sir, I think we've got something."

Jones almost dropped his tumbler while Smith started grinning from ear to ear. Westerly asked, "How and where?"

Dent looked over his notes to get the names and places correct before stating, "An officer named Villanueva of the French Anti-Terrorism Squad tracked a van, same type as ours, to a bakery shop in a small town in the south of France. When questioning the proprietor, a Mr. Fournier, Villanueva hit pay dirt. After an inspection, Fournier's van was not the one we'd been tracking but it was so similar that Villanueva pressed him. The man cracked almost instantly and confessed he'd bought his van on the local black market. As it turns out the van was part of a shipment of twenty identical vans that disappeared about eight months ago from a facility at the port of Gijón in northern Spain. Spanish authorities initially lost interest when they lost the trail, but conceded their files immediately when Villanueva called. When he got the files he knew exactly who to talk to."

Smith asked, "Who?"

Dent flipped the page in his notebook. "Valentýn Novatny. French authorities are looking for him now and will bring him in for questioning when they do. We'll have a video and audio hook-up, but the quality might be poor."

The Admiral smiled and said, "Excellent work, Mr. Dent."

Dent replied, "I would be wary of this Novatny being involved in this…not directly anyway. We have a small file on him, and the file suggests he is a facilitator not a planner."

"Bullshit! This is our guy," stated Smith. Jones nodded in agreement.

William Dent loved his time at the FBI, but hated simplistic government thinkers who wasted valuable time and precious lives jumping to conclusions. The main reason he'd left the FBI was that nobody would listen anymore.

Blame for the Twin Towers going down had been rampant in the days after 9/11, and even now it seemed as if that type of hubristic, group-think, irresponsible rush-to-judgment failure spiral would never go away. It was a shame. America, Dent thought, was doomed because of it; and also because a lot of those in power didn't care or just didn't bother anymore. As he tried to hold his tongue, Dent began to re-evaluate his time with the Slater Group; it troubled him greatly that he should be thinking about that at a time like this.

Jones began justifying his conclusions with more irreverent misconceptions and unintelligible facts. Dent couldn't stand it anymore. He lost his composure and sarcastically replied, "And this is what makes you so confident and eager to name this guy as the mastermind behind this incident? You have no concrete information, only supposition. What, feeling a bit nostalgic for the good ole' days of blame something else, anyone else, the FBI perhaps, for *9/11* are you?"

The admiral shot out of his chair. Dent turned to face his employer with a worried yet apologetic look on his face, fully aware of the egregious and unfortunate comparison he'd just made. Westerly stared William Dent up and down for a good ten seconds, then looked past his man and squared up his two guests. Both men rose to their feet as he looked back to his employee, "Mr. Dent, why don't you take a few minutes with your team. Call me when the interrogation starts."

Dent frowned. He'd stepped across a line in the sand with the admiral. Now, regardless of his analysis, or any further intelligent input he could bring to this investigation, he would be ignored. Dent wondered if his job was in danger.

~

Sebastiane awoke to the sounds of a one-sided telephone conversation and rolled off the couch onto his feet. His eyes opened slightly to a darkened room; no lights were on, and it was dark outside. Sebastiane tried to shake his head clear and wandered what time it was…and what day it was. He didn't know how long he'd been sleeping. He was starving.

Walking past the kitchen, he grabbed a piece of bread and threw it in his mouth. He then walked through the hallway and into the bathroom, and was able to hear the finality of the conversation between Maurice and whomever was on the other end of the line.

"Merci, General…Oui… Merci, René. Au revoir, Mon ami."

After splashing cold water on his face, he focused in on a small, battery operated clock sitting on the back of the toilet. Sebastiane counted backwards from the last moment he knew what time it was and realized he'd been asleep for over eighteen hours. He exited the bathroom to see Maurice grabbing his car keys off the table. By the time Sebastiane put on his shoes and collected himself, Maurice had started the car and was leaning on the horn. Sebastiane made his way downstairs to the garage, flopped into the passenger seat, shut the door, and asked, "Where are we going?" When Maurice didn't answer, he tried a different tact. "What is this flag with the blue *M* on the rearview mirror?"

"It is the team colors and flag of Olympique de Marseille," answered Maurice. "They're a…"

"Soc-er-uh, football team?"

The surprise on Maurice's face when his grandson called the sport by its proper designation, and not its repulsive Americanized moniker, garnered a brief smile from the old man. "Correct. I have supported them since I was a young man." Maurice turned and caught a glimmer of life in his grandson's eyes. Understanding the look perfectly, he asked, "Do you play?"

"Yes, but it's been awhile," returned Sebastiane.

"Were you any good?"

"I tried out for a team once. I never heard back from them.

"Well then, maybe there's hope for you yet." Another smile accompanied the playfully patronizing tone in Maurice's voice as he backed the car out of the garage.

In response, Sebastiane tried to outfox his grandfather with a light-hearted comeback, "This car looks to be as old as you are."

"This is a 1970 Citroën DS 21 Pallas. It is classic French in every way and a pleasure to drive. Also, it is not older than me, obviously, but it is older than you…and far more stylish then you'll ever be." They both laughed, allowing some light humor to alleviate the strain of the past few days.

They drove away, heading northeast along the back roads. Maurice was careful as he drove, trying not to draw any unwanted attention. Sebastiane just watched the countryside pass by in the dark. It is so beautiful here, he thought, even at night. "Where are we going?"

Maurice didn't respond.

~

Didier Villanueva confidently entered the interrogation room of the local police station and sat in the chair opposite a man he knew all too well, placed his phone and the file folder of his guest atop the table, and then sat up a little straighter in the chair. It was an act that had been repeated several times between these two men over the years.

At this point it was obvious to Villanueva, and inevitable it seemed, that he should be here and the man on the other side of the table should be there—again. His previous dealings with the man, who was looking overconfident and smug as ever, happened before he'd joined the *SDAT*. But now, Villanueva was chasing terrorists' not street thugs. He stared confidently at his opponent, encouraged he was about to wipe that ridiculously smug grin clean off of his face and stuff his over-confident arrogance right down his throat.

"Monsieur Novatny, a pleasure to see you again. It has been a long time, no?"

"Who is on the other end of that telephone?"

Villanueva ignored the question, and asked, "Do you know why you are here today?"

"Ignore my question if you will, and I will ignore your pathetic attempts to scare me—not that it's too hard to do anyway. You police are so mundane. So simplistic. Boredom is the most likely thing accomplished here today."

"I'll ask again."

"No! I will. Who is on the other end of the telephone? Please do not tell me you have enlisted the help of others to—"

"It is none of your concern." Villanueva interrupted, trying to keep his voice calm.

"I say it is. My lawyer will make sure you pay for this…this unauthorized interrogation. You haul me in here in the dead of night and keep me for hours with no explanation, for what, a crime you can't solve—yet again. How many times have you and I been here? How many? And you always lose."

Villanueva scowled. Valentýn Novatny smirked.

The *SDAT* officer opened the folder on the table and inhaled reservedly in order to collect himself. Novotny was a pain in the ass, and Villanueva was happy that the video-conferencing equipment hadn't arrived yet. The request from his American friends for a live feed of the interview couldn't be set up in time, so it was to be voice only over his cell phone.

Villanueva didn't like the new video-chat technology used in police interrogations anyway. He didn't like it when other people watched his interrogations, questioning him from behind a lens in real-time. The video camera in the corner would record everything, as it always did, but couldn't transmit live. His phone was the only option he had for his American friends, so he left the line open under the pretense they couldn't speak during the interview. He was fine with it this way. He was sure they weren't. But Villanueva had decided a long time ago while still a beat cop that post-op critique of an interview was more helpful, and more useful, than feeling as if your every move was being questioned while you did the questioning.

Villanueva asked the question again, "Do you know why you are here today?"

"Not really. Now ask me a more poignant question."

Villanueva bit, "Enlighten me."

Novatny responded with a far more genuine smirk than he had ever worn in an interview room before, "Ask me if I care."

Villanueva tried his best not to show emotion, but failed miserably. In a slightly more formidable tone, he said, "You are here today because somebody killed an American undercover agent in Marseille last night. And they used one of your stolen vans to do it. Starting to care now?"

Novatny paused, purposefully, checked his watch, and started searching for deceptions to lay upon the ground.

As he did so, Villanueva mentally thumbed through the police interrogation handbook on how to spot the *tells* of a liar. Valentýn Novatny's posture said it all…Villanueva had him.

~

Listening intently at Slater's Tampa Bay headquarters, all those present in Westerly's office heard the extended pause, presumed the same thing as the French Anti-Terrorism officer was presuming, looked at one another, and smiled.

Smith proclaimed, "He's got him."

Jones looked over in Dent's direction to gloat but got no response, just a view of the side of the technical man's balding head.

~

Maurice and Sebastiane's drive continued into and through the sunrise of another day on the winding backroads of the Languedoc-Roussillon region of Southern France. Eventually, and to pass the time, Maurice wanted to know more about Elena—if for nothing else than to keep Sebastiane's attention on something other than where they were headed. The two men talked continuously as they passed through picturesque villages pock-marking the countryside, or passed by seaside towns sitting next to the edge of the Mediterranean Sea with its distant and endless horizon of the most beautiful and bluest water Sebastiane had ever seen.

As the conversation drifted between lightheartedness and difficult memories, and as if on cue, the sky descended into stormy darkness. The cloud cover was low and ominous looking. For Sebastiane it became harder and harder to tell where the Mediterranean stopped and the sky started, and harder and harder to distinguish between storytelling for a purpose and remembering for a reason. Small, mist-like water droplets began covering the windshield. Sebastiane felt uneasy as he continued to discuss his mother with Maurice, and Maurice felt a deeper sense of loss as he listened to his grandson.

Their longish, roundabout trip had started northwest out of Laroque-des-Albères towards Carcassonne. After stopping for snacks and a bathroom break Maurice turned northeast towards Montpellier and Nimes, and then to Avignon. From there he headed southeast toward Aix-en-Provence and Aubagne.

The emotional pain due to the loss of his parents and Sebastiane's own emotional ambiguity towards his two victims built up inside him, invasively overwhelming him when he noticed a road sign that said: *MARSEILLE-15km.* But Maurice didn't turn right toward Marseille, he turned left. Not knowing exactly where they were or where it was that Maurice was taking him, Sebastiane's mind set itself adrift and immediately fell victim to the melancholy of the melodic raindrops that only got bigger and louder as the storm continued to pelt the car's windscreen. A forced sense of recrimination and guilt fell upon Sebastiane's delicate and submersed psyche. He tried to fight it off, but his state of mind was just too fragile.

He had almost killed in the past, but somehow didn't feel the same way then as he did now. All those years ago he'd acted out of rage and vengeance, seeing and finally understanding the emotional damage Heather and Sarah had been subjected to. This time was different. This time he'd acted on rage alone. A debilitating anxiety plied at his thoughts, forcing feelings of damning regret and devastating remorse to the surface thereby exposing them like a raw nerve to the bitter cold of reality. He quickly became, not depressed, but reclusive.

Maurice could see it happening, but decided not to step in. The boy needed to figure it out by himself. Even with his explanation of how the Renault family legacy worked it would be difficult at best for Sebastiane to understand—just as it had been for himself all those years ago. But maybe, just maybe, the future he had planned for his grandson would help. Hopefully his plan would grant Sebastiane an inner peace, a wanted prison perhaps, one from which he could lock up the demon from his youth; and more importantly, one with which he could forget what had occurred forty-eight hours ago. His plan might just be able to help focus Sebastiane's abilities, make them controllable, and direct them towards a different and better future. That future could also give Maurice a sense of moral justification for his past deeds, he thought, and possibly help maintain the family lineage and history as well.

This is the right thing to do.

~

"I'll ask you again. Were you in Marseille last night?"

"Are we talking last night as in a few hours ago, or are we talking two nights ago? You need to be a little more specific." Novatny was smiling from ear to ear as he continually and quite victoriously goaded his adversary.

Villanueva was growing tired of asking question after question and getting nowhere towards possible enlightenment. Novatny looked nervous, and had for hours now, thought the policeman, but never quite crossed over into the zone of inevitability; a zone perforated by an inescapable truth that always led a man to confess his sins. Novatny continually rocked in his chair and his eyes darted from side to side, but he wasn't sweating. He stammered when he talked, as limited as that was, and was constantly looking at his watch. The career criminal hadn't actually confessed to anything, not even stealing the trucks. He hadn't actually admitted to…

Villanueva sprang up from his chair and slammed his hands down on the table, "Who are you covering for? Who?"

Valentýn Novatny smiled and looked at his watch one more time. He sat back in the small, steel, uncomfortable police interrogation room chair and relaxed, satisfied that enough time was going to pass before Villanueva ever got a single truth out of him—his debt to Maurice Renault, for saving his wife and child, would be paid in full.

~

In Westerly's office, Jones and Smith jerked their heads at the speaker-phone, confused by the sudden burst of distorted sound energy blaring through the electronic circuitry. They then both looked to Westerly, dumbfounded.

The admiral swiveled in his chair to face his chief technical officer. He could see Dent was grinning from ear to ear with the satisfaction of knowing he'd been right all along.

"He played Villanueva?"

Dent replied, "Yes, sir. Seems that way."

Both Jones and Smith took out their cellphones and started calling whomever they needed to. They needed to get the ball rolling on rendition paperwork for a French national, one Valentýn Novatny.

Westerly escorted Dent out of his office while discussing alternative investigative avenues so as to help find as much information as possible to assuage the CIA over the death of one of their assets. When Westerly returned to his office chair he saw Jones give Smith a cut-throat gesture. It seemed as if the French weren't going to play ball on this one—not even for a career criminal like Novatny.

Westerly swiveled slightly in his chair to contemplate the *FI²* system's obvious growing pains and Dent's future at the head of its team, and with the Slater Group. The man was a truly gifted asset, and Westerly knew the *FI²* project could never be everything it needed to be without its creator. But the man had crossed a line. Westerly puckered his lips, deciding the least he could do was let Dent pick his own successor.

CHAPTER 38

Aubagne, France

Before Sebastiane had realized it the sun had forced away the rain, but only some of the clouds. He didn't know where he was, and didn't ask.

Maurice signaled and then turned off the main highway, gently slowing his Citroën a little ways farther down the small road. As he came to a complete stop, the hydro-pneumatic, self-levelling suspension eased the vehicle into its resting position. Maurice turned the ignition off, got out, and walked around the front of the car to the passenger door. He opened it and coaxed Sebastiane out. The boy was still staring into nothingness, not knowing where he was or caring very much either. Maurice sighed heavily, wondering again if this was truly the right thing to do. It needed to be; he needed it to be. Maurice shut the door to reaffirm his decision.

They crossed the street and came to a small, wrought-iron gate affixed between low-rise, cinderblock walls covered in dilapidated stucco and capped with barbed wire. The walls ran away down either side of the road and disappeared in both directions—one behind some trees, and the other as the road curved to the right. The gate was unimpressive. It looked to be the back entrance to some place that wasn't so important. It squeaked when Maurice pushed it open. For Sebastiane, the squeaks emanating from the gate as it was opened, and then closed, sounded as if it was laughing at him. They continued walking along a narrow path sided by rows of tall, thicketed bushes towards a figure standing within a covered doorway behind another gate about thirty meters inside the first.

The man's voice boomed at them, "Halt. This is a restricted area. Please return to your vehicle." His voice was buoyed by the clicking and sliding sounds of the recharge handle on the *FAMAS F1* assault rifle no longer slung across his chest but in his hands and pointing outwards and towards them. Then, another set of identical and far more ominous clicking sounds came from directly behind and to the left, as two more men, men in soldier's uniforms, emerged from within the thickets.

The three soldiers and Maurice all stopped to take stock of the situation. Sebastiane stopped only when Maurice's hand on his shoulder told him to. He fell to one knee as the images of Marseille exploded in front of his eyes yet again. The two soldiers behind Maurice and Sebastiane began to maneuver into tactically superior firing positions. Maurice kept his eyes locked on the soldier directly in front of him while listening for the movements of the other two as they fully exited the thickets to complete the agreed upon task of encircling their prey. Once the soldiers finished maneuvering to where they wanted to be they stopped, hands clenching a little tighter on their weapons in anticipation of a fight.

Maurice surveyed the scene, and so as not to provoke them proposed a different course of action, "I am here to speak to Lieutenant Dupuis, S'il vous plaît. Tell him Maurice Renault is here to see him."

The short, muscular sergent, now standing out in front of the covered doorway, reluctantly grabbed his radio and called the security office to inform the Officer-on-Duty that there was an unauthorized intrusion at the back gate. Less than a minute later Lieutenant Omar Dupuis arrived on the scene, breathing heavily after his sprint across the compound from his office.

Dupuis was slender, tall, and had an olive complexion. He also looked like a bookworm who missed his books, constantly pushing his glasses up the bridge of his nose. Dupuis assessed the situation immediately, ignored the old man, and focused in on the younger one kneeling with his head hung low. Dupuis presumed that he was probably the origin of the threat his sergent had called in. "Sit-rep?"

"This man says he is here to see you...says his name is Maurice Renault."

Wondering what was going on, and not knowing who this old man was, Dupuis paused to decide on a course of action. Security was still tight, but this was an old man and some punk kid who got caught breaking into the complex.

But how did he know I would be on duty today?

Dupuis asked, "Who are you? And how did you know I was here?"

Before Maurice could answer his questions, the lieutenant's radio squawked. "Lieutenant Dupuis. Phone call for you, sir."

Dupuis lost focus for a second. Not wanting to be bothered by something as trivial as a phone call while attempting to deal with a potential threat, he abrasively asked, "Who is it?"

"General René."

Dupuis's mind snapped to attention, "Put him through... Yes, sir."

"Stand down and hold for further orders."

"Sir?"

"Please hand the radio over to Monsieur Renault," ordered the general.

Dupuis was thoroughly confused as to what was going on, but did as instructed. He walked over and handed the radio to the old man, and then paused when he saw the eyes of the man he was handing the radio to. Something inside the lieutenant warned him of caution with this one. As he retreated, guardedly, the old man smiled at him.

The radio crackled to life and Maurice instantly recognized his old friend's voice. "Maurice, you know we aren't supposed to allow this kind of recruiting anymore." Maurice tried to interject, but was cut off. "I received a call from the Marseille Gendarmerie some time ago. They told me to be on the lookout for anyone who might try to enter my recruitment center under, shall we say, false pretenses."

Maurice was stone-faced and silent. He thought he had beaten the clock on the Gendarmerie's investigation.

General René could not see his old friend's face, but he could hear the silence—and it was deafening. "Don't worry my friend, I have taken care of things…Gendarmes be damned. This makes us even you and I, yes?"

"Oui."

"Good. Hand the radio back to the lieutenant."

Dupuis accepted it back at a distance, his caution grounded in his posture. He listened carefully to the instructions from the general.

"Lieutenant, you will take the young man into the holding center. He will replace the recruit who was expelled yesterday for using drugs. Lose all the paperwork. No report is to be filed concerning this incident. Other than that, everything is taken care of. Understood?"

"Yes, General."

Dupuis switched channels on the radio and talked in code for a few seconds. He then waved his hand in the air, signaling his men to get ready to move as two more soldiers arrived on the scene to take over guard duty. "You!" He pointed at the younger man, "Come with me. You, old man, go home. You are not authorized to be here. Please comply."

"A moment, lieutenant. S'il vous plaît?"

"Oui."

Maurice picked Sebastiane up, held him firmly by the shoulders, and kissed him on both cheeks. Staring into his grandson's eyes, the blank expression still smothering the life from them, Maurice smiled, forgivingly.

This is what you need.

"Good luck, my boy. And remember one thing; you are my family. The place you go to now was also my family. Do you understand?"

A blank stare was all Sebastiane could muster as he nodded and then hugged his grandfather. The embrace was a powerful one.

Sebastiane walked forward, nervously. He was flanked by two soldiers who still had their weapons trained on Maurice. Sebastiane paused to turn around and look at his grandfather one last time. Maurice nodded at him, proudly, and then turned and walked away.

The four men—Sebastiane, Dupuis, and the two guards—continued up the small path, through the inner gate, passed the muscular sergent, and stopped at the covered doorway while it was being unlocked. Continuing through the door, then up a small set of stairs, they came to be in a room that looked like a museum of sorts. The walls were decorated with elegantly framed oil paintings while small and medium-sized glass cabinets dominated the floor space and displayed all sorts of trinkets. There were also statuettes in-between them, dressed in strange military uniforms Sebastiane didn't recognize.

As they continued, the framed oil paintings gave way to framed photographs; some showed scenes of men in battle while others showed much more. Finally, the two soldiers pushed open a set of solid wood, double-doors, and the pseudo-museum gave way to a large, outdoor parade ground. The longest walk of Sebastiane's life would now begin as the double doors slowly closed behind him with a whooshing sound that prophesied change.

Sebastiane looked out and gazed upon the vast, open area. His eyes eventually came to rest on the only impediment to its flatness—a large monument with a four-foot diameter black globe set atop a six-foot-high by ten-foot-wide, white marble, rectangular pedestal. Four, eight foot tall statuettes stood at its corners; different military uniforms were sculpted over their undefined bodies. As they walked passed, Sebastiane could see an inscription on the front. It read: *HONNEUR ET FIDELITE.*

The longest walk of Sebastiane's life, all two-hundred and eighteen meters of it, finally ended when they came to the side entrance of a two-story, administrative building. There was no sign on the door. To Sebastiane it might as well have been a door to an alternate reality because all of the two-hundred and eighteen meter walk he'd just endured had consumed his every thought as well as his perception of time itself. His family, his childhood, Sarah, Heather, the last few days, it all flashed before him and overloaded his senses. He didn't know what to think anymore; he didn't know how to think anymore.

He looked through the small window in the door and all he could see was uniformed men walking in and out of offices. Turning back towards the lieutenant and the other soldiers, Sebastiane's expressionless face prayed for guidance. One of the soldiers opened the door and extended his arm towards the opening, indicating that he was to continue through it alone. Dupuis nodded in agreement.

It was only then that Sebastiane noticed a patch on the sleeve of the extended arm of the soldier. The words stitched into it were simple. The words breeched Sebastiane's mental fog, made sense to him, and he finally understood where he was.

Sebastiane thought back to Maurice's final words; and yes, they too made sense to him now. The decision to send him here, he realized, without so much as a hint of what was happening gave Sebastiane a sense of understanding through necessity. Maurice was trying to protect him by forcing upon him a future that could not only save his life but give him a purpose—a direction.

Escaping his past, especially the last forty-eight hours, was the only thing Sebastiane wasn't sure about. If he went through the door in front of him, would he be closing the door on those forty-eight hours permanently?

And, would he also be closing all the other doors he'd ventured through in his life up to this point?

Does redemption for my crime exist through there? Does regret or absolution for the paths I've taken and not taken in my life await me through there?

The lieutenant grinned when Sebastiane accepted his future and walked through the door before saying, "Bienvenue à la légion étrangère."

EPILOGUE

Overland Park, Kansas, 2004

Before Maurice approached the door numbered 1631, a small bungalow-style home in this humble, suburban retirement community, he paused. He was amazed at how it was that he came to be standing in this very spot.

Sixty years had passed since he'd seen the man who lived here; sixty years since Maurice had saved the man's life; sixty years since the man had rescued Maurice's tortured, bloodied, broken, and barely alive corpse from the Gestapo. Beyond those days long since passed, Maurice had gained and lost his wife, gained and lost the Legion, faced multiple situations that shouldn't have been, participated in some and not in others, lost his daughter and gained a grandson, and had always tried to live life the best he could considering. He'd waited too long to come here, he knew that now. The twilight of his life was casting its darkened shadow upon him, and he was glad that the darkness hadn't yet caught up to him.

I shouldn't have waited.

In the end, his journey had taken him on a cross-ocean voyage from Marseille to New Orleans, a river barge up the mighty Mississippi to St. Louis, a train from there to Kansas City, and finally a taxi to Overland Park.

Maurice reflected upon the fact of whether or not it would have been better if the man on the other side of the door had not saved his life, then just as quickly dismissed it.

Maurice walked the final ten feet to the door while straightening his shirt and bow tie, the ones Jean Francois had purchased for him before he'd left New Orleans. He rapped on the door, gently. He waited, nervously. With the late afternoon sun behind the small dwelling, and the hour of the day not yet late enough for the light over the door to be on, an unsettling darkness within the bricked alcove lingered. It was a darkness that recalled an unfortunate and unwanted part of his past.

The last time Maurice had seen the man on the other side of this door had been one of the darkest days of his young life. The torture and the unbelievably sadistic depravation he'd been subjected to wasn't supposed to be a part of war; nevertheless, it had ended up being a part of his. Maurice remembered that his last visions before waking up in a US Army field hospital were that of large barn doors exploding off their rickety, rusted hinges, and a man bursting through with his gun raised and firing away. The man killed nine SS officers and soldiers before he'd stopped firing his weapon. The Allied soldiers who had accompanied him then chased the remnants of a company of Wehrmacht out of the barn and into a field and killed them too. Those large, wooden, barn doors, thought Maurice, were far less intricately decorated than the simple door he now stood in front of. And yet, they somehow seemed to share a common bond; a bond just as significant to Maurice as the man he'd come to see. Maurice knew the man behind this door had only been trying to repay a debt equal in capacity and equal in honor.

A life for a life.

If the man behind this door hadn't returned the favor, then Maurice knew he wouldn't have met Sophia, would never have gone to Algeria, never had Elena, and never had a grandson. Would he have survived the war anyway? Maybe. If he had, would he have lived a different life? Probably so. And if he had survived and lived that different life, would he have regretted every minute of it? The door to 1631 Constance Place had opened without Maurice realizing it.

"Can I help you?"

"Pardonnez-moi, Monsieur. S'il vous plait. Est-ce la maison de Lieutenant Griggs?"

"Sorry!"

An almost inaudible shout came from inside, "Who is it, Thomas?"

"I'm not sure, Grandad. I don't know what he said. I think he is speaking French."

Another shout from inside, "Qu'est-ce?"

Maurice smiled when he recognized the hopeless attempt at asking a question in a language not practiced for over sixty years. "Your French is still hopeless my friend. It is a wonder you ever survived the Nazis."

After a few seconds, Thomas Griggs was surprised by his grandfather as he placed his aged hand on his shoulder and moved him aside, apologetically, so he could make sure the voice he'd heard coming from the front door had the same face attached to it from all those years ago.

"Well, I'll be damned," replied Jacob T. Griggs, Lieutenant, 29th Ranger Battalion, 29th Division, United States Army, retired, with a glint of tears in his eyes.

Maurice smiled at his friend, the man who had saved his life the first time—the man whose life he had saved. Both men walked forward and grasped onto each other as old men do, tightly, proudly, and comradely, and then joyously laughed as if there was something more to life than just life.

"My friend, it is good to see you. Please do come in. This is my grandson, Thomas." As Maurice greeted the young man, Jacob Griggs continued, "My boy, this here is Maurice Renault; former member of the French Resistance and the sole reason I am alive today. He saved my life during the war. And if it weren't for him, you wouldn't be here."

"Come in. Come in." Thomas Griggs greeted Maurice again, but this time with a sincerity that asked a thousand questions—and a smile that pleaded for a thousand answers.

Maurice was shown to a comfortable seat on a smallish couch in the front room while Thomas proceeded to the kitchen to put on a pot of coffee. As he poured the water into the kettle, retrieved the cups from the cabinet and the coffee from the pantry, he could hear nothing but genuine comraderie from the front room. When Thomas returned with three cups and a tray full of snacks, he saw two old men going through photo albums and laughing like school children.

Was it giddiness in his grandfather's voice he could hear, Thomas asked himself, as he proudly discussed the history of the Griggs family with their French guest? Perhaps. Or perhaps, it was just the memories and emotions of times long past that made his grandfather sound more alive today than he had in quite a while. There was also a light within his grandfather's eyes, a light that defied his age and seemed to suppress the sickness that was ravaging his body. The doctor said it wouldn't be much more than a year until things started to get really bad, and it pleased Thomas that his grandfather's suffering seemed a little less today because of this visit.

Thomas Griggs remembered back to his childhood. He remembered all the times he'd sat at his grandfather's knee listening to his stories about war, sacrifice, and honor, and been amazed by them. The stories were for the ears of a child and strayed away from the horrors of combat, but Thomas eventually came to understand how sacrifice and honor made war what it was; that sacrifice and honor were the end results of the justifications that bedeviled a man's mind while engaged in combat so that he could do what was needed to survive. Thomas smiled internally, thanking God for the chance to meet the man who had saved his grandfather's life all those years ago.

He placed the tray on the table and looked at his watch; it was almost time to go. And even though he'd never missed a single session of any of his classes at the local community college, Thomas knew that today would be different. He sat down in a seat that was as close to the two old friends as he could get, without intruding, sipped his coffee, and grinned—there was no way in hell he was going to miss any part of the stories being reminisced here today.

ABOUT THE AUTHOR

Born and raised in southern California, Jason moved to Dublin, Ireland at age 15 where he attended and completed his secondary education (High School) at Wesley College in 1990. During his time living in Ireland he traveled around Europe visiting several countries, including Austria, England, France, Germany, Greece, Northern Ireland, Scotland, Wales, and the former Yugoslavia (Croatia). Upon returning home, he enlisted in the United States Navy. After an honorable discharge, he attended the University of New Orleans and then transferred to and eventually graduated from Arizona State University with concurrent Bachelor of Arts degrees in History and Political Science in 2001. He married and returned to New Orleans, Louisiana where he resides today with his wife, a school teacher, and their two sons. He has worked as a paralegal with law firms since 2003 and writes in his spare time.

EXTRAS

Unedited excerpts from Book II of The House of Renault:

EVERYTHING PASSING BY

The Ivory Coast, 2005

Doors can be very, very strange things. Going in or coming out, you never truly know what is on the other side until you're already there. When you do get to the other side and close the door behind you, you have to accept what you've walked into—no questions asked. Good or bad, profound or obscure, it doesn't matter.

Usually, one has no objections to walking through a door. It is a necessary step during an average day, or maybe it is simply just a means to an end. You think nothing of it on most occasions and forget about it just as quickly. A door, in and of itself, is only an inanimate object with no feelings or ambitions. They are nothings, in a world of everything's.

Beware though! Doors can play tricks on you. Thinking you are simply exiting a room and entering a hallway, or exiting a house and entering the beginning of your next day, seems trivial when it occurs. But how do you know it isn't a trick? How do you know that that meaningless, mundane task of turning a handle, then pushing or pulling it open, then walking through it, couldn't absolutely be the worst idea you've ever had in your entire life. Maybe it was the best idea you ever had! Either way you have no clue, but you still walk through it without a second thought.

How many doors have I walked through in my life? How many doors have I walked through without hesitation and that have not, in some way, completely altered my sense of reality or compoundingly confused the perception of how my life was supposed to be—or might have been?

Sebastiane was staring straight ahead, asking the cold, calm darkness too many questions in the hope that the answer it couldn't give would be different than the one he knew to be true. None, whispered back at him from the void. He bowed his head to contemplate the answer, but kept his concentration on the task at hand. His thoughts, albeit highly intellectual were definitely worthy of a snooze fest in some university psychology lecture. But, they were helping him stay calm and focused on the moment.

Sebastiane screwed his eyes shut tighter on the one door he didn't want to see. It didn't help. Every time he tried to ignore it, he ended up seeing the same thing—an antique-looking, crystal ball-shaped, acrylic door knob, connected to an event horizon. Every time he reached out and turned the handle to open that door, he found himself walking through the first wooden aperture that, no matter how hard he had tried to avoid it, substantially and completely changed his life. It was the door to the room holding the seven seals of hell on earth. It was the door to Heather's room with all its memories of mischief and misery. And how horrific had it been to open that door, go through it, and see what was happening? Sebastiane shuttered violently, forcing himself to stop thinking about it.

But what about your college dorm room door, what was it, freshman year?

The mini-baseball bat that struck you in the back of the head was completely obscured because of the non-transparent nature of the metallic monstrosity usually protecting your personal things, but that unwittingly hid your attacker. There was nothing you could have done about it. You got lucky when he left you alone immediately afterwards. Because if he hadn't, it could have been death that would have tapped you on the shoulder to wake you up. Instead, there was only a little blood and a slight concussion—nothing to worry too much about. That pain-in-the-ass got his comeuppance, though, but it took you six months to pay him back in kind—far too long for your liking and far too long for Kenny also.

But wait! Was it a bad door or was it actually a good door?

Little Kenny Dominguez, all of five feet four inches and one-hundred pounds soaking wet, had been a good friend. He had enough vitality for three people, offering you something you desperately needed when you arrived in Tempe, Arizona for college. He showed you all the good hang-outs and even got you back into playing soccer. He dropped out of school after the incident and you never saw him again, but he had smiled throughout most of the nightmare and you knew he would be all right.

So, was it a good door or was it a bad door? Bad for Kenny but good for you, because after the retribution you decided not to go home and instead started spending your summer's up near Flagstaff. Old Man Nolan needed help on his ranch, giving you a place to hide from yourself while trying to excise your recent present, and most of your past. That crazy old man and his dilapidated ranch; it was just about the only good thing that had happened while you were away at college. So, the college dorm room door was a good door, right?

Sebastiane continued to parley feverishly with his sub-conscious.

Doors just lead to other doors, right? It is a constant in the universe. What door was next? Of course, Old Man Nolan's barn door. And what did that lead to!

"Two minutes," came the shout from directly in front of him. Sebastiane could barely see through the darkness, only vaguely understanding the direction from which the shout originated. Then, the shouting figure stood up from his seat, moving toward the soft luminescence of an electronics panel, and repositioned the head-phones on his ears in anticipation of what was to come. Sebastiane felt around in the dark and readjusted his own equipment. Finished, he returned to his thoughts.

What about that barn door? If you hadn't gone through it, you would never have found the bullets for the rifle, and you never would have been able to takedown

that nasty little mountain prowler before she attacked Old Man Nolan again,
would you? And then, one year later, wasn't it that same barn door where you
found Jennifer Nolan, his niece? She had her red and black, country-plaid blanket
up in the hayloft, waiting for you; her body glistened in the virgin light of the new
moon, just begging you to bathe in its radiance.

A thin, wry smile went unnoticed as it appeared on Sebastiane's face, and then disappeared just as quickly as his thought process continued unabated. He was able to recall each incident as vividly as if it was happening again; or for the first time, when the memory of such things was the strongest. Reliving each and every thing he had done helped to pass the time.

Sebastiane heard the sounds of mechanical gears turning and then felt the sting of the cold air as it rushed passed him as the aft-ramp of the Transall C-160 cargo plane began to slowly open. Beyond this metallic behemoth of a door was another void to stare out into, just as he had been staring at the darkened void of the interior of the aircraft for well over two hours now.

The first leg of the trip had taken seven hours, with most of that time spent going over intelligence intercepts and the overall plan. After a short ground refueling at São Tomé International Airport, it was back in the air for the last two hours. This leg of the trip had been spent mentally preparing for the task at hand. He was ready. But, all he could do was wait; wait and think about what this door might bring to his life?

You never know, do you?

He answered his own question knowing he would pass through it just as he had all the rest, not really knowing what was waiting for him beyond it.

Looking out the now fully opened cargo ramp door, there was nothing much to see. It wasn't easy seeing anything, let alone the stars, through the opaque plastic visor of his oxygen mask. He could just barely make out those stars as they began to fade into the light of the coming sunrise. At an altitude of 27,000 feet, day was arriving much earlier for him and the others on the plane than for those on the ground—and for good reason. The occupants of the transport plane needed to get back down to earth undetected before anyone noticed, and the *HALO* jump, High Altitude/Low Opening insertion technique he was about to endure, was the best way to accomplish that.

"One minute," came the signal from the flight deck officer.

The once shadowy figure that had shouted instructions a minute ago was now visible in the orangey-red glowing haze lighting up the inside of the aircraft. The officer was still standing at the electronics panel and still listening to the pilot in his headset. He was receiving information indicating airspeed, altitude, and the coordinates of the plane. He needed this information to calculate the time-on-target, when he'd push the button that would dim the small, red indicator lamp and light up the small green indicator light. This would inform the eight-man insertion team, of which Sebastiane was a part, and in the first position, that it was time to jump.

Sebastiane waited some more, using the time to check over his gear one more time. He was adept at waiting these days. Patience had become a definitive virtue for him, and it had come with lots of practice. He used his memories like an egg timer, passing the time while waiting, regardless of whether it was a training mission or a real mission like this one. It not only helped with the monotony, but helped to remind him of why he was here, why he needed to be here, and why he wanted to be here.

Sebastiane felt two hard taps on his shoulder and turned around to acknowledge them. The man behind him, Caporal Corso, his teammate and good friend, indicated with his thumb that Sebastiane's attention was requested at the rear of the formation. Sebastiane did so, and at the back of the line, five jumpers behind Corso, but just in front of the Sous-Lieutenant, or second-lieutenant, he saw Sergent Chef Henri holding up his hand. Henri was indicating a need to relay new instructions to his first jumper and point-man once on the ground. The non-commissioned officer

(NCO) for this specialized unit, Senior Sergent Henri Radjic started giving Sebastiane new orders via hand signals. Those signals were interpreted, and then the appropriate hand signals were returned indicating an understanding and his compliance with the change in mission parameters. About damn time, thought Sebastiane, as he prepared to jump thirty seconds earlier than everyone else. Sebastiane turned back to face his next door and waited. What was next, he asked himself, as he fell back into his psychological preparations?

Yes! Running through the front door to the house and watching the television as the second plane hit the south tower of the World Trade Center. No, I'll skip that one this time. That door was too influential.

That was the door that had brought him all the way to France, then to Maurice, then to Marseille, and then to Aubagne. That conglomeration of doors was the why he was standing here, on this particular plane, preparing to jump into the growing dawn.

"Thirty seconds."

As the deck officer turned around to punch the indicator light on the electronics panel, giving the visual signal to the jumpers they were thirty seconds from departure, Sebastiane waddled forward under the weight and restrictions of all his gear and jumped. Right behind him came the supply canister Corso pushed off the ramp.

The air was cold, and roiled violently behind the turboprop engines as the aircraft cut through the sky with amazing ease. 25,000 feet was indicated on the altimeter at his wrist as Sebastiane looked at it and his Global Positioning Satellite locator, trying to get a fix on his position. The GPS would have a hard time calculating his exact position, but it always helped to know if you were in the general vicinity of your drop zone. Besides, the visual markings of the countryside were extremely vague because the day was still trying to wake up down there. He decided to wait until he was closer to the ground to try to get his bearings.

Sebastiane decided against the standard free-fall position and made himself into a bullet shape, with his arms pinned at his sides and his legs straight back while pointing his head down towards the ground. He quickly accelerated to positional terminal velocity. By doing this, he would end up on the ground a little more than the thirty seconds head start he had on the others. The maneuver would put him on the ground and in a far better position to defend the landing zone while he waited for his arriving comrades. As he rocketed towards the earth, Sebastiane looked to the next doors in his life; the recruiting center's door at Aubagne.

You joined the French Foreign Legion.

No, that was completely and utterly wrong, he reminded himself. Sebastiane had been placed with the Legion because it was what Maurice had wanted; and was something Sebastiane had reluctantly agreed to after the fact. The walk up the parade ground and the walk down the corridor to the waiting Supervisory Recruitment Officer seemed a lot longer than the paltry two and a half minutes it took to cover the distance. Without the extensive paperwork, and a very shaky signature, the contract had been signed.

He was given a new identity with the same first name, but a different last name. It had been changed to Rousselle, and thirty minutes later he was on a bus heading back into the French countryside towards the town of Castelnaudary for his fourteen weeks of basic training. It had understandably been the right thing to do, but Sebastiane had only done so with the fullest of intentions of sliding under the radar and being as minimalistic as possible during the five years of his contract. Because, not only had he not been all that enamored with everything Maurice had told him about the Renault family's military life, Sebastiane wasn't completely sure he wanted to be a part of it even after being told he really had no choice in the matter.

Falling through the sky with nothing to do but think, Sebastiane smiled at himself for realizing quite quickly at Castelnaudary that casting aside any lingering doubts about what the Legion could do for him turned out to be the acceptance he'd craved since the death of his parents. He smiled again with an understanding that, begrudgingly of course, Maurice had been dead right to take him to Aubagne; and that Maurice would never let him live it down.

During basic training, which ended up being pretty basic—especially for someone with no military background—Sebastiane was quick to answer the call when his hand-to-hand combat instructor picked him to go two rounds with a visiting NCO. After round one, the man, his name tag said Sergent Chef Radjic, had subdued Sebastiane quite easily. After the second round, it was Sebastiane's turn as he handily subdued the sergent. The instructor had given ample warning to the visiting sergent about the skills of his best pupil, but Radjic had dismissed the warning straight out of hand. Once on the ground, looking up at the capable and quick learning recruit, the sergent had glanced over at his commanding officer, a commandant—major—and gave a head nod indicating that this recruit could make a fine addition to the parachute regiment; that is, if he passed their overwhelmingly demanding training program. The major nodded back in agreement, and that was that.

Passing twelve-thousand feet and falling at two-hundred miles per hour, Sebastiane changed his position into the more recognizable descent configuration. He put his arms out and away from his sides, holding his hands together in front of his face so that the altimeter and GPS were clearly visible. His legs were bent at the knees to help maintain balance as he slowed to a positional terminal velocity of one-hundred and twenty-six miles per hour.

The free fall continued. And that meant more waiting. And that meant more thinking—more thinking about other doors.

CPSIA information can be obtained
at www.ICGtesting.com
Printed in the USA
BVHW050018090223
658191BV00002B/267